HER COWBOY RIVAL

GENEVIEVE TURNER

Chapter 1

"WE'VE GOT A BRIDE PUKING in the lobby bathroom."

At Will's panicked announcement, Luke Merrill, manager of the hotel in which said bride was puking, looked up from his desk. "Already? The wedding hasn't even started."

He tossed down his pen. Son of a bitch. A bride puking after a wedding was one thing. A bride puking *before* a wedding was another thing entirely. "Where's Fee?"

Ofelia was his cousin and the resort's wedding planner —and the person who should be dealing with this.

"The groom's barricaded himself in the honeymoon suite. She's trying to get him out."

"Jesus." Clearly the bride and groom were well matched in terms of chaos-causing skills. Luke rose and grabbed his suit jacket from the back of his chair. So much for a quiet Saturday evening catching up on paperwork. But he was the hotel manager, which meant the buck stopped with him. Along with vomiting brides. "Get Alma into that bathroom and have her put the bride into an empty room to sober up. Fee can keep dealing with the groom. Tell the DJ to announce there's a delay in the wedding, but the bar's open, and no worries—everyone's getting their prime-rib dinner."

Luke had discovered that most wedding guests would overlook any number of disasters if they got fed, got some liquor, and got to dance. Humans were pretty simple when it came down to it. Hell, he wasn't judging—that was pretty much all he needed to be happy too.

"I already took care of all that."

Luke frowned. "Then what do you need me for?"

"There's a couple who has an appointment to see the wedding facilities."

And they had an imploding wedding on their hands. Shit. Well, Luke couldn't say hotel management wasn't exciting. But sometimes he thought he might have been happier riding with the herds on the ranch portion of the family business.

"All right. I'll take them around." He shrugged into his jacket and then dusted off a spot on his black Wranglers. Finally he pulled on his black felt Stetson. "How do I look?"

Will gave him a thumbs-up. "I'd have my wedding here."

"Let's hope they will too."

Luke found them outside Fee's office. They were both in their late twenties and already looking worried. Damn.

"Sorry. We're running a little behind today." He put on his best smile and held out his hand to the prospective groom. "Luke Merrill. I run this place, and I'll take you around today. Show you what we can do for you. James, right?"

Luke's innate charm had always served him well in this business, and now he turned it up to eleven. Being a middle kid of four, he'd learned early on that he could get attention either by being a brat or by being charming. Lil, the other middle kid, had chosen to be a brat, which left Luke to be the people pleaser. Not that he minded.

"That's right." The man—James—had a shake that was firm, friendly. "No problem about the wait."

The fiancée wasn't reassured. Her expression was screwed up with anxiety as she gave Luke's hand a brief squeeze. "Will we have time for the entire tour and the tasting? We're supposed to be meeting with Ana Chacon at the casino in an hour."

Luke never let his smile slip at Ana's name, although his mouth tasted like the inside of an ashtray. Ana had done that to him since high school—among other things.

He projected warmth and confidence, never letting that show. "You must be Sofie. Don't worry. We'll get you out of here in plenty of time. Wouldn't want to disappoint Ana."

Actually, Luke did want to disappoint her. It would piss her off so badly to know he'd showed this couple the wedding package and they'd chosen the resort. He did love riling her up. Almost as much as she loved riling him up. From the moment a mutual friend had introduced them in high school, and through their shared time at hotel-management school at Cornell, all the way up to today, she'd always given him a look that said, *You'll never impress me.*

He'd call it a friendly rivalry between them if they felt anything like friendship for each other.

Yeah, having this couple cancel on Ana because they'd chosen his resort would be delicious. But first he had to get this couple to get hitched here.

Luke rubbed his hands together, the tireless tour guide ready to show them a good time. "Let's begin outside."

He led them both to the massive lawn studded with live oaks, keeping well clear of the main ballroom where the other wedding was going FUBAR. Fee had better be cleaning that mess up.

"Most of our guests choose the lawn for their ceremony. From spring till autumn, it's just gorgeous here." He played up his drawl, let his smile go crooked. They were all friends here, and he was only pointing out the finer points of the resort as a friend. Not as a salesman. "We've even had some outdoor winter ceremonies. The lawn area will seat over five hundred. How big will your guest list be?"

"About one hundred," James said, just as Sofie said, "Over three hundred."

That disagreement didn't bode well, but it wasn't his job to make the marriage work. They only did the weddings here.

"Well, one hundred or three hundred, we can handle either. And provide rooms for all your guests." They had the wineries down in the valley beat on that—no one had to drive home from a wedding here, which meant more fun for the guests. "Now, most people like to hold the ceremony here under the main oak…"

Half an hour later, they'd had a sampling of the prime rib and salmon entrées, which they'd eaten with pretty clear relish, and Luke was plying them with cake samples. He was *this* close to closing the deal; he could tell by the way they were already envisioning their reception, pointing to where they could put the cake table, discussing what colors would work best.

Luke knew the cake would be the tiebreaker.

"Oh God." Sofie moaned with pleasure and took up another forkful of the almond cake. "This is the best cake I've ever had. Most wedding cake is…" She stopped to chew.

"Terrible?" Luke smiled conspiratorially. "I know.

4

Jasmine is a magician, isn't she?" He leaned in. "She only makes cakes for us."

Sofie's expression was pained. "You mean... I can't get this cake at the casino?"

"Well, no." Luke tried to arrange his face into something close to regretful. "But the casino and its resort are lovely too. They have the most amazing fountains."

They really did have lovely fountains. No doubt Ana would fill them with her tears when she heard she'd lost this couple.

"They're building a new spa," James said, as if trying to convince himself that was reason enough to go with the casino.

"They are," Luke said, "but we have a spa too. And we also have horses." He said it jokingly, but he was dead serious. Horses were way better than a new spa.

Sofie set a hand on James's arm. "This cake is amazing. And it would be nice to have the ceremony under the oak. Think how the pictures would look."

If Luke had Sofie convinced, then his work was done. Ninety-nine point nine percent of the time, what the bride wanted was what happened. Even so: "If you'd like an idea of what it would look like, that photo right there was done under the oak." He pointed to a picture behind them of a bride nuzzling her groom, the oak spreading dramatically behind them. The moment was both intimate and powerful.

Sofie sighed happily when she saw the picture. "So pretty."

Time to close the deal. Luke glanced at his watch. "We should get you two on the road. Ana's waiting."

Probably waiting smugly, thinking she'd win this one. Well, she wouldn't be smug much longer.

James and Sofie exchanged a look. One that said, *We've*

decided. Right?

Luke rubbed his mouth to hide his smile.

"How much for the deposit?" James asked.

Luke wore a shit-eating grin the rest of the day.

The vomiting bride had been cleared out of the lobby bathroom—and the bathroom was pristine again—and she'd been sobered up with plenty of coffee. Fee finally lured the groom out of the honeymoon suite, and if their guests thought it odd that the wedding came after the dancing had started, well, that wasn't stopping them from drinking and dancing and cheering as the couple kissed.

All Luke had to do was finish his paperwork, and then he could hit up the Stampede to celebrate. Maybe meet his friend Russ and see what the night presented them with. Russ was a firefighter, which was always handy for meeting ladies. Unless they liked cowboys, in which case Luke was already set.

He whistled as he tapped at his keyboard, already imagining how good that first beer would taste.

A knock came at the door.

It was probably Benedict, his older brother. Benedict was the CEO of the entire family enterprise—the ranch, the resort, and all the other pies the Merrills, Morenos, and Spencers owned throughout the state. He was tireless, hard-driving, and a hell of a businessman.

He was also a huge pain in Luke's ass.

"What do you need, Benedict?" Just what he wanted: whatever his brother might be dishing out this late on a Saturday.

"It's not Benedict."

What the hell? That was Jasmine, his cake genius. "Come on in."

She looked terrible, her brown eyes red and her dark

cheeks wet with tears. Her hair was caught up in one of her trademark scarves, a complex pattern of warm reds and golds that was at odds with the sadness in her expression.

"Jesus." He got up, pulled out a chair for her. "What happened? What's wrong?"

"I'm not sure how to tell you this."

He did not like the sound of that. "Do you need some time off? Is something wrong?" He pulled a tissue from the box on his desk and passed it to her.

She dabbed at her eyes. "Ana Chacon came to see me last week."

He'd known this would happen one day, that Ana would try to hire Jasmine for herself. And still he was pissed. His smug sense of triumph was squashed flat, but he kept his anger from his expression—Jasmine didn't need that.

"With your bakery going full time, I thought you wanted to keep this cake business on a part-time scale," he said. "You want to do weddings for two venues now?"

"No, I don't." Her words were reluctant and waterlogged.

Shit. Shit, shit, shit. "However much she offered you to be exclusive to them, we can match it." He didn't even hesitate as he made the offer. He'd just booked a couple based solely on her cakes. They couldn't lose her.

"Look..." She glanced to the ceiling as she dabbed at her eyes, mascara coming away on the tissue. "This is why I came to you rather than telling Fee. Because there's more than simply money behind it."

His gut turned to ice. So it was really about *that*. And no amount of money was going to smooth over *that*.

"I didn't..." He was about to say that he didn't think any of that had mattered to her, but of course it would. Her sister was involved. As was Luke's brother. "I think I understand."

He did, all too well. And knew there might be no way to

convince Jasmine to stay.

She sniffled into the tissue. "I love working here, and I don't want to quit, but ever since we heard that... that *he* was coming home, I just couldn't stop thinking about what it would be like, working here... knowing that he was too." Her voice splintered as she finished. "He *is* going to be working here?"

"Yeah, he is." Luke's jaw barely moved as he forced that out. "He's my brother."

Luke had convinced Benedict to agree to giving Josh—their youngest brother—a job when he got out of prison. That had been a hard-fought battle, but Josh deserved a second chance. And the family worked on the ranch. It was what they'd always done.

"I can't work here," Jasmine choked out. "Not if he's going to be. Leonora is my sister. After what he did..." Jasmine started crying again.

Luke passed her another tissue, his arm feeling as if it were made of lead. "I understand."

"Do you? I mean, if the roles were reversed, if it was Jackson who'd done that to Lil—"

"Jasmine, I don't blame you."

Because she was right—even though Luke and Jackson had been friends since kindergarten, if it was Jackson who had gotten blotto drunk, buckled Lil, Luke's sister, into a car, and then wrapped it around a telephone pole and nearly killed her, Luke would beat the tar out of him.

But it was Josh, Luke's brother, who'd gotten shit-faced with Leonora in the passenger seat and wrecked his car. Leonora who was lucky to be alive.

Jackson hadn't beat up Josh—that was hard to do with Josh serving five years—and he still occasionally spoke to Luke, so he was a better man than Luke was.

Jackson had been his friend.

But Josh would always be his brother.

Because of that, he'd lost Jackson's friendship, and now he was about to lose Jasmine's cakes as well.

"I know none of this is your fault," Jasmine went on. "And I hate leaving you like this, but I've been thinking about what to do, and when Ana brought me that offer... It was a solution to this... this mess."

It was a fucking mess all right.

Luke tried for a friendly smile but only got as far as strained. "You'll do great at the casino. Everyone loves your cakes, even people who hate cake. It's a great move for you."

He meant it too. None of this was Jasmine's fault.

She swallowed hard. "When you say it so sad like that..."

"Well, I am sad." He stretched his smile a little farther. "I'll miss your cakes. I'll have to crash a wedding at the casino to get some now."

Jasmine giggled even as she sniffed. "Better not. I don't think Ana likes you."

"Yeah." Understatement of the year there. "When are you leaving?"

"I'll finish out what I've got scheduled, up until the end of July."

That was more than fair—they'd definitely be able to find a replacement by then. But no one near as great as Jasmine.

"I booked a couple today solely because of your almond cake," he said. "Do you think you could do a one-off for us in January for them?"

"Sure."

They both rose, giving each other sheepish smiles. Then Jasmine came over and hugged him. "I'm sorry. But I had to."

He patted her back. "I understand. I'd do the same."

"Okay." She released him and wiped her eyes. "I've got to get home."

"Tell your family I said hello."

"Will do."

When she was gone, Luke sank into his chair and grabbed the hard rubber ball he kept in his desk drawer. He tossed it against the edge of a bookshelf, the ball bouncing right back into his hand. He tossed it again, caught it again.

Josh coming home was going to be difficult. Luke knew that. And yet it hadn't seemed real until today.

He tossed the ball again. Well, he wasn't going out tonight, that was for sure. He wasn't any kind of fit company just now.

Caught flat-footed like this, and by Ana Chacon of all people.

He caught the ball and held it, squeezing it tight in his fist. *Ana.* It wasn't her fault, he knew that, and yet he was pissed at her.

There was rivalry, and then there was undermining, and she was just plain undermining here. What the fuck had he ever done to her that she hated him, had to try to sabotage him at every opportunity? Yeah, they both ran resorts in Cabrillo, but this went beyond corporate rivalry, poaching an employee from him. This felt personal. Vindictive.

If he had to bet, Ana wasn't out tonight having fun. No, she was probably still in her office, coming up with new ways to humiliate him.

He tossed the ball back into the drawer and slammed it shut. He was planning on having it out with Ana anyway—why not tonight? He had nothing better to do.

Luke snatched up his hat and marched off to face his opponent.

Chapter 2

ANA CHACON WAS MAKING HER way through the front lobby when a floral arrangement stopped her dead.

It was wrong. There was an empty spot, right there between two sprays of poppies. She tweaked a few of the blossoms and moved a wild rose to the left.

Taking a step back, she examined it again. The hole wasn't quite gone, so she pulled the rose over farther. There. That was better.

"Ana!"

She turned to find her boss, Linda, coming toward her.

"How did the spa shoot go?" Linda asked.

"Beautifully. When we open the new section, it's going to be amazing." The area had been remodeled, mostly based on Ana's design ideas. Already several magazines had come to do stories on the new spa, one of which was *Style* magazine. And it was all thanks to Ana's hard work.

"Are you on your way home now?" Linda asked.

Ana gave a poppy one last tweak. "No, I'm headed to my office. I have some e-mails to answer."

"You are dedicated."

And didn't Ana know it. She might be the assistant director of resort operations, but she intended to lose the assistant part of that title sooner rather than later.

"I love my work," Ana said, and that was very true. Even the sounds of the revelry happening on the casino floor were music to her ears. That was the sound of her tribe's future—of schools and fire departments and senior centers and scholarships and language classes.

Ana had nothing to do with running the casino—the resort was her domain—but the sound still made her happy. So much had been lost to her people through the centuries; Ana was doing her part to ensure there was nothing but gains from now on.

"Walk back with me," Linda offered, "and we can discuss some things that have come up."

An uneasy current ran across Ana's skin. But Linda didn't look as if she was about to deliver bad news.

They went through the heavy double doors behind the front desk and into the resort offices. It was quiet at this hour, the offices dark and empty.

"I'm not sure if your mom told you yet, but we're going to bring in a consultant. Someone to take a look at our operations and give us suggestions on where we can improve and where we can cut out some dead weight."

Ana frowned. "No, she hasn't mentioned it." Her mother was a member of the tribal council, so she must have already heard about bringing in this consultant.

A consultant wasn't terrible news but... Ana could feel her lip trying to curl. An outsider coming in to tell them what they were doing wrong was *not* welcome.

But she had to remain open-minded. If this consultant could help them, that would be to the good. Ana meant to make this the most popular resort and casino in California, and if the consultant's suggestions pushed them toward that, Ana would take them. They weren't the largest resort and casino in the area, but Ana would ensure they were the most desirable one. The spa remodel was all part of her master plan.

"Well, the consultant will be observing the operations for a while, talking to various people, getting a feel for how we do things."

"As long as it doesn't interfere with our guests."

Linda unlocked her office door. "Of course not. But I wanted to talk with you specifically about some of the suggestions she'll likely make. Mostly about streamlining."

Streamlining? Ana wasn't inefficient. "Okay."

"It's not anything to worry about. It's just that..." Linda cocked her head. "You take on too much."

"How is that? All my tasks are completed and then some." Okay, maybe she'd been feeling just a tad—*a tad* —overwhelmed.

No, not overwhelmed. Maybe a bit overscheduled. Yeah, that was a better word. Just because yesterday she'd looked at her to-do list and had a spell when she absolutely could not breathe didn't mean she was overwhelmed. It had been only for a moment and it had passed. She'd gone on to do everything she'd needed to.

"That's the point," Linda said. "You do so much to run the resort, and then you take on extra work with all this charity and community outreach. That's really the job of the PR department."

Had they complained? Ana wasn't infringing on their territory. "We've talked about this. It's important that the community see a Cahuilla representing the resort. The casino benefits the tribe, and thanks to that, we can benefit the entire community. And I enjoy it."

There was a little more to it than that—Ana was very, very aware that she was a member of the tribe *and* an employee of the casino. Her mother had raised her children to be hyperaware of their position in the world—with a member on the tribal council and one working at the resort, her family was what the community saw when they saw modern Natives, which meant they had to represent their people as best they could. They only had several centuries of history they were working against here.

Ana's mother was already pretty close to perfection, and Ana's efforts at the resort and with the community outreach were her push toward perfection.

"I just don't want you to get burned out. You go twenty-four seven here. You should slow down a little." Linda sighed when Ana said nothing. "All I'm asking is that you have an open mind when the consultant makes her suggestions."

Ana pulled up a smile. "Sure. You know that improving the resort is always my top priority." Which was why she worked so hard. And she was not at all in danger of being burned out.

"That's why you're still here on a Saturday night." Linda reached into her office without turning on the lights and snatched up her purse. "But I'm not as young as you, so I'm headed home."

"Oh, before you do, did you see the employment papers for Jasmine Harper?" Ana let the tips of her smile turn triumphant. Luke Merrill was going to be so mad when he heard. So deliciously mad.

He had snatched that couple today, but that was a small victory. Ana could lose one couple—she would gain so many more with Jasmine's cakes.

"I did," Linda said. "Great job on that."

Ana was tempted to point out that the hire had been achieved in all that "extra" stuff she did for the resort but didn't. It was enough that Jasmine would be coming to work for them.

"Thank you," Ana said. "She'll be a real asset with weddings."

Linda shut her office door. "I'll sign the papers Monday, and we'll get to work on bringing her up to speed. Night."

Ana waved good-bye, then made her way to her own office, stopping by her assistant's cubical.

"Hey."

Cecilia looked up from some paperwork on her desk. "Oh, hey."

Like Ana, Cecilia had grown up on the reservation and had come back home to work at the resort once she was finished at college. She was about five years younger than Ana and more a protégé than an assistant. In a few years, Ana expected that she would have Linda's job and Cece would take Ana's job.

That thought wasn't as savory as it had been a few months ago though. Although Ana was most definitely not burned out.

"I guess everyone's working late tonight," Ana said.

"Actually, I'm leaving soon." Cece pushed the papers away and stretched. "The Torreses put in a new fire pit and they're having a party to celebrate. Are you coming?"

"I can't." Regret gave the words a coppery tinge. Ana was missing out more and more often on socializing it seemed. But there was work to be done. Always more work to be done. "I've got to finish up here." She rubbed at her forehead. "And tomorrow I have got to remember to ask Rosario if she needs a ride to church."

"Oh, I talked to Ben today—he's going to do it." Cece

hesitated. "Ana, there *is* an elder committee. They're making sure Rosario has groceries and gets to the doctor and church."

"I know." Of course she knew—she worked so hard here to help fund that committee. "I just…"

"Can't delegate?" Cece raised an eyebrow.

"Are you asking me to give you more work?" Ana asked. And she could delegate just fine. Okay, maybe she was still working on it. But she was better.

Cece laughed. "Not tonight. I've got to get going. Maybe I'll still see you? It'll probably go pretty late."

"Maybe." Ana doubted it though.

She waved good-bye to Cece, then went into her own office, firing up her computer as she sat at her desk.

She opened her e-mail and sighed. So many messages to answer and more coming every day. Wasn't e-mail supposed to make everyone more efficient? It seemed like she could spend all day doing nothing but answering e-mails. Time to do some triage.

But first some dinner. She called the kitchen, ordered a big plate of spaghetti, and was told Willie would be on his way in ten minutes.

She squared her shoulders and tackled her inbox. Urgent e-mails that should have been answered already went into one folder, stuff that didn't need to be answered but had to be saved went into the archive, and messages that could wait went into another folder, to sit until she had to move them into urgent.

Ana was good at her job, maybe even great—the resort had been rated the number one tourist destination in the county by the local newspaper three years in a row—but she was terrible at e-mail.

Just as she was down to fifty-seven unanswered messages, the new message alert dinged.

"Damn it," she muttered. Why were people sending her e-mail on a Saturday night? Didn't they understand she was trying to clean up her inbox?

She clicked on the new message, from one Chelsea Thomas. Miss Thomas was apparently the consultant Linda had been talking about and wanted to know if Ana was free to meet on Monday.

Ana gave the e-mail a suspicious stare. She didn't trust people who sent out e-mails on a Saturday night. Ana wasn't answering her e-mails—she was sorting them. But this Miss Thomas—did she want everyone to know she was still working? Ana herself might be working, but she wasn't going to flaunt it. That was just rude.

Then there was the question of when to reply. Ana could do it right now and let Miss Thomas know that yes, she too was working late on a Saturday. Or she could wait until Monday, which would tell this consultant that while Ana was happy to help out, this wasn't a "weekend urgent" thing for her.

That was why Ana hated e-mail. There was too much nuance and tone to pack into something so flatly stark.

She held her fingers high over the keys for half a moment and then set them to work.

Nice to hear from you! I'm available Monday afternoon at 3 p.m. if you'd like to meet then.

A click of the Send button and it was off. Ana went back to work on the rest of the messages, determined not to spend any more time worrying about the consultant.

A squeak echoed down the hall, probably from the wheel of a cart. Dinner was on its way.

"I'm here, Willie," she called. "Just come on in."

The tray poked into the door and she smiled, expecting Willie to be behind it.

Only it wasn't. It was over six feet of blue-eyed, dark-haired, long-legged cowboy. *Luke Merrill.*

She went hot and cold and fluttery. "You— What the hell are you doing? What have you done with Willie?"

"Conked him over the head and left him in the bushes." He lifted the lid off her plate. "Spaghetti. Are you carb-loading?"

She was, not that it was any of his damn business. A man who looked like he did probably ate nothing but protein and spent all his time in the weight room. And sneered about "cardio queens."

She'd done a long run this morning, and she was hungry enough to chew off her own arm. If he made any more smart remarks about carb-loading, she'd take a bite out of him as well.

"Where's Willie?" she demanded.

Luke set the lid aside and shook out a napkin, his movements easy. "He's fine. I saw him coming this way and figured I'd save him a trip."

"You can't do that. He can't just let you take over a tray." Not that Luke'd had to twist Willie's arm, she was sure. The man oozed charm.

"Don't fire him on my account."

"I would never do anything on your account."

He gestured her toward a chair. "I know." He gave her a look that made her toes want to curl.

Goddamn Luke Merrill. Screw him and screw all the ways he made her feel. Mad, jealous, lustful, *and* confused, which was enough to make anybody dizzy. He'd been doing this to her since high school, and the persistence of his effect on her made her that much madder at him.

She sat down and snatched the napkin from his hand. "Fine. You delivered the meal. Now go. And don't expect me to tip you."

He sat down across from her, much too large and close for her comfort. "Uh-uh. You and I have business."

"What? No, we don't." She wanted him out of her office so she could eat in peace. And get through the rest of those e-mails.

"We do. Jasmine Harper."

She couldn't help the evil grin that spread across her face. If only she had a Persian cat to stroke, because she felt exactly like a Bond villain.

No, Mr. Merrill—I expect you to die!

Okay, maybe that was a bit much. But this was still a lovely triumph.

"Yeah," he said with a slow nod at her expression, setting his hat on his knee. "We gotta talk. You can't steal my employees."

Ana suppressed the urge to roll her eyes. "I offered her more money and better benefits than you did. That's not stealing. That's the market, which you wealthy folks are so fond of."

His mouth tightened. "Yeah, because this place isn't making money hand over fist."

She batted her eyelashes at him. "Jealous?"

The smile that spread over his mouth made her stomach flip. "Nope."

Of course he wasn't. Luke Merrill had been born with a silver spoon in his mouth. He'd walked through life knowing that whatever he wanted to do on the family ranch, he could. So he'd chosen hotel management and gone to the prestigious hotel-management school at Cornell and everything.

She'd gone to Cornell too, only she'd had to work for it.

But she shouldn't be distracted by old hurts here—she'd just scored big against him.

Her stomach rumbled, so she shoved some pasta in her mouth and glared at him. *I'm eating. Go away.*

He didn't take the hint. "I'm not leaving until we discuss this."

She swallowed. "What's to discuss? Jasmine makes the best cakes in this town. I want the best for this resort, and she's it. You can't have everything. Grow up."

He tapped his hat on his knee. "It's about more than that, and you know it."

For a heart-stopping moment, she thought he might have seen through her. Seen how she resented him and wanted him all at once.

But how would he be able to see that? He was too spoiled to see past the nose on his face. "I have no idea what you're talking about," she said, her words frosty.

"Knock it off." The hat kept tapping against his knee, the blue of his eyes wintery. "You know about Josh and Leonora."

She blinked. She hadn't even thought of that. But of course he would. "You're a real asshole, you know? I didn't hire Jasmine away because Josh was coming back. I've been asking her for years now to come here. But thanks for thinking I'm that underhanded."

He shifted in the chair, but his expression remained hard. "It's not only the Jasmine situation. You try to undermine me every chance you get."

What a spoiled baby. "You're my competitor. Of course I'm going to compete."

He shook his head. "It's more than that. It feels personal."

"It's not. It's just business." It wasn't, but she'd never admit that. Besides, her personal dislike of him made it easier to challenge him. No need to worry about his feelings. "I think it only seems personal because you've never been denied anything. It kills you that someone's beating you at your own game."

"I don't like to lose."

Geez, the way he said that, with his blue eyes boring into her, the dark slashes of his brows drawn together—it felt like a promise. One that made her tingly.

"Get used to it." But that wasn't quite as sharp as she might have liked.

He leaned forward, a strand of his brown hair falling across his forehead. "No, I don't think I will."

They locked gazes for two more heartbeats, the atmosphere between them heavy.

She picked her fork up, dismissing him with the gesture. "If you've finished, you can go now. I'll make a note of your complaint."

He laughed, head thrown back, even teeth flashing. She supposed most people would find that laugh charming, but she was irritated. She hated being laughed at, especially by him.

"I'm not quite finished. I'd take you to dinner, but you've already handled that. Have a drink with me."

Of all the nerve... She could stab him with her fork and he'd probably take that as flirting. His ego was made of Teflon. "I don't drink," she bit out.

"You don't have to drink. Have a soda and shoot some pool with me. Gerry's has some great tables."

Gerry's was a bar in town known for being a couple's hangout. People went there on dates, not to pick people up. And being seen with her biggest competitor on a date or anything that looked like a date... Well, the perfection she was aiming for didn't include anything of the kind, not with its potential for nasty gossip.

"You're out of your mind," she snapped. "You just can't take no for an answer in anything, can you?" She stabbed her fork into the spaghetti, clogging the tines with noodles and sauce.

"You haven't even said no yet, and if you did, I'd honor that." His voice hit an intriguing register she'd never heard from him before. "And don't tell me it's not personal, not when you claw at me every time I open my mouth."

Claw at him. Huh. "Don't be so melodramatic." But her lungs were tight. "No, I won't go to Gerry's with you. Now please, leave my office. You're spoiling my appetite."

He rose then. "Are you going to be this difficult at the meeting next week?"

"What meeting?" Her mouth dropped open. "Oh crap. I almost forgot."

Now he was smugly triumphant. "That's right. It's for charity, so I hope you can bridle your dislike of me long enough to get us through this."

"I don't know. Will you be over your little tantrum about losing Jasmine?" She raised her eyebrow in challenge. Was that enough "bridling her dislike" for him?

He set his hat on his head, tugging the brim over his eyes. "No. But I know better than to fight with you in front of others."

"Look, you came into my office at nine p.m. on a Saturday to complain about a perfectly reasonable hire."

"I thought—I thought the Josh thing was behind it."

He looked so stricken for a moment she almost felt sorry for him. She cleared her throat. "Well, it wasn't. We're competitors, but I wouldn't do something like that." She shoved her fork into her pasta, her appetite suddenly gone. It was always fun at first to poke at him, but after, there was sometimes a hint of guilt. A hint that was growing into a suggestion lately. Which was weird, since he was still the spoiled ranching heir he always had been. She must be getting soft now that she was past thirty.

"I probably shouldn't have suspected that," he said in a low tone.

Oh jeez, now why did he have to do that? It was perilously close to an apology, and if he made a full one, complete with *I'm sorry*, it'd be that much harder to be mean to him.

"You shouldn't have," she agreed. "Now could you please leave? I still have work to do."

"Yeah, me too."

She raised her eyebrows. "You? I thought you spent every Saturday over at the Stampede."

His cocky grin reappeared. "Ms. Chacon, how do you know so much about my nighttime habits?"

"A lucky guess." That and the rumor mill, which was always churning with stories of Luke and his conquests.

He tipped his hat. "I'll see you Monday then. And I'm still pissed at you."

"And I'm still triumphant."

His smile went wry and slightly self-mocking, as if to say, *You got me there*. That was a smile that might just charm her if she let it.

But he was gone before it could.

She tried to get back to her dinner—she *was* starving—but any encounter with him always left her kind of shaky. She doubted he was feeling anything at all though, except maybe some lingering irritation. He'd get a new baker, and their wedding business would go on as before.

That was the problem with having Luke as a rival—no matter what she might score against him, his life was so charmed none of it ever stuck. And he certainly wasn't attracted to her.

So she was alone in this bonkers jealousy-attraction-rivalry thing. Which just made her madder.

She defiantly shoved some pasta into her mouth and chewed with a vengeance. Screw Luke Merrill. Screw him and all the emotional silt he churned up in her.

Her resort was one of the best in the state, partly thanks to her management, and it was only going to get better with her at the helm. After all, she'd just hired the best cake baker in the county fair and square. So Luke Merrill could take his concerns and shove them.

But her stomach continued to roil with more than just simple hunger.

Chapter 3

MONDAYS ALWAYS BLEW.

Luke loved his job, worked through the weekend most of the time—and still Monday was the worst day of the week. It was a universal law.

He took a sip of his third coffee of the morning and looked over the estimate to refurbish the central courtyard of the east wing of the resort. The hotel was done in the mission style with white stucco, red tile roof and floors, and a veranda stretched around the front of the building with a central courtyard enclosed in the middle. It brought the outdoors in from both sides of the resort, the public and the private.

But keeping a hotel looking this old-fashioned took a lot of updating. The fountain in that courtyard looked worn—Fee had told him it wasn't showing so well in wedding photos anymore. And he'd like to replace more of the landscaping with California native plants, but it would take the right kind of eye to get the effect he was envisioning.

If he could, he'd ask Ana who'd done the landscaping around the fountains at the casino. Whoever it was had done a beautiful job incorporating the oaks there. Too bad she'd probably tell him to get lost if he did.

Well, he could always ask around—Cabrillo was a small town. Someone would know.

His office door swung open without even a warning knock.

"What the hell happened Saturday night?" Fee demanded.

Fee—or Ofelia Schuler, if you wanted to get formal—was one of the Spencer cousins. She had their no-nonsense attitude but none of their natural reserve, which could make her a bit tough to chew at times.

But when she went into wedding-planner mode, she could charm the birds out of the trees. That and her mania for detail made her damn good at her job.

"I could ask you the same," he pointed out. He gave her a hard stare—she might be his cousin, but he was still her boss and Saturday had been a massive disaster.

At first it had been damn difficult to boss around his relatives. It was hard to be commanding with someone you'd eaten mud pies with. But Luke had slowly learned how to separate work from family even though he encountered the exact same people in both spheres.

Fee didn't blink. "The bride decided vodka shots would be an awesome idea before the wedding."

"Maybe someone should have stopped her?" *Someone like, say, the wedding planner?*

"I was busy with the groom, who was having second thoughts." Fee raised a hand to her hair, then let it fall. Her wavy brown hair was tamed in a bob that a flapper would have died for, and Luke guessed Fee didn't want to mess it up even though she was frustrated as hell. "He got into the vodka before he showed up here."

Luke wasn't an expert on marriage, but he'd guess that if you had to get drunk just to get through the wedding, maybe it might be time to rethink things.

"From now on," he said, "get someone to be your backup during weddings. Alma would be a good choice. You're on the bride. She's on the groom."

Fee nodded. "And if a bride and groom are that drunk *before* the wedding?"

"For now, we play it by ear. But all new contracts for a wedding include a cancellation clause if the parties are intoxicated before the ceremony."

The hotel business was millennia-old, but there was always something new to learn.

Fee tapped a pale pink fingernail against the office door. "I should have thought of that before."

"We've never had a bride and groom get that drunk before the wedding. Most of them at least wait until after the vows." He gestured to one of the chairs. "Sit. Your hovering is making me nervous."

Fee scoffed but sat down anyway. "We still have a wedding cake problem."

Luke pulled the rubber ball from his desk drawer and propped his booted feet up as he leaned way back in his chair. "Ah yes, that."

He began to rhythmically squeeze the ball in his fist for a count of fifteen in one hand, then a count of fifteen in the other.

The wedding cake problem brought to them by dear, sweet Ana. Ana, who had a great smile, even if she often smiled at his expense. And a noble nose, skin the color of dark honey, and the most intriguing mouth. Her upper lip was full with only the slightest bow, but it was the set of her lower lip that was truly intriguing. The set of that

27

mouth dared him to impress her. Her gaze was dark, and she could make it sharp enough to pierce a man if she wanted to—

"What are you thinking about?"

Fee's demand had Luke's eyes snapping open.

"Nothing." He switched hands. "Or not nothing—the baker we lost. Who can we hire to replace Jasmine?"

Fee twitched her pencil skirt into place. "There are a few people I had in mind—none as good though. I can't believe Ana would do that."

The accusation in Fee's voice made Luke twist in his chair, his fist tightening painfully on the rubber ball. "It's not Ana's fault."

"Then who's fault is it? Did you hear that she's going to have the resort featured in *Style* magazine? We're going to lose wedding business because of this."

He knew that, and he wasn't any happier about it. He released the ball, squeezed again. "It's the Josh situation."

Tension crept into Fee's posture, her expression going masklike. "Oh really?" She delicately cleared her throat. "Has anyone in your family considered the implications of Josh working here?"

Luke dropped his feet to the floor, his boot heels hitting the floor with a thump. "Implications?"

Fee wasn't cowed. "Yes, the *implications*. We lost a terrific baker because of this."

He couldn't believe Fee was bringing this up. "He's my brother."

Jasmine was only an employee. A damn good one and a friend he'd known his entire life—but Josh was blood.

"But he's not mine," Fee said, her voice chilled. "This ranch supports more than your immediate family."

He set his fist, wrapped tightly around the ball, on his

desk. "That's right. But you don't make the final decisions around here."

"Neither do you. I understand Benedict didn't want to hire Josh—you convinced him."

He worked his jaw as Fee stared him down. Luke knew that the Harpers would be against them when Josh returned home. He knew that at least half the town would be too. Hell, he even knew Benedict would be difficult.

But he hadn't expected his own damn family to be against Josh. Didn't blood count for anything? Or was it all the Almighty Dollar?

"I don't understand how it's any of your business," he said, now as coldly formal as she was. "Josh will be on the cattle operation. You run the weddings. I suggest you stick to that."

She stared openmouthed at him for a moment. "It's going to be like that, huh? You and Benedict and Lil screw the rest of us for Josh's sake?"

"Who's getting screwed? You're overreacting."

Accusing a Spencer of hysteria was a sure way to set them off, and Fee was no exception. She snapped out of her chair and stabbed her chest with a forefinger. "*I'm* getting screwed. I just lost my baker because of your brother, and God only knows how many weddings. This town is small and memories are long. How much more will we lose?"

"The decision was Benedict's. Josh has served his time—he's entitled to a job here, same as any other family member. If we can let Hank sit in that old house and get paid for doing fuck all, then we can pay Josh for herding cattle."

"Yeah, well, Hank didn't commit a felony. And the Harpers have a legitimate grievance here." Her stance softened, but her voice remained hard. "I'm not the only family member who's concerned. We all have an equal share in the ranch. We all have a voice in it." She went for the door and then paused. "But I'd still like to stick it to Ana."

Luke gave a short laugh. "Me too."

He'd also have liked to have never heard Fee's concerns. Now he'd be searching for signs of discontent in all the other family members. Awesome. Paranoia was always fun.

He rubbed a weary hand over his face. Man, this Monday was really exceeding his expectations of crappiness, and he hadn't even been here two hours.

Fee's fingers drummed against the doorframe. "I know he's your brother, but... just think about what I said."

He did, for a long time after Fee had left. She was wrong about him and Benedict and Lil being aligned together in favor of Josh. Benedict had never wanted to hire Josh—their eldest brother was still incredibly pissed about Josh's crime. And all of Josh's shittiness leading up to the accident.

Lil was pregnant and had her own problems to work out. She wasn't mad at Josh, not like Benedict was, but she wasn't his ally either.

Which left Luke to be his brother's support system. Luke knew all about never living up to Benedict's expectations—only a clone of Benedict had any chance of living up to his standards.

Yeah, Josh had fallen, but didn't he deserve a hand to help him up?

Luke hadn't thought his would be the only hand offered though.

The appointment reminder on his computer dinged, notifying him that he had a few more bites of manure sandwich to chew on this morning. He tossed the ball back into the drawer, pulled on his jacket, and checked his hair in the mirror by the door.

He knew it always pissed Ana off when he looked his best.

LUKE WAS ALREADY WAITING outside the Assistance League when Ana pulled up.

He was propped against the dingy tan stucco wall. His arms were crossed over his impressive chest, one booted foot hooked over the other, and his black Stetson hid his face.

How long had it taken him to arrange himself just so? Or had he practiced so much it was second nature? Arrogant ass.

"Mr. Merrill." It was convenient that the pronunciation of his name let her lip curl naturally.

"You can call me Luke." As lazy as a summer Sunday afternoon. "You never showed up at Gerry's on Saturday."

"Please. You never showed up there either." He'd probably headed straight to the Stampede after that and spent the night with... well, with whatever girl he'd managed to sweet-talk into his bed. Although, given his looks and charm, that probably left a lot of candidates.

Thank God Ana wasn't one of them. They both knew his invitation on Saturday was only a joke. They didn't even like each other.

"Did too." He tipped his hat back, his navy-blue eyes dark in the shadows covering his face. "Just ask Gerry. Spent hours nursing a whiskey and soda, waiting all by my lonesome for you."

Oh God, did this tired crap really work? "You've never spent a single Saturday night all by your lonesome," she hissed.

"Haven't I?" He actually managed to sound sad. Unbelievable.

She cocked her head. "You know, you're pretty chipper for someone who's just lost a valuable part of his wedding business."

"And you're pretty pissed for someone who just gained one."

"I'm not pissed." She pasted on a wide grin. "See? Happy as a clam."

"I never understood that phrase. What's so happy about a clam?"

She stared at him. "That's... you're inane."

He snapped his fingers. "Good two-dollar word."

"College must have been *so* difficult." She snapped her fingers back. "Oh no, I forgot, you were at Santa Barbara where the only major is partying."

"Don't blame me because you went to the most joyless UC of all—San Diego. Tell me, how were all those Friday nights spent studying O-Chem in the library?"

"Great, because they got me into Cornell for grad school."

"I went to Cornell too. And I had a great time." He waggled his eyebrows.

He had, which had infuriated her. She'd worked so hard, had no social life—and he had been living it up. It only made her that much more determined to be a workaholic, to prove she deserved her education and he didn't.

"I don't want to talk about college." She grabbed the door and wrenched it open before he could say anything else. But he caught the metal frame as it swung toward him and held it for her.

"After you," he drawled.

She sent him a look of fiery loathing and then gave

herself a shake. Game time. She had to stop sniping at him. She put on a wide smile as they approached the receptionist. "Mary, how nice to see you. How are you?"

"I'm just fine." Mary beamed back at them.

"You look wonderful." Luke gave Mary a wink.

Ana's fingers twitched as she suppressed the urge to smack him in the gut. He just had to flirt with everyone, didn't he?

Mary gave an airy laugh, shushing him with a happy wave of her hand. "Oh, Luke. I'm old enough to be your mother."

"That won't stop him," Ana said, all cheery tartness.

He gave Ana a slow, assessing look, his jaw working as he did. "Nope. I'm unstoppable."

Okay, now she was really going to have to work at not smacking him.

Mary clucked besottedly at Luke. "I'll have to tell your mother about you, young man. Go on—Shelly's waiting for you in her office."

"Thank you." Luke tossed Mary another wink, and her cheeks went pink.

They marched together down the hall, Luke still wearing a grin. He caught her eye and lifted an eyebrow as if daring her to say something.

"You are—" But Ana couldn't finish that, because Shelly was already coming out of her office.

"Come in, come in. I'm so happy you could make it!"

Shelly's office was done in floral chintz and white wicker, and the scent of potpourri was thick in the air. It looked more like a teashop than an office. Ana took one of the upholstered chairs, carefully moving it away from the other before sitting down.

Luke sent her a look as she did, before taking his own

chair.

"Coffee?" Shelly asked.

"Yes, please," they said in unison. Ana made sure not to catch Luke's eye.

"We've got donuts in the break room too."

"No, thank you."

Okay, their echo chamber act had to end. Ana sent him a glare this time.

He shrugged and patted his belly, which was indecently flat. "Watching my figure."

Ana bet he was, the vain, pigheaded... She forced her fingers to spread wide on her thighs and prayed he'd stop being irritating for just five minutes.

Shelly waved her hand at that. "Oh, you. Are you both comfy? I've got a pot of coffee brewing in here already."

Coffee was passed around, thanks were said, and the meeting began.

"Again, I want to thank you two and the ranch and the casino for sponsoring this obstacle run," Shelly said, taking a sip from a thin-walled cup with a gilded rim. "We should be able to raise enough money to staff the tutor program at the youth center next school year."

"Always happy to help," Luke said.

"This is our home," Ana said. "It's our duty and pleasure to give back." That at least was one thing she and Luke could agree on.

"How's the food-pantry program going?" Luke asked.

Shelly set her cup in the saucer, the better to beam at Luke. "Wonderfully, thanks to your donation."

"And how is the winter-jacket program for the homeless?" Ana asked.

"Oh, that was such a blessing to get your donation when we did." Now Ana got a beaming smile.

Ana felt a little gross parading that donation in front of Luke. But he'd started the one-upmanship. And then she felt even worse for thinking that. He really brought out the worst in her.

"Well, we do appreciate it," Shelly said. "All of it. And now you're helping with our race! This obstacle race will be quite the thing. Five miles of dangerous obstacles for our racers to overcome—ropes and walls and barbed wire and even a wall of fire." She gave a theatrical shiver. "I can hardly believe the two of you are brave enough to do it."

They swung on each other. "You're doing the race?"

Again with the echoing. At least this time he actually looked pissed. Just like she was.

"Of course I am," she said. She was a marathoner—what was five miles on a Saturday morning?

"And of course I'm running it too." His smile was entirely missing his usual charm.

She imagined he was flexing as hard he could under his clothes. He was likely counting on all those thick muscles to take him easily across the course. She knew his type—he thought those weights he lifted meant he could run too.

Oh, she was going to beat him. It would be so delicious to make him eat her dust. There was no way he was faster than her. He'd fold after the first mile. Probably had no idea about pacing.

"Well, good." She smiled evilly at him. "That will be fun. A little friendly competition."

His raised brow told her he knew it would be no such thing.

Shelly clapped her hands, thankfully too sweet herself to sense the undercurrents running between Ana and Luke. "Do you know what would be wonderful?"

Before Shelly could finish, Ana already knew it would be

nothing of the sort, not if Luke was involved.

"If you two went in as a team in the race," Shelly announced as if it was the greatest idea ever.

Ana searched for a polite way to say *hell no*. She was going to beat Luke, not work with him. A poor impulse for a charity race, but Ana didn't need to tell Shelly her intentions. She only had to wriggle her way out of this situation.

Ana pulled her expression into something reluctant and apologetic. "I don't—"

"I think it sounds great."

Ana turned on Luke, trying not to glare. "Really?" It was strangled as she attempted to keep the disbelief out of her tone. What the hell did he think he was doing?

"Yeah." A smirk played at the corners of his mouth. "Think of it, the two of us running together to raise funds for a worthy cause. Looks better than the two of us running against each other."

He was right, which made him an asshole.

And he knew she didn't want to—hell, he liked her as much as she did him—which *really* made him an asshole.

She stared at him. She couldn't say no—she'd look like the bad guy. But she really, really didn't want to say yes. It would break her jaw to get that word out.

"What do you think, Ana?"

It was the uncertainty in Shelly's voice that cracked open Ana's mouth. This run would bring in much-needed money. Ana couldn't ruin that with her own messed-up anger at Luke Merrill.

She was the face of her people and the resort here. She needed to remember that and live up to that obligation.

"Sure." She managed to sound as if she really meant it. "I think it sounds..." She looked at Luke, who watching her with a heavy-lidded expression. "Great. Just great."

Chapter 4

MONDAYS REALLY WERE THE WORST.

Ana drove back to her office, singing death metal at the top of her lungs to work out her frustration. How had she gotten stuck in that trap? And why had Luke gone along with it? She knew he didn't like her any more than she did him, for all his silly invitations to romantic bars to play pool.

She pulled into her usual spot at the resort, switched off the engine, but kept the music going, drumming her fingers in time on the steering wheel. She had to get her head together before she went back inside since she had the meeting with the consultant next.

That might also suck eggs, but she had to make sure she didn't enter the meeting girded for battle. That was the surest way to have it head south. She had to be open-minded. Receptive. And remember that this was all for the betterment of the resort.

She yanked her keys out of the ignition and the music went silent. Her fingers went still on the wheel. And finally her emotions went still—at least on the surface. She was going to need a really long run tonight to work all this out of her body.

Ana grabbed her tote and plastered a smile on her face. Always be smiling for the guests: that was rule number one.

She kept the smile on her face right up until she reached the sanctuary of her office, letting it die a natural death once she saw her desk. But when she walked in, she'd wished she'd left it on.

There, sitting in a chair and scribbling madly on a notepad, was a blond woman in her midtwenties, slim as a reed and dressed like a model.

This must be Chelsea.

Ana wasn't insecure—she was an average size, found clothes that suited her and her job well enough, and she considered her body to be awesome since it carried her on her runs so beautifully.

But next to this woman who was almost the ideal standard of beauty, the one the magazines tried to sell womankind every day, Ana felt out of place. Which was stupid, because this was her office. Her domain.

"Can I help you?" The very neutrality of the question let the woman know Ana was not happy about this.

"Oh." The woman held out her hand. "I'm Chelsea. Sorry, I'm a little early."

She was more than twenty minutes early. Ana took her hand, which was cold and bony.

"No problem. Sorry I wasn't here to meet you, but as I said in my e-mail, I had a prior commitment." Ana took up her seat behind her desk, already feeling more in control with that symbol of her authority between them.

"No worries. I was able to write up some of my notes." Chelsea's smile revealed two rows of perfect white teeth. Some dentist had no doubt gone on a nice vacation on that smile. "Do you mind if we start with what you had today? What was it for?"

"A charity run the resort is sponsoring. I'll be running in it as well."

"Hmm." Chelsea let the end of her pen hover over her lips. "I'm curious why you would be handling this rather than someone from Public Relations."

"Well, I've known Shelly, the Assistance League director, for some time now. We have a relationship. And it's important that members of the tribe be involved in our outreach efforts." Ana was proud of how even her voice was. There was no way Chelsea could argue with that.

"Yes, I can see that, but still... It's not part of your duties. Do you feel that your work in running the resort is impacted by these *extracurricular* activities?"

"No," Ana said flatly. "It isn't. Has someone been complaining?"

Chelsea flashed her ten-thousand-dollar smile. "Oh no. I'm only trying to get a handle on what you do here. Remember, I'm here to make things more efficient."

Ana flashed her ten-dollar smile, the one that only toothpaste, regular flossing, and semiannual dental visits had gone into. "Right."

Chelsea glanced at her notepad. "So, you're also running the race?"

"Yes."

"And what is the goal of that? Why does the resort need a representative actually in the race?"

To beat Luke Merrill. Yeah, that wasn't the right answer, even if it was totally untrue now that they'd been yoked together in an unholy union.

"Cabrillo is a small town. I've lived here my entire life. People know me, and I know them. When they see me representing the resort, it brings home the fact that this resort is an integral part of the community. And that we do our part to build that community."

That was an awesome answer, if Ana did say so herself.

"I see." The pen hovered over Chelsea's lips, never once touching them. "We can revisit the charity issue later. Let's move on to your other duties."

Revisit? Ana didn't like the sound of that. But she had to be open-minded. Receptive. "Sure," she chirped. "What do you want to know?"

THERE WAS nothing like a long run.

People who didn't run just didn't understand. It wasn't about pain or going from point A to B or burning calories. It was about finding that sweet rhythm when her legs moved without thought, without effort, her body and mind clear and floating as she ate up the miles. After Ana's pisser of a day, she needed that.

She was on mile eight with four more to go, on a trail that started on the reservation and wound through the edge of the valley, skirting the creek at points. The evening was soft all over, the only harshness the pull of the breath through her lungs. The sun was inching toward the mountains, painting the clouds and horizon in watercolors as it did.

A mourning dove called from a nearby tree, a whistling sort of coo that had always felt like a gentle hello to Ana. She'd passed a covey of quail earlier, the male watching her warily as she ran past his little family.

Her dog, Seth, was running at her heels. Seth wasn't any kind of breed that she could tell—he was a mutt through and through. She'd found him wandering a back road several years ago, collarless, filthy, and starved. He'd seen her and sat right down at her feet as if to say, *I've been looking for you. What took you so long?*

He had no tags, no microchip, had obviously been living rough for a while, and after a month of no responses to her *Found Dog* ads, she accepted that he was hers. He wasn't the friendliest pup—she got a few tail wags when she got home but not much else—but he loved to run as much as she did, keeping her company as they pounded out the miles together.

Running was her sacred time, and the mountains were her sacred space.

She was deep in her rhythm, nothing much floating through her mind, when Seth gave a short growl, the hair on his nape rising. Ana slowed and peered up ahead. She knew to listen to Seth when he gave a warning.

Up ahead, a coyote trotted across the trail, too far away to be any threat. Ana was always amazed at how they could look so much like dogs but move so much like cats.

Once the coyote had disappeared into the chaparral, she picked up her pace again. The wind sent thick fingers through her hair, cooled the sweat on her skin with its breath, filled her lungs with its force, and surrounded all of her like a lover would. She spread her fingers wide in a futile attempt to gather it in her hands, but it slipped through as if to tease her.

She closed her hands and put on a burst of speed, just for the pure joy of it.

Oh no, this obstacle run would be no problem at all, not for someone who loved to run like she did. She'd only have to worry about Luke keeping up. She frowned into the sunset. Did he even run? She ought to send him an e-mail. Maybe lay out a training plan.

No, she wouldn't do that. He could figure it out on his own. Limiting contact with him was probably best. She got stupid when he was involved.

Another mile went down. Just three more and then she'd have to return to the real world. She had baby duty tonight. Which was fine, but she wanted to get her head together before she tackled that.

She caught sight of a figure about half a mile up the road, coming toward her. Another jogger. A man.

Seth immediately started barking, warning the oncoming man to stay away.

The jogger slowed for half a heartbeat and then accelerated toward her.

Her breath caught and she almost stumbled. *Son of a bitch*.

This trail was usually deserted, and anyone she did meet was even less interested in interacting than she was. They didn't *charge* at lone women, that was for sure. She had Seth, but would that be enough to convince this man to move on?

Then she realized who it was and stopped dead.

Luke Merrill, wearing a blue workout tank and black athletic shorts, was running toward her. On *her* route. Well, she didn't have to be afraid anymore. Just annoyed.

"Kill, Seth," she ordered under her breath.

Seth gave her a puzzled look since she'd never taught him that command. Then he took up barking again.

"It's all right," she told the dog. "He's..."

Not a friend, that was certain. A rival? That was better, but still not quite right. "He's okay," she finished grudgingly.

Seth quieted down but stayed close by. As Luke pulled to a stop himself, Seth watched warily. Because he was a dog with impeccable taste, he didn't even wag hello. She'd have to give him an extra treat tonight.

"Come here often?" Luke asked, his breathing accelerated. He set his hands on his hips, all of him glowing with exertion.

She pulled her braid over her shoulder and played with the ends. "All the time. But you don't."

He raised his hands. "It's a public trail."

True. But she still didn't want him on it. "How convenient we met. It's almost magical."

Almost as if he'd meant to run into her out here. Devious bastard.

He grinned. "Isn't it? Nice dog, by the way." His smile died. "We need to talk."

"About what?"

You didn't say that to someone unless you were in a relationship, and they most certainly were *not*.

"Our training plan."

"*Our* training plan? We're only running it together, not training." She tossed her braid over her shoulder. "I don't need a training plan. It's only five miles." She wasn't some hobby jogger here. He ought to be worried about himself, not her.

"Five miles filled with obstacles we'll have to get over and through." He shook out his shoulders, no doubt the better to show off his pecs. "Do you even lift?"

"Do you even run?"

"I'm here, aren't I?"

She snorted. One jog did not a runner make. "How about you do your thing and I'll do mine? And pick a different route. This one is mine." And he damn well knew it, which was why he was here.

He crossed his arms. "Why do you hate me?"

What an arrogant, conceited ass. "Who says I hate you? Just because I'm not bowled over by your wealth, your ranch, or your charm doesn't mean I hate you." She crossed her own arms, mimicking his stance. "Maybe I'm just not that into you. But your ego translates indifference into hate."

He irritated her, he infuriated her, and yes, she enjoyed beating him when she could, but that wasn't hate. Not even close. She'd have to care more about him for it to be hate. Which she didn't.

He tilted his head. "You think I'm charming?"

When he'd said he was unstoppable, he wasn't kidding. "No, I don't," she said. "Which is my entire point."

"I don't know. Sometimes, when you look at me, it feels deeper than that." His voice shifted registers. "It feels personal. Targeted."

Now she felt targeted, because... Well, she didn't like him was all. It wasn't anything deeper. "I don't look at you."

He shook his head. "Okay, Ana."

"Okay, *Luke*."

"Now see, every time I open my mouth, you react like I'm attacking you."

She did not. "You were needling me!" She curled her hands into fists and growled with frustration. God, why did he always bring out the worst in her? "Look, it's only a charity race. As long as we survive..." She shrugged. Actually, only as long as *she* survived—and she wasn't worried about that a bit.

He gave her an assessing look. "That's not the Ana Chacon I know. You don't want to win?"

Well of course she did. But it was for charity—she couldn't admit that. Besides, the thought of winning had been more enjoyable when it would have been him she was beating. Crossing the finishing line *with* him, even if they were first, held less appeal.

"That's not the point of all this," she said, raising her nose a smug inch.

"Well, I'm less noble than you are." His tone said he knew perfectly well she was lying. "We should come up with a strategy to train—and to win. You're not stupid; you know running alone won't cut it."

"Wow, thank you." The compliments just kept on coming from him. His reputation as charming really was hard earned. "*Not stupid*—I'll have that engraved on a plaque and hang it in my office. News flash, since maybe you didn't realize, but your dudebro meathead lifting routine won't cut it either."

"'Dudebro meathead.' Why, Miss Chacon," he drawled, "you'll turn my head. I already know that, which is why we should train together. You know running, and I know strength training. Together we'll be unstoppable."

Unstoppable. She liked that bit. The together part, not so much.

"Think of how great the publicity would be for the both of us," he went on. "Front page of the local section, the two of us crossing the finish line together."

That was a nice image to picture. And it would be free media coverage. "It would be pretty great."

"Plus you owe me for stealing my baker."

Of all the— "You know, I almost said yes until you said that."

"Ana." He caught at her arm—her wrist really, and just the edge.

It was like touching a downed power line. Her skin felt as if it might lift from her bones.

She'd known him since high school, but he'd never once

touched her before. Not even close. He probably shouldn't ever do it again, considering her response.

She yanked her arm away and rubbed at her wrist, trying not to gasp as her lungs refilled.

"Holy shit." It was less than even a whisper from him as his eyes widened. "Holy shit."

Jesus, he had felt it too? That hadn't been only her brain going apeshit there? She kept rubbing at her wrist, trying to find some explanation.

"What was that?" he asked.

"Probably just static electricity." It had to be. Or maybe their irritation with each other had ignited or something.

"The hell it was." He reached for her hand. "Let's try that again."

She pulled her arm out of his reach and took two steps back. Seth growled.

Yeah, she didn't need another shock like that. Her heart might stop the next time.

He looked at her for a moment, his eyes going an abashed shade of blue. "I'm sorry," he said. "I shouldn't have done that."

She didn't let go of her arm. "No, you shouldn't have."

"I won't do it again."

He'd spent well over a decade knowing her and not touching her—she believed him. "Okay." She gave her wrist one last rub and then released her arm. It was already feeling more normal.

He rubbed his neck in a gesture so uncertain, so unresolved, she hardly recognized him. "Forget I ever said anything about training together. You're right—it's a bad idea. I'll see you the day of the race and we'll... figure out something. Don't worry, I'll stay off your route."

He turned around and began to jog away, his calves straining as his legs pumped.

She blinked after him, putting a hand to Seth's neck as she pondered what Luke had said.

Unstoppable. Front page. Crossing the finish line first.

"Wait."

He stopped instantly, turning to give her a questioning glance.

"I want to win," she said.

There. It sounded just as bad as she'd thought it would, but she'd admitted it.

"I want to too." He sent her a sheepish smile.

Well, weren't they a pair?

She tilted her head and studied him with a narrow gaze. Sheepish, apologetic, uncertain—who was this Luke Merrill? She could almost like this version of him.

She lifted her chin. Not only did she want to win, she wanted that story in the paper Luke had been talking about. *See,* she could tell Chelsea Thomas, *personal community outreach efforts* are *worth it!* And she'd prove to her boss that she wasn't taking on too much. Ana could do it all and she would. Including winning this race.

"So," she asked, "how are we going to win this? Because I want a half-page picture of us in the paper the morning after."

His grin came on slow but was devastating all the same. "We run a few days a week, which you're in charge of."

"I can handle that." Some kind of modified 10K plan ought to work, with the fact that they'd have obstacles involved worked in somehow. The Internet would provide as it always did.

"Will we run together?"

There was an intrigued, teasing hook in his question. She ignored the pull of it.

"Yes. So I can check your form and pacing. What's your part then?"

"Lifting the other days of the week. Can you do a pull-up?"

Her cheeks went hot. "Uh, no." Was that something regular people were expected to do? That was only a torment from high school gym, right?

"Don't worry, we'll get you there." He sounded very certain. "Do you do any kind of weights?"

"I do yoga sometimes." Which wasn't exactly *weights* but was more than running.

"So do I."

God, the thought of this bear of a man coming into a studio with a mat under his arm, twisting that body into a pretzel for the next hour...

"Okay." She wanted to fan her cheeks, but that would be a dead giveaway. "Should we do that at your gym or mine? I can get you a guest pass or something, I'm sure."

He laughed. "I work out at home."

She tensed. His house? "Oh."

"Someone's always there," he assured her. "We won't really be alone."

She would have been less worried about that before he'd touched her. Something weird had occurred, and she didn't want to repeat it even by chance. Still, he'd promised it wouldn't happen again.

"I was more commenting on the fact that you have an entire home gym," she said.

"Only way to work out." Such a meathead answer. He probably also had a weight belt and carried around a gallon jug of water, grunting like a woman in labor as he did his sets.

Well, she'd find out, wouldn't she?

"Fine," she said. "We run together, we lift together, and do our own thing for yoga." She drew the line at watching him do contortions. "What time do you want to meet for sessions?"

"I usually work out first thing in the morning."

She shook her head. "I can't. I've got baby duty in the mornings." And tonight too, which was why she ought to be sending him on his way.

"Baby duty?" He raised an eyebrow and looked pointedly at her stomach.

"Not my baby. My sister's." She didn't feel like explaining further, and it wasn't any of his business anyway.

"Okay. How about after work?"

"I work late," she warned.

"So do I. After dinner then?"

"We are not eating dinner together."

"I wouldn't dream of it."

"Fine." She felt a little guilty about being so snappy about dinner, so she said, "You can finish my last three miles with me."

His mouth twitched. "I'd be happy to."

Running with someone else was strange. She hardly ever did it since part of the appeal was the solitude. She had Seth, but that was different. Seth didn't ask for conversation.

But neither did Luke, to her surprise. He wasn't exactly a graceful runner—he had too much muscle for that—but he was game. He'd probably never be a marathoner, but by the time the race came around, she'd have turned him into a decent runner.

And it sounded like he was going to get her to do a pull-up. She'd never before thought of doing one, but since he'd raised the possibility, she wanted to. Really, really badly. Why hadn't she ever thought to do pull-ups?

Probably because you didn't need to do a pull-up to run.

For all that Luke was quiet as he ran, she couldn't slip back into her headspace. She couldn't concentrate on the wind or the mountains or the birdcalls with him by her side —he kept pulling her attention toward him. Not on purpose, but it still unsettled her.

The last three miles ended quickly enough even though she slowed her pace for his benefit. And he never had tried to talk.

When they got to her truck, she opened the door for Seth to hop inside. Then she turned to Luke.

"We start tomorrow?"

He was sweating, all of him flushed from the exercise. She couldn't help but stare at his legs. And his arms. And his chest. Normally he was in Wranglers and a button-down, so this was... novel. A very muscly, hairy, sweaty sort of novel.

She swallowed hard. It was no big deal, seeing him like this. She'd be seeing this often as they trained together, and soon enough it *would* be no big deal.

Right.

"Yep, tomorrow evening." He quirked an eyebrow as if he knew she'd been checking him out. "See you then."

He jogged away as if he hadn't a care in the world.

Ana wasn't quite so sanguine as she got into her truck to head out to baby duty.

Chapter 5

ANA RAN HER FINGER DOWN the page of the textbook, trying to find a suitable question. Ah, that one would work. "What is the name of the mechanism by which DNA is copied?"

Her sister, Sara, frowned as she took up a spoonful of pureed peas and pushed it into her daughter Lorelei's mouth. "Oh, I know this," she muttered.

Lorelei spit the peas back out, a thick stream of green rolling down her chin like a second tongue.

"Baby girl, that is so gross," Sara said, scraping it off the baby's chin and shoving it back into her mouth. "Semiconservative replication!" she announced with triumph.

"That's right." Ana looked at her own meal with less enthusiasm than before. Lorelei was cute, but her eating habits not so much. Ana shifted her elbows on the kitchen table and began to search through the textbook for another fact to quiz Sara on. "You know," she said, "cramming the night before isn't supposed to help much."

"Maybe not, but you know how I am. Actually, could you

watch Lori tonight for a little bit? I know you were up with her last night and I hate to ask you again—"

"I can't. I've got a… a meeting." Damn. Ana hated letting Sara down, but she couldn't cancel on Luke. "Maybe Mom?"

"Mom's got a council meeting. They're supposed to be voting on the final proposal for the new school." She shoved more peas into Lori's mouth, and the baby just as quickly spit them back out.

"I don't think she likes those," Ana said.

"She's not even a year old. She doesn't know what she likes." Sara sighed. "It's okay if you're busy. I'll figure something out."

There wasn't even a hint of accusation in her voice, which only made Ana's guilt that much thornier. Sara's husband, Joe, was deployed, and Sara was working on her associate's degree. If not for Ana and their mom, she'd be on her own.

"If I could cancel, I would," Ana offered lamely. She'd given that same line to Sara last week when her sister had needed to write an essay and Ana'd had to finish up some paperwork that was due in the morning. She couldn't work and watch the baby—Lori could climb like a champ. One minute you'd leave her playing with her stuffed dog, the next she'd be using the bookshelf as a ladder. It was nerve-racking. "Maybe Luisa?"

"No, Luisa's going to the council meeting too." Sara waved off Ana's suggestion with the hand holding the spoon, wafting the smell toward Ana's nose. Ugh. No wonder Lori kept spitting it out. "Don't worry about it."

Easier said than done. And Ana had wanted to go to this council meeting—they'd been working for a school of their own for so long—but she'd completely forgotten about it when she'd scheduled with Luke. She never used to do that;

she'd have to start double-checking the calendar on her phone before she committed to things.

Oh well. If everything went to plan—and Ana kept pushing the resort to new heights—Lori would go to that school. A school run by and for their people. That was worth Ana missing out on council meetings and parties and a social life.

Their mother came into the kitchen then. Her hair was pulled back over her ears, the gray swiped through it as if by a paintbrush. She wore a long skirt and blouse, with heavy silver jewelry at her neck and ears.

Ana never failed to be moved by the sight of her mother like this. Consuelo Chacon was everything Ana hoped to be someday—respected, wise, and influential. Someone who'd never double schedule a workout during a council meeting.

"Did you eat, Mom?" Ana asked.

"A little something before I leave would be nice."

Ana dished up some chili from the pot on the stove and then cut a nice thick slab of warm cornbread, setting it on the edge of the flared bowl. When she set the meal before her mother, Consuelo placed her hand against Ana's cheek. "Thank you, mija."

Ana leaned into her mother's touch for a moment, the palm warm and gently callused, the rings on her fingers cool and smooth. With a smile, she pulled away to let her mother eat.

"I'll be late tonight," Mom warned. "Ken wants to discuss some water-use issues after the meeting."

Sara raised an eyebrow. "Oh, is that what the kids are calling it these days? 'Water-use issues?'"

Their mother laughed. "No, he really does. But if he were to invite me for dinner later this week, then no, we won't be talking about water use then."

Ken was a good guy, and Ana was happy for her mom. When her father had his fatal heart attack right before Ana started her senior year of high school, her mother had gone on as before, mostly because she'd had to. And she'd done a tremendous job of keeping their family intact and safe.

But there had been an odd note of suspension in her mother's personality after, which was only now slowly dissolving.

"Tell Ken I said hi." Ana winked. "And I promise not to spy on you if you have dinner at the resort."

The clock on the oven caught her eye then. "Sh— Crap. I've got to get going."

"Where are you off to?" Mom asked.

Sara gave Ana a look.

Ana took a deep breath. What she was doing with Luke wasn't scandalous—but her mother probably remembered all the times in high school Ana had ranted about him. "Um, remember that charity race? For the Assistance League?"

"Sure." Her mother blew on a spoonful of chili, steam curling around her. "It's wonderful that you're doing that."

"Well, Luke Merrill is doing it too, and Shelly thought it would be nice if we ran as a team."

Her mother's spoon dropped back into the bowl. "Oh." She set a hand to her cheek, tilting her head as she studied Ana. "You don't think that will look odd? Him being who he is?"

Ana waved a hand. "It's purely a business thing. You know, the two resorts can come together to help the community and all that."

Her mother took up her spoon again. "Well, don't forget that he's still your competitor. Watch what you say around him. We don't need outsiders knowing our business."

"I know." Ana was planning to keep him at arm's length,

both personally and physically. Especially since her brain seemed to short-circuit when he touched her.

"I figured you did." Her mother gave her a fond smile. "But a reminder wouldn't hurt."

Sara twirled the baby spoon between her fingers. "I'm curious. You used to say he was the most arrogant, underserving jerk you'd ever met. And now you're doing this with him?"

Ana sighed. Now that her mother had established Ana wasn't crossing any lines with Luke, the teasing would begin.

"That was high school. Things are different now," Ana insisted. Sure, she disliked him intensely, but it was a professional dislike, not teenaged rage.

"If you say so," Sara said, sarcasm gilding the words.

Her mother frowned. "I know he manages the other resort, but I don't know this boy." Her mother meant like she'd *know* someone from the reservation. "What has he done to you?"

Oh geez. "He hasn't done anything to me. He's just... annoying."

That didn't do a thing to erase her mother's skepticism. "I don't know. Perhaps you shouldn't be alone with him if he's so terrible."

"He's not that kind of terrible. It's purely a business thing, this stuff between us. Anyway," Ana said loudly, trying to bring the conversation back on track. "Luke and I are training together. We want to win."

"That sounds more like you," Sara said. "The wanting to win part."

Her mother nodded. "I sometimes worry about how driven you are."

Not this again. First Linda telling her to slow down and now Mom too?

"I've got to feed before I leave," she said, cutting off the discussion. She planted a kiss on Lori's soft black hair, avoiding the pea-smeared fists milling in the air, and slipped outside.

Dark was falling fast, the remaining light chasing after the sun as it disappeared. Seth roused himself from the back deck, following as she made her way down the red paving-stone path to the barn. Tex nickered a greeting as she approached. She gave him a pat in return before tossing him a flake of alfalfa. Tex was too old and lame to be ridden anymore, but she'd learned to ride on him, so he'd more than earned his retirement. She kept resolving to find a new horse, one she could take out on the trails here, but she never could find the time.

The two nanny goats, Mabel and Hazel, came up for their dinner too. Ana shook out some goat pellets into their buckets and then checked everyone's water. Bruiser, the one-eyed barn cat, came out to wind around her legs and try to trip her as she did. Ana dumped some wet food into his bowl to keep him from trying to break her neck and then checked on the chickens. They'd already roosted for the night, tucked up on their perches like stately matrons from an oil painting.

She trudged back up to the deck to feed Seth and get him settled for the night. She'd tried to keep him in the house at night—she didn't want him to tangle with any coyotes or, God forbid, mountain lions—but he'd been so unhappy he'd howled at the door all night. For all that he was her dog, he was still independent.

She gave him two scoops of the pricey dog food—yeah, he was spoiled, so what?—then fluffed his bed. Unlike most dogs, he didn't dive head first into his bowl. Instead, he stared at her with his deep brown eyes as if asking her for something.

"I never really hated him," she told the dog. "He just made me so mad. And still does."

Seth simply kept staring.

"It'll be perfectly fine tonight," she assured him. "We're only working out. Yeah, we'll be sweaty together, but not that kind of sweaty together."

The dog gave a long-suffering canine sigh, then finally turned to his food bowl.

"Well, I don't care if you believe me," Ana said. "Nothing at all is going to happen."

Seth never looked up from his food, clearly unconvinced.

LUKE LINED up the nail and then pounded it home. He ran a hand across it, making certain it was flush. Yeah, that would do. Hang some drywall, do some painting, and this apartment over the garage would be brand-spanking-new. Or almost new.

"He's not gonna be home for another six months."

Luke let the hammer slip down in his grasp and turned to face Benedict, who'd appeared in the doorway. "I want it to be ready in time."

His shoulders came up toward his ears, his fist tightening on the hammer, all of him preparing for Benedict to start sniping.

His older brother looked around, his hands on his hips. "Huh."

Benedict was only a few years older than Luke, but

sometimes it seemed more like a decade. Perhaps it had something to do with the lines around Benedict's eyes and the ones chiseled into his forehead, or the set of his shoulders, as if he were always carrying some heavy weight.

Or perhaps it had something to do with Benedict behaving as if he'd been born old.

Had this been any other project, Benedict would have grabbed a tool and jumped in to help. Or take over.

Not for this one.

Benedict couldn't forbid Josh from living in the Big House on the ranch. He might run the family enterprises, but the house was Luke and Lil's domain, Benedict having retreated to the pool house some years ago. Now that Benedict and Pilar had gotten together, he was probably going to find a more permanent place.

Luke wasn't going anywhere though, and he meant to make sure there was a place for Josh when he came home.

He turned back to the plywood sheet he was hanging and selected another nail. "Was there something you wanted?"

Benedict didn't say anything for long moments. "You're pissed at me."

It was more complicated than that. Nothing so simple as anger churned in Luke's gut when he looked at his eldest brother—it was a complicated mix that had been brewing for years.

Resentment made up the biggest part. And then guilt. And of course love.

"I'm not pissed." He slammed the hammer against the nail, the head slipping as it hit, bending the nail into uselessness. Son of a bitch.

Luke worked on prying it out as Benedict went on behind him.

"Look, I only... I want us all to be ready if Josh fucks up again. You seem to think he's been reborn in prison, and maybe he has... but we need to be prepared if he hasn't."

That was too fucking much. "No, you want to set him up to fail. You wouldn't even have given him a job if I hadn't begged for it. You'd forbid him from this house if you could. You'd cast him out of this family if it were up to you." His grip tightened on the hammer, his bicep flexing hard as he wrestled with the nail. "But it ain't up to you, and that kills you."

"Luke, look at me."

Benedict never could leave well enough alone. He couldn't simply seek Luke out to give him a lecture—no, Luke had to look him in the eye as he did. Benedict was such an asshole sometimes.

When Luke turned, Benedict's expression was a mix of fury and sadness. "I don't want him to fail. He's my brother, same as yours. But I ain't in your position, Luke. I've got to protect this entire family and all our holdings. We've got thousands of people relying on the family business. Relying on me to steer that business. And if I've got to protect their interests even against my own brother's... then that's what I'll do."

"Have you been talking to Fee?" Luke demanded.

Benedict hooked his thumbs into his pockets and rocked on his heels. "She's spoken to me, yes. Along with other family members. I'm the head of the business. It's my job to listen and react to their concerns."

What a bullshit corporate answer. This was their brother they were talking about.

"So everyone's against Josh then? Before he's even out." Luke shook his head.

"Don't make it about that." Benedict jabbed a finger at him. "I gave him a job, didn't I?"

"After I begged," Luke said. Benedict better not pretend that was some act of charity on his part.

Benedict rubbed hard at his forehead, and suddenly his brother looked so, so tired. Weary and tipping toward exhaustion. "I can't only think about Josh here. There's more at stake."

Luke wasn't going to be swayed by this act of Benedict's. His brother had never been tired a day in his life. "Well, I *can* think about Josh. It seems like I'm the only one who will. And if that puts us at odds..." He swallowed hard and took his stand. "We'll be at odds."

Benedict's expression went stark. "It doesn't have to be like that between us. Josh isn't even here yet."

"But I'll be ready when he is. Ready to help him start a new life. Reborn." Maybe nobody else believed in Josh, but Luke would. He'd be the link back to this family, to the real world, for Josh. He wasn't like Benedict; he wouldn't abandon his brother for *business*.

"If that's how you feel then," Benedict said with soft resignation.

A long silence pulsed between them, Luke still holding tight to the hammer as Benedict studied the unfinished floor.

The moment dissolved when Benedict asked, "What's going on with Lil and Silva? He's not here and she's... depressed."

Now there was something they could agree on—their dislike of the bull rider who'd knocked up their sister.

"I don't know. She hasn't said anything to me about it. Maybe she kicked him out." Luke certainly hoped so. Lil had money and a supportive family—she didn't need some asshole she barely knew barging into her life, even if he was the father of her baby.

"I heard he was kicked off the tour."

Luke reared back. "What? Shit, I never heard that. So where is he now?"

"I don't know. But with the kid coming, it's better they get along." Although Benedict sounded as grudging as Luke felt.

They exchanged a look filled with silent understanding. Well, at least they were agreed on kicking Silva's ass if he put a toe out of line. Male bonding through violence—there was nothing like it.

Maybe once Josh was here they could all unite together in brotherly outrage against Silva. That was one possible solution. Problem was, Josh wouldn't be home for another six months.

Speaking of that— "Lil and I are gonna visit Josh this weekend. I'll ask her about it then."

Benedict didn't offer to go with them, didn't ask Luke to take a message... nothing. Not that Luke had expected anything else.

So he decided to push Benedict a little further. "We're gonna have a full house here in six months," he said. "Me, Lil, Silva, the baby, and Josh." He gave Benedict a glance. "You could always move back and make it a baker's dozen."

His brother laughed. "No fucking thank you. Once Pilar is done with school, I'm getting a place off the ranch."

"Really? I never thought you'd move away." The thought of Benedict moving off the ranch tickled in Luke's head. Maybe it wasn't such a bad idea, with Lil starting her own family here. Luke sure as shit didn't want to keep a baby's hours, even if the baby was his niece or nephew.

"Well, maybe just the farthest corner of the ranch."

Benedict stretched one of his legs before him, his boot heel scraping across the plywood of the bare subfloor. "I heard the casino hired away Jasmine."

"Yeah." Luke wasn't going to bring up Josh's role in that. "We'll get somebody else. Did Fee bitch to you about that too?"

"Yeah. And she mentioned Ana's part." His brother pierced him with a too-probing look. "You ever get the feeling Ana hates you?"

All the fucking time. "I don't know. Maybe she's just prickly."

"Maybe. But she's friends with most everyone I know. Except for you. You guys were in school together—was she always like this?"

In school, she'd been unapproachable and all the more intriguing for it. Goddamn Luke if he hadn't wanted to impress her. And he never once had yet.

Maybe if he got her to do a pull-up, she'd stop acting as if everything he did was expressly designed to piss her off.

And she wasn't totally unapproachable. There had been that weird thing when he'd touched her wrist, as if there were lightning beneath her skin and it had struck him when he'd touched her. He'd have to be careful of that when they were training together.

Luke cleared his throat and his thoughts. "Ana just doesn't take any shit. You ought to understand the type."

Benedict gave an amused nod. "Yeah, I do."

"She can't hate me that much—we're doing this charity run together. As a team."

"Excuse you?"

Luke leveled a stare at his brother. "Is that a problem?"

"She only works for our biggest competitor. And you're teaming up with her?"

The aggression in Benedict's tone had Luke's teeth grinding.

"It's not like she's using this to commit corporate espionage." Luke had had to force her into it; she didn't have some master plan to spy on him.

"How do you know?" Benedict's chin jutted forward. "She's as competitive as all hell, and I wouldn't put it past her to cook something up to get at us."

"I forced her into it," Luke ground out. Which made him sound like an asshole, but at least he wasn't a *paranoid* asshole like his brother.

"Still, we're a privately held company," Benedict said grudgingly. "I'd like to keep things private, especially from anyone connected with the casino. I don't like the thought of her being alone with you."

Luke rolled his eyes and hefted the hammer again. Benedict *had* to order everyone around like they were idiots, didn't he? It made Luke want to kiss Ana senseless right in front of his brother just to rub it in.

Of course, if he did that, she'd knee him in the balls. Hard. But it'd probably be fun up until then.

"Don't worry, all our secrets are safe with me. We're only going to talk about training anyway."

"You'd better. And I can't believe Ana's doing this," Benedict said. "She always looks so... put together."

Not when Luke had caught her on her run. She'd been sweaty, windblown, in a tank that barely covered her jog bra and short shorts that had revealed every inch of her gorgeous legs. With miles and miles of bronzed skin that his hands had itched to run over.

Okay, that was it: no more of that mental lusting. Luke would cut that out right now.

"She's a marathoner," he said. Which wasn't the same as

an obstacle race, but she wasn't some woman who was afraid of the outdoors.

"Really? How'd you know that?"

Well, this was embarrassing. "Oh, somebody told me. Somewhere."

Luke couldn't admit that he kept an ear out for any tidbits about Ana and had heard through the local grapevine about her running exploits.

"Huh. She's got the body for it."

Luke's hand tightened on this hammer, and he forced his fingers to relax. Benedict was only making an observation. And he was his brother.

And Ana Chacon really did hate him.

Luke fished a nail out of the bucket and set it in place of the one he'd ruined, giving it a few good whacks. "We start training today. She's coming here to work out with me."

He heard the scrape of Benedict's boot behind him, a meditative sort of noise. Benedict was cogitating, which he did a lot.

"Well," his brother said, "at least she's never made a secret of the fact she dislikes you. If she does start buttering you up, we'll know she's only pretending due to some ulterior motive."

Of course. Because Luke was just that unappealing.

"Maybe you're wrong about her," Luke said. "Maybe she really does like me and just can't admit it."

Even as it left his mouth, it felt ridiculous. Ana didn't do stuff like that. If she liked a person—and there were plenty of people she liked—she wasn't afraid of demonstrating it.

She'd never shown Luke any hint of that.

Benedict shook his head. "You arrogant so-and-so. Got to have every woman love you, huh?"

Luke grinned. "Better than having every one of them hate me."

A snort from Benedict. "That's not happening. And maybe you're right. But Ana always struck me as the kind of woman who always said what she meant. And never hid her true feelings."

That was exactly what Luke was worried about.

Chapter 6

ANA WATCHED THE DOGS CHURNING around her car, her fingers on the door handle and her brain trying to decide if it was safe to come out.

The pack was all wagging their tails, but dogs in a group behaved differently than a dog on its own. And she didn't know these dogs. But the Merrill family wouldn't let dangerous dogs greet visitors—would they?

Just when she'd decided that no, they wouldn't, the front door of the mansion opened and Liliana came out.

Lil was Luke's younger sister by a year, energetic, a bit tomboyish—and very definitely pregnant. Like, she wasn't about to "pop," gross as that phrase was, but there was clearly another human being residing in her midsection.

"Go on," she ordered the dogs, who did the doggy slink of remorse past her before disappearing behind the house.

Ana opened the car door and climbed out, grabbing the bottle of Lightning Blue sports drink she always drank on her runs. "Hey." This was a little awkward, coming across Lil. She and Lil had never really been friends, but Ana liked her. Lil didn't seem like she took any shit. It was just too bad she had Luke as a brother, and it was going to be kind of hard to explain Ana was here to workout.

"Sorry about the dogs." Lil's smile was hardly a smile at all. More like an approximation of one. "Luke's dogs are idiots."

"No worries." Ana rubbed her hands down the front of her shorts. Usually Lil was more... friendly than this. "Are all those Luke's?" Because that many dogs was getting close to hoarder numbers.

Lil squinted after the pack. "No. Not all."

A beat passed, and Ana pondered how best to bring up her reason for being here.

Lil gestured to the house. "Sorry. You should come in. Things have been..." She shook her head. "Yeah. Sorry."

Ana didn't ask her to elaborate. The pregnancy and the rumors that the father was here and then gone and then here again were probably explanation enough.

She took a deep breath and followed Lil inside. She'd been to the Merrill house once before. Maybe back in high school? She couldn't quite remember when or why.

It was decorated in a manner meant to be homey, with overstuffed sofas and family portraits and bouquets in mason jars. But with the size of the place, it didn't quite work. It was as if they were trying to disguise the fact it was a mansion but didn't quite make it convincing.

Lil went through the living room and started down a hall.

"Um..." Did Lil know why Ana was here? Where was she going?

"Luke told me you were coming," Lil said. "His gym is this way."

Interesting—Lil had called it Luke's gym. So no one else in the family used it then. Which meant that even though

Lil would be in the house, Ana and Luke would be pretty much alone.

As long as he didn't touch her, everything should be fine.

"Thanks." The next step would be to ask Lil how she was doing, but the answer to that was sure to be fraught. What had been in the paper today? That accident at Oak Truck Road—they could talk about that.

"You guys are doing this obstacle race, huh?"

Or they could talk about that. Ana would have rather brought up the accident. "Yeah. For the Assistance League."

"Shelly's so nice."

"She is. And we're happy to help her. You know. For charity."

"Charity won't keep Luke from trying his damnedest to win," Lil said. "Here we are." She knocked on the open door. "Got a visitor for you."

Ana poked her head past Lil into the room.

Whoa, Luke hadn't been kidding when he'd called it a gym. The floor was covered with black rubber mats, one entire wall was mirrored, and there were all kinds of machines and barbells and weights.

Luke was standing in the middle of it all, his hands on his hips. He was dressed much as he was when he'd been jogging, only this time... It was different somehow this time. He was comfortable here, which made him—languid. Dangerous.

She felt the sparks again, weaker than when he'd touched her. But definite sparks.

"Thanks, Lil." His voice even sounded deeper. He gave Ana a challenging lift of his brows as his sister left. "You ready?"

She didn't think she was, at least not for him like this. The weights would be a piece of cake if she could just ignore how jumpy he made her. Of course, she made him just as jumpy if she'd interpreted his "Holy shit" from the other day correctly.

"Of course. What will we start with?" She sounded like a breathy idiot, which she most certainly was not. She was very smart and had excellent lung control.

He looked around the room, and she noticed he wasn't quite as loose as he'd first seemed. His shoulders were knotted, and the skin was pulled tight over his jawline.

Something was going on here, with him looking so tense and Lil so subdued. But it really wasn't Ana's concern. She was only here to get sweaty with him.

Wait, that sounded wrong.

Luke gestured toward the treadmill. "Warm up for ten minutes. Nothing fast, just to get your blood flowing. I'm already warmed up."

Which meant that *his* blood was flowing.

She rolled her eyes at herself, where he couldn't see. She had to quit that.

She climbed onto the machine and turned up the speed and the incline. She kept her gaze firmly on the treadmill readout, even though that was a sure way to go crazy, waiting and watching those red numbers. Better to go crazy than to watch him though.

She couldn't hear him over the treadmill motor, so she had no idea what he might be doing behind her. And the mirrors were behind her too. If he was watching her...

She bit back a curse as she stumbled, grabbing the bar before she face-planted into the moving belt.

Concentrate. She had to concentrate.

As soon as the display hit 10:00, she smacked the Off button. She let the motion of the belt carry her to edge and then she hopped down, turning as she did.

He was still behind her, but he hadn't been watching. Instead, he was staring at the squat rack with a faraway look, his fingers curled into his palms.

Whatever he was thinking about, she'd guess that it wasn't weight lifting.

"I'm done," she said.

He turned his head and blinked at her. "Sure." He looked to the rack, then back to her, or rather to her feet. "Uh. Squats. We'll do squats. Just body weight for now." The tension was still in his shoulders, and he wouldn't meet her eyes.

"Okay." She knew how to do a squat. That was easy enough. Except— "Where should I be?"

"Um—" He gestured to a spot before the mirror. "There. There is good."

This was... it was weird. She'd never before seen him like this, all tight and jittery. He wasn't wearing his charm at the moment, and she would have sworn he never took it off. Interesting. If he were anyone else, she would have asked if he was okay, if he wanted to put this off to another time.

But this was Luke, whom she didn't like. So she went to the spot he'd pointed out, planting her feet. She put her hands on her thighs and began to lower her hips. He was watching from behind her, which made it ten times harder. Her thighs burned as they came parallel to the floor, her heels lifting from the ground. *Don't fall, don't fall, don't fall* —she snapped back up before she landed on her ass and embarrassed herself.

She looked over her shoulder at him. "Well?"

"Uh, no." He was frowning now, but at least he looked less out of it. The sight of her ass popping out at him must have snapped him out of whatever funk he was in.

"No? That was a squat." She knew that much at least. Even if she couldn't do a pull-up.

"You squatted." He wagged a finger at her. "But that wasn't a squat. Watch me." He set his fist into his other hand, right over his heart, and his hips fell back just as if he were sitting in a chair. His quads did... Jesus, his quads were *thick*. "Chest high. Eyes up. Thighs parallel and ass to the grass. You might want to spread your legs a little wider."

Spread her legs wider? Her pulse hammered between her temples, and heat unfurled beneath her skin.

She was beginning to think Seth had had a point earlier.

No. She caught herself before she could shake her head. Seth was a dog and had no idea what he was talking about. She could do this.

She inched her feet apart, just slightly wider than her hips. "Like this?"

"Yep. Now go slow."

Their eyes locked in the mirror, but only because she was using him as a focal point to keep her head up. This time her heels didn't rise as her hips fell back, but her thighs were not only burning this time—they *wobbled*.

She felt graceless and uneasy in her own body, not at all how she was when she ran. A glimpse of herself in the mirror showed that her expression was sourer than she'd expected. Quickly she smoothed it out.

"How was that?"

He'd crossed one arm over his chest and had a finger at his chin, looking quite serious. "Better. But you've got to go lower. And go slow until you get the movement down."

She tried again, going slow, not feeling quite so much like she was going to fall forward, but now feeling as if she were going to fall backward. She didn't see how this might be *better*. But still she asked when she was done, "Better?"

"You..." He dropped his arm. "You need to go lower. Um..." He tugged a hand through his hair, clearly frustrated, but trying not to show it.

"How much lower?" She really did not want to fall here. The rubber mats weren't that soft and would leave one hell of a bruise. If anyone saw that, she'd have the worst time trying to explain it away.

"Well, you see, I was with Luke Merrill..."

Nope, she definitely did not want to deal with that.

"Here." He came closer. "Come down until you touch my hand."

She looked behind her and saw his hand stretched out. A target for her ass.

"You want me to set my butt on your hand?"

A wicked glint entered his eye, but he only said, "No, just come down to where my hand is. The butt touches are entirely optional."

Ah, there was his charm. She'd almost missed it.

"Okay." She was not going to touch his hand. She'd only look in the mirror, watch carefully to see if she was going far enough—

She snapped out of the squat as if she'd been scalded. She'd accidentally touched his hand—brushed it really—but even that tiny contact fired up her nerve ends. She took two quick steps away, pivoting to face him as she did.

He raised his hands, his eyes wide. "I don't—I don't want to be a jerk about this, in case there's some deeper reason you don't like to be touched, but this isn't going to work if I can't."

She hadn't thought this through. Of course he'd have to touch her, if only briefly. And there was no deeper reason for her to jump when he did—something about him simply made her brain short-circuit. She crossed her arms, her shoulders trying to meet in front of her. "There's not."

God, now he'd know exactly what effect he had on her. And it would serve her right if he took advantage to tease her about it. She hadn't exactly been kind to him.

"So it's just me?"

She nodded, focusing on his feet. Better to look there than see the triumphant glint in his eye.

"And it wasn't static electricity last time?"

That had her head snapping up, because it wasn't in the least sarcastic. He was... sincere, which was an odd tone from him.

"Then what was it? Because it's not logical that we both"—she gesticulated wildly at him, trying to express the inexpressible—"flip out when we touch," she finished, although that didn't really cover it either.

He simply frowned at her as if she'd switched languages and his ears couldn't keep up.

"This is stupid," she said and took the two steps to close the distance between them before snatching up his hand. She'd meant to finish with, "See? There's nothing," but the words died in her throat. Because touching him wasn't *nothing*.

The sensations weren't as severe as before—thank God —but there was still a humming beneath her skin, a feeling of something winding up.

He had calluses on his palms, probably from the weights. She rubbed her thumb on one, leathery and tough. She never would have guessed his hands were so weathered.

She turned his hand over, studied the other side. His knuckles were misshapen, the tendons strong and prominent. It wasn't a beautiful hand, not by a long shot. And yet it fascinated her.

"Have you ever broken your hand?" she asked. She should have remembered something like that, shouldn't she? Not that they were friends or shared a circle really, but a broken hand deserved a mention somewhere from someone.

He snorted. "Honey, I'm a steer wrestler. Of course I've broken my hands."

"A steer wrestler? How come I never knew that?" Broken hands, steer wrestling... How had he hidden all that? And what more lurked in the shadows of his past?

He shrugged. "I was never good enough to go pro."

Suddenly she realized that she was practically caressing his hand. But at least she didn't feel like she was going to come out of her skin anymore.

Progress.

"Well, looks like that cured our little problem," she said with careful carelessness. She dropped his hand as if it had been totally natural for her to grab it in the first place. And hold on after.

"Did it?" There was his sarcasm too. No, she definitely hadn't missed *that* from him.

She stared at him. No way was he still feeling all that craziness as she'd held his hand—his brain would have melted.

"It did for me. You'll just have to deal." She put her back to him and set herself up for a squat. "Let's go."

"Do you need my hand again?"

Her mind went someplace deliciously filthy. She cleared her throat. "No. I think I've got it."

"If you're sure. Just holler if you change your mind."

Okay, he was being deliberately provoking now. "I won't," she bit off. "How many of these do I need to do?"

"Fifteen reps, three sets."

She held his gaze through the mirror the entire time, her mouth pinched as she aimed her defiance at him like a laser pointer, right between his navy-blue eyes. He must have known what she was doing, since with every rep, his smile grew wider.

This was why she disliked him. He needed to keep doing that, and then there'd be no way she'd short-circuit if he touched her again.

"Fifteen," she announced triumphantly. "What now?"

"Very nice." His smile settled into something smaller and a touch more acidic. "Your... form was great."

"Thanks," she said, all snide condescension.

His smile tipped closer to real amusement for a moment, then he said, "Kettlebell swings. Done those before?"

"What's a kettlebell?"

"That's a no then." He picked up an ugly gray lump of metal with a handle attached to it. "This is a kettlebell."

"Okay." She took it from him, careful not to brush her fingers against his. He was being annoying enough to kill any subconscious attraction she had to him, but better safe than sorry. And that thing landing on her toe would hurt. "What do I do with it?"

"We'll do a kettlebell swing." He picked up another one, letting the weight hang between his legs.

She was reminded of those ridiculous false testicles people put on their trucks—Truck Nutz—and had to hold her breath to keep from giggling.

"Like this," he said and did a sort of half squat, snapping his hips forward as he swung the weight up to chest height.

The thing looked like a scrotum and he was thrusting his hips to swing it around. It was glorious, the sheer profane absurdity of it.

"Could, uh, could you show me again?" The fact that she wasn't on the floor laughing was a miracle.

"Sure." The weight hung low and heavy between his legs, then *pop* with his hips—that was her favorite part, that sassy thrust of his—and the weight was swinging in front of him. "You're driving with your legs and hips."

Oh, she just bet he was. "Um, maybe one more time?"

His expression cleared, twisted into dawning awareness. "Are you mocking me?"

"Nope." She let her own kettlebell hang between her legs. If this was what it was like to have testicles, she could see why manspreading was so popular. "I thrust my hips, right? A good, hard thrust?"

He stuck his tongue in his cheek. "Yep. Nice and hard."

Well, at least he had a sense of humor about this.

She lowered her hips and then thrust up, trying to use the motion to swing the weight before her, only her arms just weren't that into it and wanted to quit halfway through. She let the weight sink back down. Okay, that wasn't so funny when she was actually doing it.

"That was terrible." She didn't need to wait for his opinion to know that.

"It wasn't bad. At least not for your very first attempt." He cocked an eyebrow. "But maybe next time try to watch my form instead of giggling."

"I never giggle." Which wasn't true; she'd just never done it with him. She took a breath, clearing her mind and concentrating on her body as she got into position. "Okay."

She dropped the weight between her legs, readying herself. She started to snap her hips forward, but something felt off, and she—

He touched her hip as he said, "You need to—"

But the rest was lost as she jumped at the unexpected

touch, the kettlebell swinging in a wild arc away from her and landing right in his face.

He dropped to the mat at the exact same moment that the kettlebell did.

She gasped, putting a hand to her mouth. *Oh God, oh God, oh...*

She dropped to her knees next to him, searching his face. If she'd killed him—but could you kill a man with a kettlebell?

Well of course you could if you him in the right spot hard enough.

But that wasn't what she'd done here. He was still conscious, one hand held to his eye and his knees pulled up to his belly as he rolled back and forth. Okay, he was alive, but clearly he was in pain. A lot.

She swallowed hard and set a light hand on his knee. "Luke?"

"Jesus fucking Christ," he groaned.

"Is anything broken?" Maybe she should call for Lil, but what Lil might do that Ana couldn't, she didn't know. But nothing seemed like a piss-poor response to his obvious agony.

"Only my pride," he said. "And maybe my eye socket."

Her spine collapsed. She'd broken his eye socket. That was... God, what kind of monster broke someone's eye socket?

"Can I see?" she whispered. If it was broken, she definitely didn't want to see, but she had to face up to what she'd done.

He lifted his hand from his eye. Instead of the bloody horror show she was expecting, it was only red and swollen. Really red, and it would get really swollen, but no shards of bone poked out.

"Can you... does your eye still work?" Real clinical of her, but it got the point across.

He opened the lid slowly, blinked a few times. "Yeah. Yeah, I can see."

A relieved smile spread across her face. That was good. A functioning eye was great. "Did you black out?"

"No." He stared up at the ceiling, his expression going blank.

"Do you want to?"

"No." He wet his lips. "Tell me: how bad is it?"

She stared at his eye, trying not to let her mouth twist up. "It's... you'll have a pretty good shiner by tomorrow." Wasn't that important to men, the ferocity of their black eyes?

"A pretty good shiner," he repeated. "Well, thank you for that."

She couldn't say anything, since it had totally been her fault. She didn't like him, but she didn't want to wound him. At least not physically.

He pushed himself up onto his elbows. "Hey," he said when he caught sight of her face. "This was my fault. I tried to correct you while you were swinging. I scared you. I was dumb, and I paid for it."

She lifted her hand from his knee. His graciousness was making her feel that much more guilty. "No, I should have been in control of the weight. It was my fault."

A beat passed between them as she stared at the floor, half his leg in the corner of her vision, and he breathed into the silence, the sound tight with aching.

"Let's share the blame," he said finally. "We'll both be more careful in the future."

"Okay." Suddenly, she was immensely tired, the air itself feeling too heavy for her to bear. This was going to be much,

much harder than she'd thought. But she'd already agreed, so: "What's next?"

He hauled himself to his feet and held out a hand to help her. When she was upright, his battered face was right next to hers and she winced at the sight.

"I think we should call it quits for today. You know, before you target anything more tender," he said.

That sounded good to her. "I really am sorry."

He waved that off. "I know. I'll call you about the run later this week."

She slunk off, trying not to let her thoughts linger on the sight of the damage she'd done to him.

Chapter 7

ANOTHER MONDAY AND ANOTHER CRAPTASTIC day in the books. Ana sighed as she slid into the booth across from Jackson Harper. She desperately needed to unwind after today, hence her calling Jackson and asking if he wanted to get together. No matter that she had several hours of work to do when she got home; she needed this.

Jackson gave her a tight smile, his cheeks staying flat as his mouth pulled at the edges. His features echoed his sister Jasmine's: deep bronze skin, a mouth continually quirked up in half a smile, set off by a somewhat pointed chin. But while Jasmine's eyes were light brown, Jackson's eyes were the most extraordinary shade of golden-green. If Ana hadn't been friends with him since forever, the sight of those eyes would make her gasp each and every time.

"What's with you?" she asked.

"Nothing." He rolled his beer from one hand to the other. "You look tired."

She shrugged and took a sip of her soda. "I'm not any more tired than usual. I just... I needed to get away from work for a bit."

"I know the feeling. Why didn't you want to meet at Gerry's?"

"A long story." She didn't want to talk about how Luke had ruined that place for her, without even actually being in there with her at any point.

"How's your *training* going?"

"Fine." She'd told Jackson right after she'd agreed to train with Luke. Jackson was touchy around the subject of the Merrills, and she wanted any nasty surprises to come from her. Other than making several pointed comments about her change of heart, he'd left the issue alone.

"We've only met the once so far," she said. *And I gave him a black eye.* But she hadn't breathed that to anyone. Not that it would be a secret if they saw Luke's face.

She'd been waiting all week for Luke to call her so that they could go for a run. She'd even postponed her own run for a few days in case he contacted her. But he never had.

Maybe after she'd smashed his eye socket in, he was over this whole training-together thing.

"Huh." Jackson drained the last of his beer and raised a hand to get the waitress's attention.

"Are you and Luke still friends?"

The hand he'd raised fell. "What?"

"You heard me." She and Jackson had been friends almost as long as he and Luke had been friends. She and Jackson had been in the same first grade class—she'd accidentally bloodied his nose with a basketball at recess one day. When, much to her panic, he'd burst into tears, she'd announced, "You can't cry at me. We're friends." And they had been ever since.

But when Jackson had introduced her to his friend Luke, she hadn't been impressed. And they'd managed to keep the circles of their friendship from intersecting.

His jaw worked as he stared at the table. "We're not... *not* friends." He pulled at the corner of the bottle label. "We talk. It's just not like before." He caught the waitress's eye and pointed to his empty bottle. "What's it to you? You hate him."

He never once met her eyes.

She shrugged. "We're doing this race together." Which wasn't exactly a denial, but high school was ages ago.

"For work." He nodded his thanks to the waitress as she set his beer before him. "Aren't you worried about how this looks, you and Luke hanging out together? What did your mom say?"

"To be careful around him."

"Good advice."

Ana gritted her teeth. Luke had once been good enough to be best friends with Jackson, but now he had to *warn* her about him?

It was ridiculous to think Luke might seduce trade secrets out of her. He wasn't attracted to her, and she wasn't attracted to him. Never had been.

Except when you were getting all hot and bothered in his home gym there.

She shook her head. Everyone's paranoia was infecting her. This was only about the charity run. Doing this with him wouldn't hurt her standing or her family's in the community. And she had nothing to fear from Luke.

Jackson aimed the neck of his bottle at her. "My turn now. You might not hate Luke, but you sure don't like him. Why is that? At least I have an excuse."

She didn't want to think about why she disliked him. *He's spoiled, too charming, everything comes so damn easy for him.* She sounded like the one with the problem when she put it like that.

"I thought you said you were still kind of friends," she pointed out, hoping to sidetrack him. "But now you don't like him?"

Jackson sighed. "All right, radical honesty time: I fucking hate Josh. If he showed up here, I'd be hard-pressed not to beat the shit out of him." He rolled his knuckle slowly, almost lovingly, along the tabletop. Ana shivered. "And Luke... Luke was like my brother, man." His voice caught on that and then hardened again. "But after what Josh did to my sister, my hate for his brother crowded out my friendship with Luke." He shrugged, the motion jagged. "I'm not happy about it, any of it, but it is what it is."

For all that his words were calibrated to be final, his tone was anything but.

"What really happened?" she asked.

He slid her a look. "You know the story."

"I read the papers, but I never heard the story from someone connected with Josh or Leonora." Here in Cabrillo, there was always more than one way to tell a story. The newspaper would tell the bare facts—or depending on who was writing the story, add their own interpretation—and then there were the nuances, the details, the layers that came from everyone else's perspective.

She wanted Jackson's specific perspective on this one. She'd never asked him before, out of solidarity, but the accident had happened five years ago. Asking now wasn't so unreasonable.

"You *are* connected with Leonora," he said.

Cute evasion, but it wasn't going to work. "Us sharing a great-great-grandmother wasn't quite enough of a connection."

Jackson grinned. "That mean I can't call you coz?"

"You're stalling." She leaned back and crossed her arms, putting on her "talk or else" expression.

His gaze cut away to his beer, his thumb rubbing the label into fragments. "It's damn painful, that's why. Josh and Leonora were out drinking, at one of Cody Stark's parties." He took a rough breath. "Luke and I were there too."

"Jesus. I never knew that." That definitely had not been in the papers. But why would it be? Cody threw big parties —half the people their age in Cabrillo would have been there.

But not Ana. Drunk people made her nervous. Alcohol was a fool's game. It made you stupid, and Ana hated feeling stupid. She'd never touched the stuff, which hadn't made her too popular in college.

Luke had been popular in college.

She set her jaw and refocused on Jackson.

"Anyway, we both saw how drunk Josh was," he was saying. "We agreed we'd get his keys, keep the two of them from leaving. And then we got distracted. The two of them slipped out." The label on his bottle was obliterated now. "And Josh wrecked the car."

Which meant that both he and Luke felt responsible. Although Luke never talked about his brother, at least not to her, so she might never be able to verify that last. But she could guess.

Jackson tapped the bottle meditatively against the bar. "Leonora was in the ICU for a week and then the hospital for a month."

Ana did know that. They'd brought food for Mrs. Harper during that time. The whole family had been so terribly shaken. Ana felt sick just remembering. She swallowed that down. "But she's better now," she offered. "She got that job at the library."

"Yeah, she can work—at least at certain jobs, but she can't drive, thanks to her spells. Her short-term memory is spotty and she... The brain injury changed her. She's not the Leonora I grew up with. I love her, and she's still the most awesome person I know... just a different kind of awesome."

She understood why he wanted to hurt Josh. If anything like that happened to Sara or Lori—God, she couldn't even finish that thought—she'd feel exactly like Jackson did.

And Luke shared some of the bitter guilt that was souring Jackson's expression.

"Have you talked about this with Luke—the sense of guilt you both share?" Weirdly enough, Luke was the only person in a position to really understand what Jackson had gone through.

"What the fuck?" He shoved the bottle away. "I'm not guilty. It's all Josh's fault."

She sighed. She should have known Jackson would shut down when she tried that—he wasn't a touchy-feely kind of guy. "I'm only suggesting that you and Luke might want to sit down and talk about what happened. Not to be friends again but to clear the air."

"Maybe. What do you care? You've never brought it up before now."

"Like I said, I'm doing this race with him. And I was curious about your history."

"Well, now you know." Clearly, the matter was closed. "How's work?"

"Okay. They brought in this outside consultant to see if there's any room for improvements in the resort. She thinks all this community stuff I do is worthless." Ana put community stuff in air quotes, rolling her eyes as she did. She could let all her annoyance unfurl here, in front of Jackson. There was no need to be politic with him.

"She said that?"

Ana pondered that. "No, she didn't say it outright. More a feeling I got. Anyway, I want to use this charity race to prove that it does have its place. That stuff matters."

"I agree."

"Thank you, but I need to get her to agree. Which is why I want to win this race." Now it was her turn to play with her drink as she thought through some difficult stuff. "Do you think I take on too much?"

Jackson had no investment in any of it—her work at the resort, her work for the tribe, her helping her sister—so he'd be the best neutral viewpoint on the issue. Which she desperately needed.

"Do *you* feel like you take on too much?"

"Before Linda or this consultant said anything, I would have said no. But now... Well, I'm noticing things. Like I'm missing out on stuff I really want to do because I've already scheduled an event. I have to keep telling Sara no on babysitting. And sometimes I look at my planner and I can't breathe." It was more than sometimes lately—it was nearly every day. And along with the not breathing, she wanted to cry. "I'm wondering if it's really an issue, or if now that they've put it in my mind, I'm making it an issue."

"Honestly..." He searched for the words. "I was pretty surprised when you called and wanted to meet up. You haven't done that in a long time."

"Really?" She went over the past few months, trying to find a meeting with Jackson there. "We met up... Oh God, you're right. It's been at least six months. I'm sorry; I've been a bad friend."

Jackson flashed her a smile. "Yeah, I've been crying into my pillow thinking you hated me. Look, I know you've been busy. I completely understand. But I'm glad we were able to get together."

She flashed her own smile. "Me too." Maybe she should cut back some, if only to have time to catch up like this. She was almost rejuvenated enough to tackle the work still waiting for her at home.

Jackson glanced at the door and then did a double take, going rigid.

"What is it?" She twisted in the booth to see for herself.

Luke was walking into the bar.

When he saw her, his expression bloomed into a smile, his big hand coming up to wave at her. She found herself smiling back, her own hand mirroring his. She'd given him one hell of a black eye—it gleamed a deep purple even under the soft lights of the bar—and still he'd lit up when he'd realized she was there.

But he must have seen Jackson then, because his expression went stiff and his wave ended up being halfhearted.

"Hey," he called across the room.

"Hey yourself," she said.

He turned, ready to disappear into the crowd.

"Why don't you sit with us?"

Jackson made a strangled noise behind her. She ignored it. He'd said they weren't *not* friends. So they could all share a drink as something other than friends. And maybe Luke and Jackson would take those first steps toward speaking with each other again.

Besides, the sight of Luke's shiner was making her feel guilty all over again.

Luke walked over slowly, coming to stand at the edge of their table. "I don't want to interrupt."

"You're not."

Jackson kept quiet.

Luke looked from her to Jackson, then back again. "If you're sure."

Ana gave Jackson a pointed look. If he didn't want Luke to sit with them, he'd say so. He wasn't afraid to call bullshit when he smelled it. Were they not *not* friends or what?

And why do you care?

Because I care about Jackson. This is hurting him.

Jackson cleared his throat. "Yeah. We're sure."

A beat of silence, and then Luke was sliding in next to her. Which of course he would—he wasn't going to sit next to Jackson—but she was still caught off guard.

He must have recently showered since the smell of soap and shampoo clung to him. He eased his hat off, setting it on the table between them, and his dark hair was slick and damp.

She scooted over to make room, tossing a strand of her own hair over her shoulder as she did.

A beat passed between them all. Luke was big and close, seeming to take up too much space. She stared at the scarred tabletop, trying not to regret her crazy impulse, while Jackson stared at his own beer.

"Sooo, how was everyone's day?" she chirped just a bit too brightly.

The tension cracked but didn't disappear entirely. Luke might have been laughing silently next to her, judging by how his shoulders shook, and Jackson had a half smile aimed at the bottle in his hand.

"Fine," Jackson said, shooting her a look from beneath his brows.

"Good. Good to hear." She kept up the fake cheer, hoping to keep hammering at the awkwardness.

"Mine was awful," Luke drawled, "but thanks for asking."

The waitress came over then. "Hey, darling," she said to Luke. Clearly they knew each other. Were *fond* of each other.

"Sweetheart, I am so glad to see you," Luke said. "My favorite person here."

If Ana had had a fork at that moment, she would have driven it right into his thigh. Deep into those thick, hard muscles girding it. He just had to flirt with everyone, didn't he? God forbid he drop the charm act ever.

"I was so glad to see you walk in." The waitress gave him a smile that had happiness, invitation, and memories with it. It was the most speaking smile Ana had ever seen.

And Luke probably heard every word.

Ana forced her jaw to relax. It wasn't any of her business. She had enough monkeys and circuses on her hands without getting worked up over Luke.

The waitress then looked between the three of them, her happy expression fading.

Suddenly Ana remembered who the waitress was. Betsy or Birdie or something old-fashioned like that—she was maybe a year or two younger than Sara.

Right now she looked as though she smelled something bad.

"Can I get a root beer?" Luke asked.

Betsy pulled a forced smile. "You know, we've got space at the bar."

Luke blinked at her, but Ana instantly knew what she meant by that: Luke didn't have to sit with her and Jackson. And honestly, why would he want to? It was well known she and Jackson didn't like him.

"Uh, that's okay," Luke said. "I'm fine here. With a root beer."

Betsy's eyes narrowed as if she sensed some gossip here.

Ana could just imagine what stories might make the rounds tomorrow.

"Your usual then?" Betsy asked.

He nodded. "Thank you, darling."

His usual was root beer? That was so unexpected, Ana didn't even bother to close her mouth, although she had to look ridiculous.

She was so used to being the only person not drinking it was a head trip to have company. The dynamic between the three of them shifted, her and Luke not drinking on one side, with Jackson and his beer on the other. Silly that alcohol had so much power, but it did.

Luke shifted the angle of his shoulders, changing the space between him and Ana. "How was your day?"

She smiled at his "Fifties TV dad comes home" tone. "It's not over yet."

Jackson cleared his throat. "Ana here is worried about burning out."

Her cheeks heated. "Aren't we here to talk about fun stuff?"

Jackson gave her another look from beneath his brows. He knew this wasn't a chance meeting between three old friends like she was pretending.

Luke shifted, his leg brushing hers. She didn't flinch, but her insides went sideways for a moment.

"Sorry," he muttered. "Okay, let's talk about something fun."

Another beat passed. Ana could see why they'd never all hung out together in high school. That and the fact that she'd hated Luke.

The waitress came back then, setting a glass before Luke. She set a hand to her hip, cocking it. "Is your eye okay?"

Heat and pressure built in Ana's eardrums, and she ducked toward her own drink, hiding her face. This was going to be bad.

"It's fine," Luke said stiffly.

Her skin prickled with guilt. It must still hurt. The bruise looked nasty. She could only imagine how it felt. Her fingers went to her own eye, tracing the ridge of her brow. If she touched Luke's eye like that, he'd probably howl like Seth when he was stuck in the house.

"How did it happen?" the waitress asked.

Ana gripped the edge of the table, bracing herself for the story. God, she was either going to look like a klutz or a horrible bitch. Before Luke had given her that smile when he'd come in, she would have preferred looking like a bitch. But a klutz didn't look any more appealing.

"I can't talk about it."

Her head snapped up. Luke hadn't been spreading the story all over town? She could hardly believe it.

Betsy was taken aback. "Wow." She put a hand to her throat. "God, I hope it wasn't anything too terrible."

Just a kettlebell wielded by a total idiot.

"It wasn't," Luke said, his voice deeper than usual. "Thank you for this."

The waitress recognized that as a dismissal and left.

Now Ana had to think of an organic way to bring up the fact that Luke hadn't said anything to anyone and ask him very casually why he'd done such a thing. But before she could—

"How did you get that shiner?" Jackson asked. He tipped the neck of his beer toward it, as if Luke didn't know exactly where it was.

"If the person involved wants to say something, they can. But I won't incriminate them. It was an accident."

He was trying to protect her, which was nice, but Jackson was going to guess right away. Luke wasn't too good at concealment, and she'd been squirming the entire time.

"It was me," she blurted out. "I did it." She jutted her chin at Jackson, daring him to make a joke.

He didn't, but the twinkle in his eyes said he was holding back a laugh. "Can I ask how it happened? Or is that top secret?"

She and Luke looked at each other. Did he want to describe what had happened? Did he expect her to?

He raised his brows, lobbing the question to her.

"It was a kettlebell. I was swinging it, he startled me, and it hit him in the eye." She made a dismissive motion with her hand as if this were all something that totally happened in the normal course of some kettlebell swinging.

"I was knocked on my ass too. Got a big ole bruise there," Luke drawled, a wink in his voice.

"Man, I knew she disliked you," Jackson said, "but not this much. I guess I didn't have to warn her about you."

A bubble of protest rose in Ana's chest, but she held it back. The two men were speaking to each other. Almost joking with each other. She didn't want to sever the thin thread spinning between them.

"You could have warned *me*," Luke said.

"I thought you were smart enough to recognize the look on her face whenever you came near. It's called disgust. But maybe you don't see that often from the ladies."

"Can't say I do. I'll have to rely on an expert like yourself to identify it in the wild."

"Asshole. You know I see that face even less than you do."

They shared a look filled with an easy amusement. Ana had no doubt they'd used that same look many, many times before with each other. She hadn't expected them to simply bust out their complicated feelings about what had happened with Josh and Leonora, then hug it out, but this was a better start than she'd hoped for.

She slouched in her seat, trying for inconspicuousness so that they'd keep on. She didn't even mind that they were both kind of laughing at her.

There was one last beat of that feeling between them, familiar, happy, content, and then they both looked away and the atmosphere dissolved once more into awkwardness.

"I've gotta go," Jackson said, pushing away his half-finished beer. "Got a long day tomorrow. See you."

He slid out of the booth without even a wave and disappeared before Ana could ask him to call her later.

She sighed and twirled her straw through the ice floating in her soda. And suddenly remembered that Luke was still there, boxing her into this corner of the booth, his big body not exactly looming but definitely a tangible presence. Anyone coming up on them might think they were having a super sappy date.

Now she really had to get away from him before Betsy—or anyone else—caught them like this.

"Um—" she started right as he said, "Want to get out of here?"

She blinked up at him. "Not together."

He closed his eyes for half a moment, chagrin twisting his expression. "Sorry, I meant do you want to head home? I'll walk you to your car. I know you don't want to hang out with me and you've still got work to finish tonight."

This was the point where politeness insisted that she say, *No! Of course I want to hang out with you.* But she was tired and uncomfortable being alone with him. Only this time it wasn't solely because she disliked him. The irritation she usually felt with him was muted, replaced by something with a much deeper note.

"Yeah, I'd better head out." She rummaged through her purse, using it to avoid seeing his reaction to that.

"I've got it," he said as the dry, papery sound of money hitting the table reached her ears.

"Thanks," she mumbled into her purse.

Carefully keeping her gaze away from his, she made for the exit.

THE NIGHT WAS COOL, the sky studded with hundreds of stars. Luke took a moment to appreciate it as he crossed the parking lot, Ana a few paces in front of him. Her hair swung with her strides, the yellow-orange of the parking lot lights catching on it and sliding crazily across the strands.

She was still in her work clothes, the pencil skirt hugging her hips, her blouse tastefully pronouncing her a young professional, and her heels causing her calves to tighten into sharp relief. But even with her getup, her stride was rangy, as if she were eating up the miles on the trail.

The several lengths she put between them didn't bother him—he knew she was feeling a little mixed up about whacking him in the face, then seeing him here—and then inviting him to sit with them.

He was feeling mixed up himself. She'd given him a black eye and yet he still wondered what it might be like to kiss her. To run his fingers through the heavy black silk of her hair as he tasted her.

But that wasn't ever happening.

"Where's your car?" he asked.

"It's a lifted black F-150."

He looked around the lot. "Yeah, that doesn't really clarify anything."

She hit the fob on her keychain, and a truck two rows down chirped back at her.

"That solves it," he said.

They trudged toward the truck in silence, the only sound the whistling whoosh of cars barreling down the 398, racing through Cabrillo toward Pine Ridge. As they neared the truck, he cut around her and opened the door.

She studied him for a moment, her eyes like chips of obsidian under the parking lot lights. "You're quite the gentleman, aren't you?" Clearly she thought that a sin on his part.

"My mama always taught me to be polite." But that wasn't all of it—he'd had a suspicion opening the door for her would set her off, so he'd done it. He had to admit, her sniping at him was comfortingly familiar.

Her fingers wrapped around the door handle, and she set her foot on the running board but didn't climb into the cab. "You haven't told anyone what I did to you."

Her gaze landed on his bruised eye, and it pulsed at the phantom touch.

"I don't kiss and tell."

"It wasn't a kiss."

"Darlin', you bruised me coming and going with that swing." He hadn't been joking about the bruise on his ass. "What was that about back there in the bar?"

She hadn't called him over for the pleasure of his company for all that she'd smiled when she'd seen him. If she'd been on her own, Luke would have found himself drinking alone. But Jackson's presence had changed her reaction somehow.

She met his gaze openly, almost boldly. "Jackson told me

what happened the night of Josh's crash. That you two were there."

He took in a shaky breath. That wasn't something he and Jackson ever talked about, not to each other or anyone else. He leaned over her, searching her face for her verdict on what had happened. Because he damn sure felt guilty about it. "And?"

"You used to be friends."

She'd heard the story from Jackson and she still asked that? "What's that to you? It's for me and Jackson to work out."

"Which neither of you were doing."

"Maybe not working it out was our solution." Friend-ships died all the time. And even if his and Jackson's could have survived through the past five years with Josh being in jail, it certainly wouldn't have survived Josh coming back. Luke suspected a lot of his current friendships weren't going to survive that.

Little Miss I'm Stealing Your Baker herself had been the catalyst for that particular realization.

"That's not a solution, it's avoidance." She hauled herself into the driver's seat, her shoulders tight and her mouth flat. "Whatever. I did what I could. The rest is up to you two. Speaking of avoidance, are we going to run this week?"

Luke blinked at the change in subject. He still didn't quite understand why she cared enough to intervene, but it looked like he wasn't going to find out.

"Yeah, we should." He rubbed the back of his neck. "Sorry I didn't call, but this week…" There weren't words to encompass the shit storm of that week. Which was why he'd wandered into the bar all on his own, intending to nurse nothing stronger than a soda. He just couldn't handle walking into the house and dealing with everything all over again.

"Hang on." She pulled out her phone and called something up on it. "I need to check my calendar."

"What was Jackson saying about your being burned out?"

"Nothing." She shook her head, her hair swinging across her neck. "Don't worry about it. I'm going to give one hundred percent to this race."

That wasn't what he'd been worried about, but he let it go. "How about a run together Monday, lifting Tuesday and Thursday, and another run Friday and Sunday?"

"Uh…" She frowned at the phone. "I…"

"If it won't work, we can do something else."

"No," she said sharply. "I'll make it work." She tapped decisively on the phone. "There. You're in there."

"Okay." He pondered telling her she could cancel if she needed, but decided not to. "Drive safe."

"You too."

He shut the door and watched as she pulled onto the highway, her taillights washing his world in red.

He put a hand to his brow and rubbed without thinking, then winced when pain stitched through his eye socket.

Ana had marked him but good.

Despite her confession to Jackson tonight, Luke still wasn't going to tell anyone who asked that she was behind his black eye. Like he'd said: he didn't kiss and tell.

Especially if he had the hope—the thinnest sliver of one, but still a hope—of someday kissing the lady in question.

Chapter 8

ANA BLEW OUT A LONG BREATH, shaking her hands like a prizefighter before the gloves went on.

An hour alone with Luke Merrill on a trail. She could do this. She knew she could.

She swooped down into a hamstring stretch, her braid tumbling over her head as she gave her left hamstring one last push. It had been bugging her lately, and she'd have to start foam rolling again if it kept this up, an activity she absolutely loathed. The Inquisition had really missed out on not using foam rolling as one of their preferred tortures.

Seth lay at her feet, clearly bored. He was ready to run and probably thought all this stretching stuff was nonsense.

Luke was waiting quietly beside where their cars were parked on the back road, staring at the dirt between his feet. On the other two runs they'd done this week, he'd been quiet. Distant. Which suited her fine—she'd needed the mental break from everything in her life in order to be able to tackle it all again the next day.

But today he wasn't just distant. He was tense. Closed off. His mouth was flat and his eyes were slits, the ring of bruising around his left eye now a sickly greenish-yellow. *Don't even think about talking to me*—that's what his expression said.

He was dropping the charm with her more and more. Which shouldn't have been attractive, but it was. That must have been his superpower: to make everything attractive. She supposed it wasn't the attraction part that was surprising—it was that she found him less annoying this way. Maybe because she understood his current expression all too well. It struck her as real in a way his charm never had.

He wasn't trying to woo her, and during their workout sessions in his gym, he hadn't once touched her. Which had been a relief. No need to worry about smashing him in some other delicate spot.

With his expression, it looked like there would be no conversation from him. That was fine with her, although she did like to talk to Seth when they were alone. But she couldn't look like the crazy dog-talking lady in front of Luke.

"Ready?" she asked, grabbing her bottle of Lightning Blue.

Seth jumped up, his butt wagging. Oh yeah, he was ready.

Luke only nodded, then set to jogging.

The first five miles went by easily. She felt great, her legs working with hardly any sense of effort, and he kept the pace with no signs of tiring. He didn't say anything at all, simply kept his face forward, the lines bracketing his mouth grim as his arms pumped, his legs working like pistons. It was an almost poisoned determination animating him.

He wasn't mad and he wasn't talking, but the emotion rolling off him was still messing with her mind. The glances she kept sending him to see if his attitude would crack were breaking her rhythm. So as they approached the illegal motocross track the Herman boys had dug out there in the middle of nowhere, she said, "Want to talk about it?"

Only silence came in response. Damn. Maybe he was mad at her. But she hadn't done anything this week that might have set him off. If hiring away Jasmine hadn't pissed him off enough to stop talking to her, nothing she'd done after should have done it either. And she shouldn't care so much if he was. His attitude was his own problem.

"Talk about what?" he said finally. His voice was as flatly aggressive as his expression.

Seth pulled back his ears, catching Luke's tone and not liking it.

Ana could let it drop, could simply answer *whatever* and let them get on with their silent, angry run. Instead, she doubled down. "Well, you don't look so good. Besides the eye."

He raised a hand as if to touch it but let his hand fall before he did. "I've had a hell of a week."

Finally, finally, his anger broke, harsh exhaustion leaking into his voice as his shoulders slumped.

"Worse than when I gave you a black eye?"

"Hard to believe, but yes." His feet pounded on, his arms pumping in time, his biceps hard arcs beneath his skin. "You know Lil is pregnant?"

"Yeah, I figured that one out." Hard to miss, even if Ana hadn't heard the gossip.

He lifted the hem of his shirt and mopped his brow, all without breaking stride. His stomach was obscenely flat and etched with muscle. An anatomy student could have used him to study musculature. Her brain went into a weird fog.

He snapped her right out of it when he said, "Lil's on bed rest."

Ana put a hand to her mouth, her feet slowing, clouds of dust rising as her toes dug into the sandy road. "Oh my God. Is she okay?"

"I think so. It's more precautionary." Luke didn't bother to slow down, and she had to sprint to catch him. "But the father of her kid has moved in to take care of her."

Ana had heard about him, or more accurately, she'd heard the story about him and Lil having a make-out session at the Stampede. "Wow. It's amazing that you're upright," she said dryly.

He slid her a fondly exasperated look, silently saying, *I know it's ridiculous. Just indulge me.*

If he was expecting her to hold his hair back as he emotionally vomited, he'd picked the wrong girl.

"I still don't see how that's worse than a black eye," she said. Because really, bodily harm versus a man taking care of the woman he'd impregnated? Easy choice there. "I'm guessing that you don't like this..." Her mouth twisted as she searched for a word. "Boyfriend?" she tried. But that was kind of high school. "You know, English really needs a word that's classier than baby daddy. Something shorter than 'father of her child' that you can use in polite company."

"Yeah, that seems like a problem science should have solved by now."

He didn't say anything more, just kept on grimly jogging. But she wasn't finished here. "So?" she prompted.

"So what?"

As if he didn't know. She sent him a look and asked slowly, spelling out each syllable, "Do you like the boyfriend?"

"No, I don't," he said with hard precision. "But Lil wants to try to work it out. And it's her life." He said that the same way he might say, *It's her funeral.*

Ana supposed that Lil could do whatever she wanted, with or without a man, backed as she was by her family's money. And their love. Even Ana had to admit the Merrills tight-knit unit was admirable.

But apparently money couldn't buy everything—or at least not tolerable brothers-in-law.

"That sounds like a crappy situation," she said.

"That wasn't even all of it this week," he said. "You know Bea?"

"Your cousin? Yeah." Bea was a professor in San Diego. Very smart and very tightly wound. "What happened to her?"

"She had some craziness with some hippies happen on a camping trip."

"Hippies?" That wasn't something Ana heard every day. Were there even any hippies anymore? *Where had all the hippies gone?* Apparently they'd gone to wherever Bea had taken her camping trip. "Do I want to know what happened?"

He began to laugh, almost against his will. "It's..." He laughed harder. "Actually, it's a hell of a story. I can hardly believe it. She's fine, but there was a pot farm and an illegal encampment and a brush fire. And the hippies, of course."

Ana tried to process all that. That wasn't a camping trip or "some craziness with some hippies." That was a certified disaster. "God. That sounds like the camping trip from hell."

"Yeah." His amusement fled as his mouth twisted sourly. "She also slept with one of my best friends."

"Jackson?" she screeched. *Jackson and Bea?* That was... No way. No flipping way. She would not have guessed that in ten hundred thousand million years.

Jackson and Bea? Her mind twisted in on itself as she tried to imagine that. No. Just... *no.*

Luke sent her a puzzled look. "Not Jackson. I have friends besides him."

Well, look at him, all pissy because she didn't think he had any friends. "Sure you do." She shoved her tongue into her cheek because she couldn't resist adding, "Friends who sleep with your cousin."

He chewed on that as they jogged past a massive live oak, the shade beneath it a welcome respite from the sun. There was nothing like an oak tree for providing a cool spot.

"Russ is a good guy," he said finally. "I just hope Bea realizes that."

"Wait, first you're pissed, and now you want them together?"

"Well, yeah."

She rolled her eyes. "That makes no sense."

"It's just, like, a reflex, when you're pissed when a dude sleeps with one of your relatives."

"Oh, of course, how I could I forget. The He-Man-Woman-Haters reflex—we learned about that in biology."

He covered another laugh with one of his big, capable hands, his eyes crinkling in a way that made her heart feel funny. "Anyway, once I had time to think about it, I realized that Bea and Russ would be great together. And she ought to realize that too." His smile turned sly and smirky. "Russ is planning something kind of big to prove it to her, actually."

"Is it a good kind of big?"

"It involves firefighters."

Damn. Big *and* firefighters? She'd like to see that. "Then yeah, that's probably good."

Ana nodded to herself as she tried to imagine what the surprise might be. But somehow she wasn't totally convinced a bunch of firefighters might actually do a striptease—

"You're into firefighters?" Luke was giving her a skeptical, assessing look. As if he was a little bit offended that she might be into firefighters.

"Who isn't?" Although that wasn't really true—she wasn't *against* firefighters, but she didn't want to admit what really turned her on. If she said cowboys made her weak-kneed, he might think she meant him.

"Firefighters are a perennial favorite, I guess," he said.

He sounded so forlorn she had to laugh.

"Not being a firefighter hasn't hurt you any when it comes to hooking up," she said. "Come on."

Again, she wasn't going to hold his hair back for the emotional vomit. He was a big boy. He could buck up.

A very big boy, a naughty voice reminded her.

Luke flashed a smile at her, his easy charm back in full force. "All right, you got me there."

Surprisingly, she didn't want to smack that smile off his face. Which was interesting. "Okay, so you like this firefighter buddy of yours," she ticked off, "and you hope your cousin ends up with him. That's actually not so bad."

He tilted his head, pondering the road ahead of them. "You're probably right."

"Let's talk about your sister's boyfriend then."

His expression went sour again, his fists tightening as he punched at the air in the same cadence as his steps. "He's a bull rider."

She imagined he'd pronounce *serial killer* the exact same way he'd said *bull rider*.

"Oooh," she said, mostly to poke at him.

"And he's Brazilian."

"Double ooooh."

He gave an exasperated huff. "Seriously, can you quit with the oohs?"

Well, she definitely wasn't if it got him this wound up. "Come on, a Brazilian bull rider is pretty awesome. Women want him, and men want to be him. Isn't that how it goes?"

"Yeah, well, he didn't knock up your sister."

"Your sister having a baby isn't the worst thing in the world. Lori, my niece, is amazing."

Luke made a gesture of dawning comprehension, the other hand on his hip. "That's the baby you were watching the other day."

It wasn't a secret, but her insides still squirmed that he'd figured that out. "That's her."

Ana worried that he'd keep on asking about Lori—not that any of it was a secret, but she simply didn't want to discuss her family with him. That would be too much like being friends.

Thankfully he dropped it, instead bending over to stretch his legs, breathing as hard as she was. They shouldn't have just stopped like that; they needed a proper cooldown. Her legs were already tingling.

Ana checked her GPS, shaking out her legs as she did. "We can turn around here."

They weren't quite halfway, and she didn't usually let herself cheat like this, but she was suddenly ready to get away from him. Maybe because he'd revealed he had bad days just like anyone else. She'd rather think of him as perpetually unfairly blessed.

Luke nodded to her in response, and they set off the way they'd come.

After several minutes of silence from him, she figured they'd play the quiet game the whole way back. Which was fine with her.

But as they were passing the oak again, he said out of nowhere, "So you have a high-stress job, you do tons of charity work, and you help your sister out with babysitting?" He gave her a penetrating look with those navy-blue eyes. "No wonder you're burned out."

That was ridiculous. "I'm not burned out." She was nowhere near. "And my sister needs help. A baby needs attention twenty-four seven. All day and all night. She's the one who's burned out."

Ana's voice went to a high, fretful register on *burned out.* But only for Sara's sake, not her own.

Luke was frowning, his movements tight and thoughtful. "I never thought about it that way."

Such a man's answer. "How many babies are in your family? And you never thought about it?"

She knew for a fact that the Merrills and Morenos were crawling with babies. And it sounded like Luke hadn't once lifted a finger to help with any of them. Well, if she'd needed something to turn her mood with him back to angry, there it was.

"There are a lot of babies," he said. "I should have thought about helping more, and I didn't."

She snorted. "Words are cheap." Ana didn't give her sister words—she helped however she could.

Luke shrugged, half angry, half resigned. "So I'm an asshole. You've always thought that."

That... that kind of hurt. She punched the air herself, trying to dispel that feeling.

He wasn't an asshole. Not really. *Asshole* was maybe too strong. Spoiled, thoughtless about certain things—that fit. But maybe not asshole.

She gave herself a shake. What was happening to her? The Ana of a month ago would have said asshole fit him just fine.

Ana cleared her throat. "You ought to think about these

things more," she said prissily. Because he should, but now she felt weird telling him that.

"I will. And you should think about slowing down."

So they were back to that. She'd have to thank Jackson for his big fat mouth when she saw him next.

But his suggestion wasn't so easy to dismiss. It worked its way into her brain, forcing her to chew on it. To ponder her increasing stress over her to-do list. To remember all the things she'd been forgetting that she'd agreed to do. To face the things she really, really wanted to do but always had to say no to.

Maybe she should slow down. Or at least cut a few things out. Maybe.

But not yet. Not with the consultant sniffing around. Ana knew her greatest weakness was that she was competitive and pigheaded—she *knew* that—but she still had to prove to Chelsea Thomas that Ana's way of doing things was perfectly valid.

Ana shied away from exposing all that to Luke. Or to anyone besides say, Jackson. Jackson had no stake in her work or her charity endeavors or her family, so she could confess to him why she ran so fast. Why she was frightened of never slowing down.

Luke, however, was intimately involved in this charity race. If she told him finding time for these workouts—*doing* the workouts—was exhausting her... he could back out of the race from some noble impulse to save her.

She didn't need saving.

But she was so tired. And he'd opened up to her. About a lot of things. She could maybe explain why her life had to move at this speed for the time being.

"I can't slow down," she said, keeping her gaze firmly before her. "At least not yet." She took a deep breath, trying to decide if saying this next was wise or utterly stupid. "There's this consultant at work."

That wasn't giving too much away. Lots of places hired consultants. Hell, he might already know about it.

He didn't say anything at first, so she risked a glance at him.

His body was pumping like a magnificent organic machine, propelling him forward with steady power. He wasn't a graceful runner, but there was something brutally gorgeous in the rhythm he set.

He turned his head toward her and caught her staring. "Go on," he said. "I can tell there's more."

Even though his tone was neutral—maybe even tilting toward supportive?—Ana wasn't certain if she wanted to continue. But she'd already decided to start it; might as well keep on.

"The consultant's been brought on to make suggestions. You know, where we can streamline, where we can improve, better business practices." She rolled her hand at all the stuff Chelsea Thomas was supposed to stick her nose into.

"Ah." In that one syllable of his, she heard everything she'd felt when getting the news about the consultant.

Ana took a steadying breath. Encouraged, she went on, "One of her suggestions is that I'm doing too much. That I take on too many community projects." Again, there were no trade secrets there. He knew she did community outreach—that was the entire point of this run. "It's the PR department's job, she says."

The worst of it was, Ana couldn't refute that last. But she also couldn't shake the sense that she had to do these things.

"But you're really good at community outreach," Luke said. "And at running the resort. Do they want the best or don't they?"

Well. Ana knew that of course, but to hear it from someone who really understood—from her rival even—was... awesome. Terrifically awesome. Her chest lightened even as her lungs burned with effort. She felt as if she might run forever on the energy that compliment gave her.

"The consultant might be right though." She ground her teeth, but it didn't prevent the next words from slipping out: "Things are escaping from me lately. Either I forget, or I can't make room, or... or I just don't want to do them. There used to be more than enough time, and now... there just isn't."

Was that sensation burnout though? Or if she magically had more hours in the day, would everything be fixed?

"So you don't want to cut back and prove her right," Luke said.

That was pretty insightful for someone who didn't know her well.

"I don't think I can cut back," she said. "Who will take up the slack?"

"What does your family think?"

That I should cut back. Her mother hadn't exactly said that, but the meaning was there.

Only, Ana wasn't certain if her mother was correct.

Luke didn't know her, not that well, and wasn't her family. He was an outsider, but he also was uniquely suited to know exactly what her job entailed. He was neutral on this in the best way. So maybe his advice would be valuable.

"Do you think I should cut back?" she asked carefully.

Not that she would necessarily follow any of his suggestions, but she wanted to know what her life looked like from the outside.

"I think you should do what *you* think is best," he said.

"Not necessarily what makes you happy," he clarified, "because sometimes that isn't what's best."

She focused on a willow by the side of the road as she pondered that. The tree was short and squat, innumerable branches reaching pell-mell toward the road. It wasn't pruned or neat or even really pretty... but it was surviving. It was getting the job done.

What was best? Honestly, what she'd been doing seemed best. Until recently, when it didn't.

Unfortunately, she couldn't see what she should be doing instead. Couldn't see what might be best now.

"You... you have a very unique role in this community," Luke was saying. "No one can do exactly what you do, the way you do. I hope this consultant understands that."

"Me too."

He grinned at her and then turned sober. "The casino is..." He gestured in frustration. "Well, I don't have to tell you what the casino represents."

No, he didn't. "I never really expected you to say that."

The casino was a mixed bag to the outside world. To most people it was a place to play—drink some, gamble some, see a show, and maybe have a nice dinner while you did. They went for a few hours to have fun, to escape the grind of the everyday.

For others it was a den of sin, a place that stole money from people with a gambling problem. To them, the casino represented the worst kind of immorality.

And for still others, it was a place of resentment, a place where the tribe amassed wealth they didn't deserve. Wealth that they believed rightfully belonged to them. Or someone else. Or anyone other than the tribe.

Ana saw all that. She'd had people put all three of those attitudes right in her face.

But she wanted people to see more of what the casino meant to her and her people. What it could mean to the community when the casino gave back. Which was why she did everything that she did. There was so much more to do —if she slowed down, would any of it ever get done?

Luke took a deep breath, as if gathering himself for something difficult. "Look, for all that you try to fuck with my business, I respect the hell out of you. And I have no illusions. The ranch supports pretty much my entire family, but if it disappeared tomorrow, it would be no great loss. We'd all find something else to do." He cleared his throat awkwardly. "But with all that the casino supports... you couldn't say the same."

She couldn't speak for long moments. There was so much in his speech, so much to unpack—she couldn't do it all right now. She'd have to take it apart later, when she was alone.

But first: "I have to win this race," she said. "Then I can slow down." She needed him to understand that.

Once she'd crossed the finish line, she'd catch up on her sleep, look at her to-do list without having a panic attack... all kinds of things.

Perhaps that was best at the moment. Get through the race and this consultant's visit, then reassess. The tightness in her chest eased as she pondered that. Yes, that was probably the best path at the moment.

"I'll do everything I can to get you over that finish line first," he said. "Not that you need that much of my help."

She supposed not. Although— "Being able to do a pull-up would be amazing."

He grinned. "You're addicted. You'll have a pull-up bar in your office soon enough, just busting out those bad boys every chance you get."

"I might." It was a tempting image, even if she never could really do that. Maybe in her bedroom at home though. Sara would laugh and laugh to see that, although she'd probably stop once Ana busted out some pull-ups.

They were about a quarter mile from the cars, and Ana realized the hour had passed like it was nothing. Her chest was achy, beyond the usual burning from such a long run... because she was sad. Sad that their time together was over, which made her blink at herself.

She'd always disliked him. She'd always thought he disliked her. Which raised the question: "Why did you want to partner with me on this? Why are you helping me?"

He didn't say anything, his expression turning inward. He snagged his truck keys from his running shorts, hitting the fob to shut down the alarm. And not responding to her question.

"Do you even know?" she prompted. She wanted some kind of answer before he left.

He jingled the keys in his hand, his shirt clinging damply to his chest. He looked... well, sweaty and flushed, but also incredibly hot.

She was suddenly more than aware she was in the exact same sweaty, heated state, and something pulsed deep within her.

His jaw went tight and he finally spit out, "You would always poke at me. Act like I irritated you just by existing. And I wanted to poke you back."

"This is about poking me?"

His gaze met hers, intense as a midnight sky, and she pulsed again. "Not anymore. And I wasn't joking about wanting to win."

She swallowed hard, trying to find her bearings. "I know that. You're as competitive as I am."

That's what this was about, right? Winning?

His expression shifted, and suddenly she could breathe again. He smiled without humor. "Which is probably what makes us such great rivals."

Rivals. That was the best way to describe them, even though they were teamed up here. Once the race was over, they'd be right back where they'd started. She'd be able to do a pull-up and he'd be a better runner, but those were superficial changes. The ridges on their personalities, their lives, the jaggedness that kept them from being easy with each other—that wouldn't change.

Rivals. The word fit. But it suddenly felt too tight.

Chapter 9

LUKE YAWNED AND STRETCHED IN his chair, throwing his pen on the desk in his bedroom. He rubbed his face hard, trying to erase the past five hours of work. He was finally caught up on his paperwork, it was Sunday, and he could go put his feet up if he liked. Although there was one last thing he'd been meaning to do today.

He walked out to the front porch, the afternoon heat mellow instead of scorching. Setting his hands on the railing, he took a moment to breathe deeply and savor his opportunity to do exactly nothing. There was a hint of spring left in the air, of flowers madly expending themselves before the summer heat came to dry them out.

Luke shooed two of his dogs off the glider, then threw himself down on it, the springs creaking as he did. Time to get to that last thing he had to do. He pulled his cell phone from his pocket and waited.

Josh was allowed to make phone calls on Sunday afternoons, and Luke always made sure he was available then. He didn't hear from Josh every week, but he was ready every week just in case.

He was lucky this week: the phone started ringing after only a few minutes. Luke picked it up on the second ring.

"Hello?"

There was a painful burst of static that made him wince. And then, very faintly, he heard a *hello*. Static poked through the syllables, but it was clearly Josh's voice.

"Hey, brother," Luke said, one corner of his mouth tipping up. He hated having to talk to Josh through this crappy connection, but hearing his voice, knowing that his brother was still there, was still coming home someday... Well, that made him happy.

"Hey, hermano."

Luke's smile took over his entire mouth. If Josh was making jokes, that meant he was feeling better. Josh used to be jokester of the family—there wasn't a prank he hadn't tried to pull on someone, somewhere, at some point.

Luke tucked his free hand behind his head, the glider swaying with his movements. "How's it going?"

"All right." Josh's voice was thin, maybe because of the terrible connection, the words halting and flat. Maybe his brother wasn't feeling better.

"Well," Luke said with forced cheer, "just five more months until you're home again. Actually, less than five."

Nothing answered this except for more static.

"Aren't you excited?" he asked when Josh still hadn't said anything.

Luke swung his feet to the floor, his chest tightening. Josh was still so... so blank. If Luke had been hoping his brother might come more alive as his sentence came to a close, his hopes were being dashed with this call.

"Not really," Josh finally said. It was as gray as his earlier words. And frighteningly sluggish.

"What the hell do you mean? You're not excited to get

out of there?" If getting out of prison wasn't getting Josh excited, then Luke didn't know what would.

He thought of the apartment over the garage, all the gleaming newness he'd installed for his brother, his push to get Josh back to something like his old self. But a self without the carelessness of before. Without the almost pathological need to not give a fuck about anything.

That part of Josh could stay behind in prison.

Josh released a long exhale, which created its own kind of static, distinct from the rest. "It's hard to explain. You haven't been here; you wouldn't understand."

Luke didn't know what to say to that. It was true, and therefore he couldn't refute it. Luke decided to change the subject instead. "I got the apartment above the garage all ready for you. New carpet, new paint, new furniture—it looks awesome. And not just because I did it."

He waited for Josh's laugh. He'd take even a politely forced one at this point.

"Luke, I really appreciate it…"

"But? I hear a but in there. Is there something else you'll need? Tell me and I'll get it for you." Luke could do this, could pull Josh back into the family and back into normal life. He only needed Josh to meet him a little way there.

"No, that's not it. I'm not going to need stuff when I get out of here." There was an odd tapping noise—maybe Josh's fingers against the pay phone. "What I'll need is… Well, I'm going to need more than just a place to stay."

"I got you a job too." Luke tried to keep his irritation at Josh's lack of gratitude out of his voice. A job, a place to stay, no need for stuff—Josh was set then. "Was that what you're talking about?"

The tapping grew louder, taking on a sharp, angry cadence. "No, that wasn't what I meant either. Look, like I said,

I appreciate all this, but adjusting to life outside is going to take me some time. I've got some things I've got to make good on, both with myself and with others. That's what I meant."

Luke's stomach twisted into a cold knot. "You mean Leonora?" he asked, shock making his voice low and harsh.

Josh deciding to mess around with Leonora again was bad news. Jackson wasn't going to take that well, and Luke wouldn't blame him.

After their failure to stop Josh and Leonora from getting into that car, both he and Jackson had a shared burden of guilt in this. Jackson's guilt meant he'd do anything to defend his sister this time.

Luke's guilt meant he'd do anything to save his brother this time.

What he and Jackson shared put them on opposing sides in this clusterfuck. Which was one of the shittier aspects of the situation.

Luke pinched the bridge of his nose, took a slow, head-clearing inhale. *Please don't mean Leonora. Please leave that woman alone. Don't make it worse for everyone.*

"Yes, Leonora," Josh said. "And some other people. She wasn't the only one I hurt."

Fuck. Josh careening around town, apologizing to everyone he'd ever pissed off—which was going to be a hell of a list—he was sure to get his ass kicked. Luke couldn't take on the whole town while trying to keep Josh out of trouble. Again.

Maybe Josh would forget about it when he got home. Maybe this was just some prison thing he had to promise to do. Luke tried for a joking tone. "Did you get into that self-help stuff there?"

"Yeah, I did." There was a strength in Josh's voice that

Luke had never heard before. "But there's only so much I can do from here and so much more to be done."

That new note of resolution was promising, but Luke still didn't want Josh near Leonora. But that was something to worry about once Josh was actually here.

"Whatever I can do to help," Luke said, "just let me know. You know I'm here for you, right?"

Josh had to know that he wasn't alone, that when he came home it wouldn't all be gossipy whispers and cold stares. And not only from people in town. After his conversation with Fee, Luke was beginning to suspect that even family members might do the same.

No need to mention that to Josh though. His brother had probably already figured out where Benedict stood—Benedict hadn't been shy about telling Josh exactly how he'd felt when Josh had been sentenced. But Fee and whoever else had spoken to Benedict about their reservations... Well, Josh likely didn't suspect anything about them. Luke certainly hadn't.

"I know," Josh said, "and I appreciate it." He coughed faintly. "Thanks again for coming to visit me. I know it's a long drive."

"Not too long to come see you." Luke only wished he could make the drive more than once a month. "Speaking of the drive, I had a chance to talk with Lil on the way back about this baby situation."

There was a rustling, as if Josh was shifting position. "Oh yeah? What'd she say?"

Luke did some mental calculations. "Let's see, it's been about three weeks since we saw you. The day after our visit, she went to the doc—she was telling you about that."

"Uh-huh."

"Well, her blood pressure was a little high, so the doc put her on bed rest."

"Shit. Is she okay?"

The story was so goddamn convoluted at this point Luke wished he didn't have to be the one to tell it. "She's fine. I think." She'd certainly been acting like her usual self, which meant she'd been bellowing like a mule at being stuck in the house. "But Silva moved in here to take care of her."

That was fun, coming home every night to a bull rider playing house with his sister. The Big House had never felt more cramped. Thank God Luke had the excuse of meeting Ana to slip away.

"I thought they were fighting," Josh said with wry amusement.

"They were. But now they're not." Luke let his tone say exactly what he thought about that.

"If they're working things out, that's good. A kid needs its dad."

That reminded Luke: "There's another piece of news— it's definitely a girl. Let's hope she's not a terror like Lil."

Josh's answering laugh made Luke smile. This was good, that he could laugh about family stuff. It boded well for when he was back in the real world.

"Anyway," Luke said, "I'm only preparing you for the chaos waiting for you when you get home."

There was a long stretch of silence—or rather, static. "It'll be a while before that happens," Josh said.

After five years in prison, Luke wouldn't guess that a few months would be *a while* in Josh's mind. Luke hated to admit it, but sometimes Josh seemed more like a stranger than his younger brother.

Luke didn't want to have to learn Josh all over again once he was home. He wanted the old Josh back, just minus all the parts that had gotten him into trouble before. Luke wanted to laugh and joke with his brother again, play all the pranks no one else would. Lil was fun, but it wasn't quite the same.

"Still," Luke said stiltedly, "it'll be a full house."

There was a long stretch of nothing, only the static buzzing across the line indicating that the call hadn't been disconnected.

"Are you ever going to tell me about your black eye?" Josh finally asked.

Luke squirmed, setting the glider to rocking again. "Maybe."

Ana had told Jackson, which meant it was probably fine for Luke to tell everyone, but he still felt guilty at the thought of exposing her role. Which was silly—she was totally the one at fault, if there was even any fault to be assigned.

He touched his brow bone. There was no more pain, and the bruising had faded to a sort of mustardy yellow-green. Now he looked more like he'd fallen into Lil's eye shadow rather than having gone ten rounds with the heavyweight champ.

People were definitely intrigued by his refusal to name names though. It was all anyone ever asked him about these days no matter how tight he kept his lips.

He took a deep breath and tried to be matter-of-fact. "I was having Ana do some kettlebell swings. She got startled and lost control of her swing. And the kettlebell ended up smashed into my eye."

Pretty simple story on the face of it. It was only his and Ana's entanglement in the incident that made it juicy.

"What startled her?" Josh asked.

My touching her. It startled me too. Luke tried to think of a plausible reason for Ana to be startled that didn't involve his hands on her. "Uh, the phone rang. And I wasn't paying close enough attention anyway."

Luke actually *had* been paying close attention, just to the wrong body part. If he'd been staring at her hands as hard as he was her ass, his eye would be a normal color right now. He touched it again. It really was a hell of a story.

"How's the running going?" Josh asked. "I know how much you *love* that."

Luke didn't love running, didn't even enjoy it really... but running with Ana was different. Which probably wasn't good.

Okay, maybe it wasn't the *running* with her. It was the *talking*. Not that they really talked about anything major. Mostly small things about work—nothing sensitive—about people they both knew—which was a fair number of people —and what was coming next in their training. If Luke had to guess, they were silent more than they talked. But there was something in those silences. Something self-aware. And growing.

"It's fine," he said shortly.

"Sure sounds fine," Josh said. "How's work?"

"Work is..." Luke shrugged even though Josh couldn't see. "It's work." He been more focused lately on getting the apartment ready and sussing out who Benedict might have been referring to when he'd said some of the family didn't want Josh around. And his workouts with Ana. Work had been in the background of all that for the past few weeks.

"I've been thinking about this job on the ranch," Josh said suddenly.

Luke went rigid. "Why? Did someone say something to you?"

After all Luke's work to convince Benedict, after

standing up to Fee, after telling Benedict that he'd fight for Josh... Josh couldn't back out of the job. There was no way that Luke was letting him do that.

"No. Should someone have?" Josh asked.

His brother was going to figure it out at some point. The story of Jasmine's departure was fairly well-known. It was exactly the kind of scandal people were hungry for. The Merrill family had provided quite a bit of that when Josh had first gone to jail, and it looked like they were going to provide more when Josh came home. Hooray for them.

"There were some incidents," Luke bit off. "Nothing to worry about."

Jasmine was gone and Fee and the rest of the naysayers would come around. Luke wouldn't believe that they'd really put money over family, not when push came to shove. Once Josh was home, once everyone saw him again, saw that prison had changed him for the better, it would all be fixed.

"If it involves me, maybe I should." His brother's words were quietly measured.

That caught Luke short. Josh's motto before had been, *Not my problem.* Even when it sometimes was.

He took a breath, braced himself to hit Josh with the full story. "Okay. Well, Jasmine Harper decided she couldn't work for us anymore if you would be working at the resort. So she went to work for An—the casino."

No need to drag Ana into this—it was already complicated enough. Although Fee had just the other day when not one but two couples had booked weddings at the casino instead of at the ranch. That had been a fun conversation.

There was a long beat of silence from Josh and then: "Shit." That was almost lost in the static. "I'm sorry, Luke."

"It's... It's no problem. We'll figure it out." He wasn't

certain if he was reassuring his brother or himself. Or maybe the both of them.

Although they hadn't figured it out yet—Fee still hadn't found a new cake baker. Every time Luke brought it up, she'd have some new excuse for why she hadn't. Which was starting to piss him off.

Maybe the problem of Jasmine's departure wouldn't be so easy to solve. But Josh had said he was sorry, so Luke had to reassure him. It really wasn't Josh's fault. At least not this time.

So Luke kept his tone upbeat as he went on. "Don't worry about the job either. You might have heard from Lil that Benedict isn't too keen on it. But I talked to him and brought him around."

More like wore Benedict down until he gave in. But hey, Luke had gotten his way in the end.

"Oh, I already talked to Benedict," Josh said.

"What? When did you talk to Benedict?" As far as Luke knew, Benedict hadn't even been to the prison once.

"He came up to see me about two months ago. We talked about the job—he wasn't happy, but then he never is. Anyway, he said I can have the job but I had to prove myself."

Well, goddamn it if that wasn't exactly like Benedict: going up in secret to see Josh, promising him the job without telling anyone, telling Josh that he was on probation. Classic Benedict.

Luke ground his teeth and tried not to let his anger leak into his voice. "That's... Well, I'm glad you two got to talk."

He wasn't at all; he wanted to go pound some sand.

There was the sound of some kind of alarm from Josh's end of the connection: loud, rude, and nerve shattering.

Jesus. If Josh had to hear that every day... but in a few months, he wouldn't. Best to focus on that.

Soon enough, his brother would be returned to him. And things would settle into a new, better normal.

"I've got to go," Josh said. "Tell Ana I said hi. And compliment her on the black eye for me."

"Sure thing. Talk to you later."

"Later, bro."

Luke hung up. That call had been... illuminating. His eyes hurt from all the light that had been shined in his face.

He rocked for a few moments, watching one of his dogs as it tried to dig up a gopher hole. That idiot dog hadn't caught a gopher yet—he just kept making bigger holes.

That was an all-too-familiar feeling. Luke tapped his phone on his thigh, waiting for his riled-up emotions to settle. But they wouldn't.

He sighed. He was a damn fool for what he was about to do, but he did it anyway. He unlocked his phone, brought up the number he called most often these days, and hit Send.

"Hello?"

"Hey." He smiled wide at the sound of her voice, at the slight edge of irritation she sometimes wore with him. "I know it's not our scheduled day, but do you want to go for a short run?"

Chapter 10

ANA SET HER HANDS ON her hips, the fabric of her running shorts cool and slippery under her palms, and narrowed her eyes at Luke. "Okay, here's what we're going to do."

The afternoon was warm, but not overly so. A good day for a run, although she hadn't planned for this. When he'd called, she'd been contemplating a write-up of the new spa features. She'd been meaning to finish the thing for a week, but somehow the write-up refused to read as anything but "utterly boring" no matter how much she tweaked it. A run sounded so much better than trying to think up twelve different ways to say "beauty."

Plus it had made her heart do a little flip to hear his voice. Only because she was so bored and looking for some procrastination though.

Luke paused in his stretch, holding his heel to his butt as his quads did very interesting things. "I thought this was just for fun."

"We can train at the same time. Besides, I don't really have time to do workouts for fun. I was going to have to cancel on you Thursday anyway." Yet another evening that she'd double-booked, having forgotten that she was supposed to speak about college to the intertribal youth association.

But she didn't want to think about that right now. She only wanted to run.

"Want to talk about it?" Luke's expression held a tinge of sympathy, which was exactly the right amount she needed.

"It's only the usual." She tilted her head. "Do *you* want to talk about it?"

A man who wasn't really into running didn't call up on a Sunday afternoon asking for a pleasure jog if something wasn't wrong.

"Not really," he said.

Fair enough.

"Well, if we're not going to talk, let's run." She clapped her hands together. "We're going to do fartleks today."

He sputtered out a laugh. "You made that up."

"I'd pick something less... flatulent if I were going to do that. It's Swedish or something. It's speed work, but it's fun."

He set his hands on his hips, his skepticism way too cute. "Speed work, but fun. Now I know you're bullshitting me."

"Hey, you called me up for a fun run. They're called fartleks—do you really think they'll be that serious?"

"All right," he said with absurdly heavy resignation. "What are we going to do?"

"We pick a point up the road, any point—doesn't matter how far away it is." She gestured at some far off place to illustrate. "Measuring exact distances isn't important here. We pick a point, and then we run as fast as we can toward it. After we recover for a bit, we pick a new point. We quit when we've stopped having fun."

She supposed she could have also called it the Sprinting

Game, but fartleks was more fun. And she'd gotten a little rise out of him, which was always worth it.

"I still think it needs a better name," he muttered.

Oh look at him, being much too much mature to appreciate something with fart in the name. He wasn't fooling her.

"What's in a name?" She shrugged. "You can call it Zombie Survival Chase if that makes you feel more manly." She pointed out a busted recliner someone had dumped in the chaparral. "We'll run to that. And I'll beat you."

She took off immediately, giggling when he shouted after her. *Too slow, Merrill. Can't catch me.*

Seth barked at her heels, wanting to join in the game. Luke came pounding after her, coming closer and closer, his breathing rough behind her as he gained on her. Her skin prickled as she imagined him catching her, his arms wrapping around her as he lifted her from her feet.

She wouldn't let him do that, but she could have a little fun here.

She slowed a hair, just to mess with him. Lured like she'd intended, he came closer, putting on a supreme effort to catch her judging by the rhythm of his breathing. She slowed another fraction, letting him come that much closer.

Come on. You know you want to try.

He was going to attempt to grab her—she could sense him gathering for it. The air was charged with his intentions, with the reach of his hand toward her. His breathing changed, took on a tinge of triumph. He thought he had her.

Bingo.

She put on a burst of speed, putting several lengths between them. She laughed all the way to the recliner as he sputtered with frustrated rage behind her. When she passed the recliner, she turned to walk backward—the better to see him as she taunted him—and called out, "Come on, slowpoke."

"You can't do that forever," he panted, his cheeks red and shining. "Sprint like that."

She raised an eyebrow. That was cute, coming from someone who was six foot two and carrying at least a hundred pounds of muscle. "Can't I?"

"Prove it."

God, he was an arrogant ass. "You just ate my dust. Because I made sure you were going to eat it."

"And I'm saying you can only pull that trick once."

"And I'm saying I can do this all day."

He gave her a slow, wicked smile. "Darlin', there are so many other interesting things you can do all day."

She'd just bet. "I like you better when you turn the charm off."

"But you do like me."

She shook her head—his ego was steel-plated and utterly resistant to deflation. But she was going to do her best to poke a hole in it today. She pointed down the road. "We run to that boulder next."

Before she'd even finished saying *next,* she was racing off since she wouldn't put it past him to start before her. Hell, she'd be sad if he didn't.

He made a noise that was half curse, half grunt and took off after her.

That time she tried to slow down more naturally, to make it look more like fatigue. She let him come closer than before, until he was near enough for her to sense the heat of his body—and then she all out sprinted away, breathing too hard to laugh, but tickled all the same.

Oh yeah, she could totally do this all day.

"Goddamn it," he roared from behind her.

"You're wasting your breath," she trilled, laughter and breathlessness making the effort difficult.

Again she slowed, teasing him with her nearness. Again he couldn't resist trying to grab her. And again she raced away, laughing.

"I know what you're doing," he called as she approached the boulder.

"Oh yeah?" She hoped he did know. She hoped it burned at him that she was taunting him and he couldn't make her pay for it. "You might, but you still can't catch me. And I win again."

He caught up to her, his chest heaving and his eyes dark. Oh, he was so deliciously pissed. "You can't do this forever."

"Oh, can't I?" She'd just done it twice, and she felt good enough to do it the rest of the afternoon.

"No," he huffed out. He grabbed for his knees, sucking wind.

Poor baby. He'd tried to go too fast and his little body couldn't handle it.

But she knew hers could.

She did it five more times, taunting him in every sprint. Once, he even managed to brush her arm, but no more, which was all part of her plan. She was utterly in control here, and there was nothing he could do about it.

This was the most fun she'd had in a long time.

On the sixth sprint, the two of them dashing for a stand of eucalyptus, he called to her, "You're getting tired. I can tell." But the words were panted out between sawing breaths —clearly he was the tired one.

She was amused by his sad attempt at reverse psychology. "Doesn't matter if I am. I could be asleep and you still wouldn't catch me."

As she ran on, she felt fleet, sly, graceful—he'd never touch her, not unless she let him.

A hawk called from high above, harsh and piercing. She looked up and saw that there were two of them, wheeling around each other in a graceful dance. She always wondered what the story was behind a pair of hawks flying together. Were they mates? Or just—

A large arm snared her waist and pulled her back against a hard, hot chest.

Her feet slowed and she sank against him, his breathing a feral beat in her ear, his scent sharply enticing. She was achingly aware of her pulse in every inch of herself: her fingers, her legs, her lungs, even the roots of her hair, waves of heat spreading in the wake of the current of her blood. Her very cells seemed swollen with life and want.

She turned in his arms and tipped her face up to catch his expression, to test his response, to see if it mirrored her own. They were both flushed and sweating, chests heaving. His expression was open, intense. Hungry.

She knew the feeling.

They breathed together for long moments, the force of it making them sway with each other in a kind of dance. His eyes were the most mesmerizing shade of blue, and his mouth looked good enough to eat. She ran her tongue along her lips, trying to ease the rawness there.

"I really want to kiss you," he said. There wasn't a lick of charm there—it was naked and stark and abraded her good sense.

"I want to too," she said, breathless not just from the chase they'd been through.

She waited for him to lower his mouth to hers, to follow through on the promise flaring in his eyes. Her nipples tightened at the image, rubbing against his chest, which was as rock hard as the arm he had slung across her lower back.

But he didn't. He held there, with too much space between them. His only response to her confession was to swallow hard and lick his lips.

She was reminded of how wrong this was by his inaction. She gritted her teeth and put her hands on his chest, leveraging more space between them. Some mind-clearing, thought-clarifying space. "We... we don't even like each other," she said.

"I know."

If he kept talking in that growly voice though...

She shook off her instinctive reaction. Okay. They both needed some reason injected into the situation. "It's only natural," she began, "when two adults do physical things together that they might have... urges. But it's not anything deeper than that—than an urge—and they don't have to give in to it."

He pursed his lips and squinted at her. "You sound like a sex-ed teacher."

Maybe she had. "The only thing I remember from sex ed was 'Pet your dog, not your date.'"

He laughed, shaking the both of them as he did. "Yeah, sex ed was pretty terrible."

"Poor Mrs. Garaldi. You could tell she didn't want to have to teach it. I think it killed her to say that stupid line."

"Well, Mrs. Garaldi was a stone-cold fox. She was probably getting plenty of awesome sex, while the whole time she was telling us not to."

Now she squinted at him. "Wait, you were attracted to the sex-ed teacher?"

He made a sharp, scoffing noise. "Of course I was. She

was hot. Also, I was a sixteen-year-old boy. I could see melons at the grocery store and get a hard-on."

She leaned her shoulders out, her waist and lower body still snared against his. "I never needed to know that. How am I supposed to buy melons now?"

He gave her that grin of his, the one that said, *Ain't I a stinker?* But then he turned serious and released her.

She took two steps back and wrapped her arms around herself, shivering as the wind touched her sweat-slick skin.

His body was stiff as he watched her for a long moment. "Look," he said finally, "I know all the reasons why we shouldn't." He ran a hand through his hair, leaving it in spiky disarray. "I've got a shit ton of stuff to deal with since Josh is coming home, and it's…" He simply shook his head.

"Right." She nodded jerkily. "I'm glad you understand."

"But while I've got you here," he went on, "know this: Mrs. Garaldi wasn't the only woman I wanted in high school but couldn't have."

That got stuck in her throat, made it hard to breathe. "You shouldn't tell me that," she choked out.

"I know. And I won't again." That was a vow, more steadily spoken than anything she'd ever heard from him before.

She should have been relieved. Should have nodded, accepted it, and agreed with it.

Instead, she wanted to hear about him wanting her again. Again and again, until her ears were filled with it.

And then she wanted to kiss him.

This was bad. Very bad.

Chapter 11

THE CALENDAR ON ANA'S OFFICE computer blurted out an alert.

She looked up from the spa write-up—which she still wasn't happy with—and sent the monitor a hard look, but sadly that didn't shut it up. Punching the button on the mouse did the trick though.

Now that she was using the sound alerts to remind her when she needed to do something, the stupid thing never stopped chirping at her. Her annoyance levels were reaching critical, but she'd be more annoyed if she missed something important. Lesser of two evils and all that, but the cheery electronic bing was starting to sound pretty evil.

And all right, she was also ticked because it was reminding her of a meeting she did not want to have. Chelsea Thomas was stopping by in five minutes, and Ana already had a knot of cold dread in her belly.

For the past three months, Ana had seen Chelsea around the resort, asking questions, poking into things, and e-mailing Ana occasionally with requests for figures and data. Ana knew her turn was up for an interrogation, but today really wasn't a good day. She was exhausted, and her body kept insisting that it was a really good idea to kiss Luke, when her brain knew good and well it was a really bad idea.

Their workouts of the past few weeks had been done with a minimum of talking and zero touching. Their almost-kiss was ignored hard enough to generate its own force field, but that shared force roped them together all the same, even as they tiptoed around it.

But she couldn't worry about that—her attention was already too divided here. She rolled her shoulders and shook out her hands, trying to unseat some of the exhaustion—and thoughts of Luke—that were clinging to her.

She gulped some coffee from the mug on her desk and grimaced at how cold it was. Hot coffee was a thing of beauty, iced coffee was pretty nice too, but cold coffee was just awful. But there was no time to freshen it up. She began to pull up the spreadsheets she knew Chelsea would ask for —every conceivable bit of information about the spa and salon and restaurants and the weddings and all of it. It was Ana's job to ensure the guests' experience was seamless, but it took a lot of stitching to get there.

"Knock knock."

Chelsea said it instead of actually knocking, which unreasonably annoyed Ana. Maybe because it was cutesy and Ana suspected that in her heart of hearts, Chelsea was anything but.

"Come in," Ana said. "It's so good to see you."

Ana wouldn't say that the hospitality industry was built on deceit per se, but carefully placed illusions were always necessary. The little bottles of soap and shampoo that seemed so much more luxurious than at home, the robes in the rooms, the staff who seemed to be ready to answer your every whim and yours alone—it wasn't entirely a lie, but it wasn't quite the truth.

So she told Chelsea she was happy to see her and didn't feel even a twinge of guilt.

"I've been looking forward to meeting with you again." Chelsea was dressed in an electric-blue skirt that skimmed her hips and a baggy gray knit sweater that somehow emphasized how thin she was.

"Coffee?" Ana offered. "Or maybe tea or soda?"

"No thank you, I have some cucumber water here." Chelsea posed herself in her chair—the set of her limbs was exactly that carefully arranged.

Ana took another deliberate sip of her coffee. "If you're sure." She didn't trust anyone who survived the day only on cucumber water.

Chelsea arranged her folio—leather bound, with cream paper—on her lap and pulled out a gleaming black pen with a gold clip, uncapping it decisively. "I am."

Ready to get down to business, Ana set her cup down. But as she did, her jaw cracked open wide, and to her horror, she yawned like a toad showing its tonsils, only just covering her mouth in time. Stupid exhausted body.

"Oh my," Chelsea trilled. "I hope I'm not boring you." Her smile clung to the edge of politeness by its fingertips.

"Hardly." Ana's smile was less polite. "I was at a funeral last night."

Rosario Garcia had passed away and the funeral mass had been at the little Catholic church on the reservation. Afterward, everyone had gone to the tribal hall for stew and the bird singers had come, singing bird throughout the night to honor Rosario while the women danced. Ana had listened most of the night, the songs mixing with her dreams when she finally fell asleep.

It had been sad, yes, but there had been a sense of deep contentment too as they all came together to say good-bye and thank you.

"I'm so sorry," Chelsea said, her gaze softening.

"It's all right." Losing an elder was always difficult, but Ana didn't want to get into that with Chelsea. "What do you need from me?"

Chelsea was all business again, her pen coming to attention. "Well, as I've been speaking with the other employees, I've received some conflicting information as to what your job entails."

Ana already knew where this was heading. "I'm the assistant manager in charge of resort operations. I believe I already e-mailed a description of my duties."

"Yes, but it's clear that you're involved in many other things besides the resort operations. Some people seemed confused about who they should report to."

Ana's hand tightened on the mug handle. That was misleading. Ana never told anyone else what to do, at least no one who wasn't directly under her. There was nothing to complain about there. But if there was an opportunity to reach out to the community and the PR department wasn't already on it, Ana wasn't going to let those opportunities slide.

She wasn't acting outside her authority; she was picking up slack.

"Let me know who's confused," Ana said, each word snipped off as if by scissors, "and I can help clarify matters."

Chelsea's pen tilted toward Ana. "I was thinking we could try something else first."

Judging by the expression on Chelsea's face, Ana guessed she wasn't going to like this.

"It would be helpful if you could keep track of everything you do in the course of a day. And that includes things you do outside the resort. For example, the training you're doing for the charity race—that would count."

"But that's all unpaid. I'm not counting that as work-work."

"Yes, but it does benefit the resort, if indirectly. I'm wondering if we should take a look at everything you do and reassess where your energies are going. Perhaps we need some new hires. Or to reassign some of your duties."

Reassess her energies. Ana swallowed down her instinctive response to that. "I'm handling my duties just fine," she said. "I was instrumental in the spa redesign, in hiring the new wedding cake baker—who is exclusive to us—and I made contacts at *Style* magazine, which will run a story on the new spa. I also recently organized the wine festival, which brought in several hundred guests, and we were voted best resort in the county by the newspaper this year and last."

Chelsea couldn't argue with Ana's results. And if she wanted to, Ana had even more accomplishments to trot out.

"You are a valuable asset here," Chelsea said. "We just don't want you to burn out."

Since when did a company care if its employees were working *too* much? Ana sensed there was something off here, but she couldn't quite bring it into focus.

"That's touching," she said. "But there's no worry of that."

Again with the lie that wasn't quite a lie. After all, once the charity race was done, she had every intention of slowing down. Once she had less on her plate, she'd stop having these crazy, panicky, suffocating moments when she looked at that overflowing plate.

"Great." Chelsea drew out the *r* the same way Tony the

Tiger did. "But to humor me, could you fill out the schedule? Only for a week or so."

She passed across a sheaf of printouts with a day's worth of hours blocked off. There was even a place to mark off when and how long she slept.

"Wow. Thank you." The fog of insincerity floating between them was thick enough to choke a horse.

"Don't mention it."

They smiled at each other for a long, sharp beat.

Then Ana said, "Well, don't let me keep you. I've got to get started on my homework."

Chelsea waggled her fingers in farewell. "I expect you to get an A."

As soon as the door closed behind the consultant, Ana let the papers and her smile fall.

Boy, she really wanted to punch something. Thank goodness she had a workout scheduled tonight with Luke.

She turned back to her computer to the write-up she'd been wrestling with for weeks. Chelsea wanted her to delegate? Fine, she'd delegate.

Ana marched to her door and looked out. "Cece?"

Her assistant poked her head over the cubical wall. "Yeah?"

"I've been trying to write up something on the new spa for ages, but it's just not working. It needs fresh eyes. Do you think you could take a look at it?"

Cece's expression lit with pleased surprise. "Sure. I'd love to."

"Thanks." Ana smiled at her. "I'll send over what I have so far."

She ducked into her office, trying not to feel too smug. Well, she could already put "Successfully reassigned task" on Chelsea's little schedule.

LUKE PUSHED OPEN the back door to the Big House, catching it right before it slammed into the wall. He still remembered his mother yelling at them whenever they forgot and let the doorknob gouge the wall. His mom had retired to Cambria, but he continued to treat the house the same as when she'd lived in it.

Something smelled damn good. His stomach gurgled as he walked into the kitchen where Lil was preparing dinner. Maybe she'd let him sneak a bite.

"Hey, Lil."

Her back was to him as she worked over the stove, her apron strings tied in a messy bow at the small of her back. The strings dangling from the end of the knot grew shorter and shorter each day as she made room under the apron for her growing belly.

"Hey." She turned, and the size of her smile nearly knocked him over. "How are you?"

"Good," he said slowly. "You seem really happy. Happier than usual to see me."

She didn't answer—instead, she closed the distance between them and wrapped him in a bear hug.

"Oof!" he grunted out. Lil had a grip on her. He patted her back. "I'm happy to see you too."

And he was, but he hadn't been expecting such a vigorous welcome.

"I'm not on bed rest anymore!" She punctuated that with another squeeze.

"Great." He kept patting her back. "Could you let me get some air?"

She released him but kept hold of his arms, grinning up

at him. Luke hadn't seen her this happy in a while now. She seemed her old self again.

"I'm so glad to get back to my life," she said.

Which raised the question of who was coming with her back to that life. "And Adriano?"

His sister's face lit with an emotion he'd never seen from her before. She looked almost *serene*. "We've worked it all out. He's staying and we're..." A wondering disbelief took hold of her voice. "We're in love."

Luke could only blink at her. She was in *love*? *Lil*? His hard-charging, roughneck little sister? She hardly even did relationships, much less love.

But she must have been, because Lil wouldn't say it unless she was 110% sure.

"That's... that's awesome." It was, and he was happy that Lil was so happy, but he felt... left behind.

Benedict had Pilar and now Lil had Adriano. And Luke had—

He wouldn't even allow himself to think her name. No matter that they'd almost kissed, that he spent more time with her than anyone else in his life at the moment... hell, no matter how eagerly he looked forward to seeing her... he wouldn't do it. He wouldn't put the burden of his need on her, even in the privacy of his own mind.

"We should have a barbeque," Lil was saying. "To celebrate that I'm off bed rest and to introduce Adriano to the family." She rubbed her hands together, probably already thinking up a menu.

"Yeah." Luke's tongue was numb as he said it. "Yeah. You should invite Bea and Russ. I think she'd like to show him off."

Well, at least he could still sound halfway normal.

"Oh my God, can you believe it?" Lil asked. "But I called that before they even left."

He raised a skeptical brow. "You did not."

Luke had been the one to arrange for Russ to help Bea on her trip. Lil hadn't known anything about it.

"Did so," Lil countered. "Ask Bea."

He *had* talked to Bea—he'd been the one to meet her in the hospital after the trip had gone terribly. Bea had been fine though, just shaken. "She said you called him Fireman Goofy—which, if you really knew Russ, you'd know he's anything but—so how was that predicting them getting together?"

Sometimes following Lil's train of thought felt like running off a cliff.

"I called him Fireman Goofy because I knew it would send Bea into a panic. And when Bea panics, she does interesting things." Lil twirled her hand through the air as she pronounced *interesting*. "And then there was the one-night stand thing between them too," she said as a rapid afterthought.

"Huh. Right, so it was your calling him Goofy that set everything off and not that incidental detail?"

"Yup." She gave him a brazen grin, daring him to do anything but find her adorable.

Which of course he couldn't do. He laughed and pulled her in for another hug, not quite so tight as hers because of the baby. "Never change, Lil."

She squeezed him back. "I love you too, bro."

Maybe his siblings pairing off wouldn't be so bad. Although the empty sensation in his middle didn't exactly fade at the thought.

Adriano walked in then, giving Luke a wary look.

Luke released his sister. "Hey."

It wasn't aggressive, but it wasn't exactly welcoming. He was glad that Lil and Adriano had worked things out, but he wasn't quite ready to admit that to Adriano. It wasn't like he and Luke had fallen in love.

"Hey." Adriano's greeting was just as flat. But when he caught Lil's eye, they exchanged a look that made Luke want to squirm.

He turned his face away, needing to give them some privacy.

"I'll just be off then," he called in their general direction with a halfhearted wave.

"You don't want dinner?" Lil asked.

It smelled amazing and it killed him to say it, but: "No, I've got plans." He didn't, but he didn't want to play the third wheel tonight.

Moping sounded pretty good, so he went to his room to do exactly that. He flopped onto his bed. After a minute or two, he got sick of feeling sorry for himself. He needed something to do.

He pondered calling Ana. It was a Friday night, but she was probably at home. Probably working. They couldn't go out or anything—the two of them sharing a cozy meal wasn't happening—but they could...

He drew a blank. If they weren't working out, he had no excuse to call her. And "I just wanted to talk to you" wasn't an excuse.

He could call up a friend. He had plenty of friends. Except that the person he wanted to talk to wasn't his friend anymore thanks to what Josh had done. So calling Jackson was out too.

He rubbed his thumb across his forehead, trying to smooth out the lines there. Trying to figure out what he ought to be doing.

Fuck it. He pulled out his cell phone. He wouldn't call Ana, but he could text her. That was pretty innocuous. If she didn't want to reply, she didn't have to.

What are you up to?

The reply buzzed back only a few seconds later. *Working.*

He smiled. She was around and she did want to talk. Then he read her text again and shook his head. She was a dynamo at her job and everything else she did, but she never stopped. It made him tired just to think about everything she did. *At work or at home?*

Home. What are you up to?

He wanted to write, *Feeling sorry for myself and wishing I could actually meet up with you.* Instead he sent, *Nothing. Just being bored.* Which was still kind of pathetic. But hey, it beat what he first wanted to send.

If you're bored, then you're boring. That came a second after he hit send. She might say she was working, but she was answering him back fast.

He sent back, *Thanks, Mom.*

Her reply took a little longer this time. *So, because you have nothing to do, you're bugging me?*

Bugging was kind of an unkind way to put it. But it was true enough—he always had liked to poke her. *Yep.*

She'd said she was at home, but he wondered exactly what that meant. He knew she lived with her mom and sister, but he'd never seen the house himself. Was she in her bedroom, lying on her stomach with her work spread before her, her legs kicked over her head? Or maybe she was at the dining room table, having taken it over. She might even have her own office there. Her desk at the resort was organized, but not really neat. Would her desk at home be the same? Or did she let that one get messier?

His phone buzzed again: *Did you reach the end of your Netflix queue? Like, you really have nothing to do?*

He couldn't help but smile as he imagined how she'd say that. He could almost see the expression she was wearing right now: halfway to rolling her eyes, but also halfway to smiling. For all that she was scolding him, she'd answered his texts and kept on answering them. Which raised the question: *Why are you working so late on a Friday? Didn't we talk about burnout?*

Another long pause. Maybe he'd pushed too far with that. But then she replied: *Yes. But I had another meeting with the consultant yesterday.*

He shifted on his bed, pondering how to respond to that. The consultant stuff was obviously a sore spot, but Ana wouldn't be able to tell him much about what was going on and he didn't want to make her uncomfortable by asking the wrong thing. *You didn't say anything about it when I saw you.*

There. That was neutral. She could go on and say how she felt, or let it drop.

I was still working out my feelings. And working out my rage on the body bag.

He remembered that from last night, although he'd pinned it down to simple determination on her part. She didn't just work out—she attacked the exercises. *Yeah, if that had been a real live human, he'd be hurting today.*

Hopefully that would make her smile a bit. Yeah, he was bored and wanted to distract himself, but more than that, he wanted to amuse her. To give her a few moments of happy distraction.

It didn't work though. Ana sent back: *She wants me to track everything I do all day. So I'm trying to get all this work done so I won't have anything to track over the weekend. Except our workouts.*

He could imagine how someone as independent as Ana felt about having to report on her movements. Probably about the same as he would feel.

Let me understand, he wrote. *In order to minimize how much work you have to report to her, you're doing more work?*

No, it's the same amount of work. I'm just trying to do it faster.

That was nuts, but he wasn't going to argue with her. *And I'm interrupting you with my boredom.*

Yep.

But she didn't tell him she had to go. So he decided to tease her a little. After all, he did like poking her.

Sorry my boredom is annoying you. Maybe you should suggest something for me to do?

Another long pause. Shit. Maybe he had misread the situation and she just wanted to get back to work.

But then the phone buzzed again and he busted out laughing at her message: *Was that a proposition for sexting?*

Oh yeah, she wanted to play.

Can you really have sex through texts?

Sure. You can have any kind of sex.

E-mail sex?

It'll take longer, but yes.

Now he was really laughing, doubled over on his bed as he tried to breathe. Jesus, she was funny. And quick.

She went on: *With e-mail sex, you fill my inbox with your hot musky spurts of manly essence.*

As you wish. E-mail's sent. Watch out—it might be a little sticky.

There was another long pause, and he watched the phone eagerly, anxious for her response. Needing her response, really. His fingers were tight on the phone as he practically willed her to continue the game.

Then she wrote: *My mom just called up the stairs asking if I was okay because I was laughing so hard.*

What'd you tell her?

That I was having phone sex with Luke Merrill.

Sexting. Nuance matters.

I have to say, it's been pretty disappointing so far. You haven't even sent me a dick pic.

That made him do a spit take. *Why the hell would I ever take a picture of my own penis? I see him every day. I don't need a picture to remember.*

I've never seen your penis.

Shit. He went very, very still. Of course she wasn't asking to see it, and she didn't want to… but the possibility was a bubble right in the middle of his brain, expanding and expanding, making him light-headed and his limbs tingly—

And then it popped.

They were playing a game. Nothing more. So he made another joke: *He looks like pretty much every other penis you've seen.*

He sent that, then couldn't resist the next: *Only bigger though.*

You call him "he"?

Yeah. He's pretty much my best friend. Always there, always up for a good time.

He tucked a hand behind his head and grinned at his own wit. She was going to love that one.

It took a full two minutes for her to write back: *I can't breathe I'm laughing so hard. Your texts are going to kill me and they'll use them as evidence at the homicide trial.*

Don't go into the light. I still need you for this race.

See? There? I'm dead. I hope you're happy.

He was. He really was. Bantering like this with her had been exactly what he'd needed. And he hoped that she was happy too—the "laughing fit to die" was probably a good sign of that.

Reluctantly, he typed out: *I'm happy that you're happy. And I'll let you get back to work now.*

He'd bugged her enough for one night, and he had no doubt that she had a mountain of work to get through.

Yeah, I've still got a ton of stuff to do. Thanks for the break though.

He smiled sadly at his phone. He'd been expecting her to say just that—hell, he'd purposely left it open for her to —but it still ached a bit to know the game was done. *No problem. And if you need another, you know where to come for some more of that hot text love. I'll spurt it right into your messages.*

Thanks. You're super generous.

I know.

Talk to you later.

Later.

He switched off the phone and tucked both hands behind his head, contemplating his ceiling.

Chapter 12

ANA WANTED TO PUNCH LUKE in the face. Instead, she glared at him in the mirror, wishing she had lasers coming out of her eyes. Her rage alone wasn't quite hot enough to burn him.

"Come on," he barked. "You got five more of these. Don't get lazy."

"I'm not lazy," she hissed. And he damn well knew it— he was only trying to goad her.

She was doing box jumps, which she passionately loathed. The step she was supposed to jump on was a little higher than her knees, and she had to explosively leap and land atop the step—safely, of course. Her legs were trembling, the muscles burning with fatigue, and she wanted to throw up.

After she punched Luke of course, for being such an asshole drill sergeant. Punch, then throw up, and finally fall down with exhaustion. Yeah, that sounded like a good plan.

"Ana," he chided in a deep voice.

"Fuck you, fuck you, fuck you," she chanted as she

lowered to a squat, then jumped as hard as she could for the box. She landed heavily, her body swaying, her arms wheeling to keep her upright. But she didn't land on her ass or her head. Thank God for small miracles.

But there were still four more to go. She groaned and jumped back down.

"Such language," he said with mock horror.

Whatever. She'd heard worse from him, and his fake pearl clutching was only meant to get her angry enough to do four more jumps. She'd thought that she liked him better without the charm, but she was wrong. She wanted it back if it meant she could quit these stupid box jumps sooner.

But that wasn't happening, and she wouldn't give him the satisfaction of seeing her give up.

She clenched her fists and gritted her teeth before dropping into another squat. She did the last four with her rage at him propelling her, rocketing her to the top of that box over and over again.

"There," she said, jumping down after the last one, her legs ready to collapse under her. "I did it."

She tried to send him a triumphant glare, but her knees gave out just then, her quads throwing in the towel on her. Her last thought as the floor rushed toward her ass was *This is going to be embarrassing.*

But her butt never hit the floor. Instead, his arm snared her waist, pulling her against the support of his body, catching her before she could fall. He was rock hard and solid as a wall. And disconcertingly warm. And he smelled great, even with the sweat.

"I got you," he said, low and ticklish.

Okay, maybe this was worse than hitting the floor. He'd been so careful not to touch her since their almost-kiss, and now he was *holding* her. She took a shaky breath, adrenaline making her pulse jittery. And her legs still felt awful.

"You all right?" he rasped into her ear. His voice had an odd tremor, as if he might be frightened under his calm.

"Sure," she panted. She let her head fall against his chest since even her neck felt wobbly. His arm tightened around her. "It's just... My legs really hurt."

She felt like such a dweeb admitting it, and the fact that her voice was breaking made it so much worse.

"I know." He'd been shouting at her a moment ago, but those two words were surprisingly soft. "But you only get stronger if it hurts."

She sighed. "Yeah. After this, I'd better get really strong. Like She-Hulk or something."

He laughed silently. With him holding her so close, his breath in her ear and his chest against her back, she was pulled into the laugh too.

"I've got a surprise for you," he said.

"What? No more box jumps ever?" That would be an awesome surprise.

He released her carefully, making sure she could stand, then turned her toward the pull-up bar. "Box jumps are still on the menu. No, your surprise is that you're going to do a pull-up today."

"How is that a surprise?" Her pulse took up a ragged tattoo. She didn't think she was ready. Not for the main event, not yet.

"Come on. I know you're dying to do it. And I think you're ready."

"Are you sure?" She stared at the bar, her tired body beginning to revive. Maybe she could do this.

"We've been working toward this for three months." He

considered that, started again. "No, *you've* been working hard for this for three months. It was all you. And you're going to do one today, a real one."

She wanted this. She wet her lips as the pull-up bar filled her vision. She wanted so badly not to fail this time, to not need his help to pull her chin all the way up to the bar.

But she wasn't sure. Last time she'd felt so weak as she'd done it, as if she were pulling with all her might and getting nowhere. After all those box jumps today, she was so wobbly right now that if she grabbed the bar, her arms might only stretch like rubber bands.

"You won't help me?" she asked.

"Nope. It's going to be all you." He put his hand around her elbow, a soft touch that held a question and reassurance all at once. "You ready?"

She nodded. If she wasn't ready, she'd die trying. She walked over to the pull-up bar and craned her neck to look up at it. She had to somehow get her chin over that, using only her arms, shoulders, and back.

Luke made it look so easy when he did it, but she knew from her failed attempts how hard it was. Her lats began to tingle at the memories.

"Can you get up there?" he asked.

She tested her legs. Yeah, she had one more jump left in them. She nodded and then dropped into a squat.

Imagining her legs exploding with power, she propelled herself toward the bar. Her hands wrapped around it, the metal cold and rough beneath her palms, her shoulders locking as they caught her weight.

Okay, she was up. Now for the hard part. She took a deep breath and centered herself. She could do this. A faint burn was already setting up in the muscles of her arms, but it wasn't too bad. Her belly muscles pulled tight as she braced herself, as she prepared her body to help her here as much as it could.

And then she began to pull. First with her biceps, curling her arms as she did. Then engaging the deep muscles of her back and shoulders as she moved past what her arms were capable of. The muscles burned in earnest now, smoldering with the effort she was putting in. Her core was tight as a drum, her lungs too stiff to draw air. But she was still pulling.

Her forehead passed the bar. Just a few more inches. A few more. So few. She was so close.

Her arms began to shake, the tremors of exhaustion settling deep in the tissue.

No. No, she could do this. But she wasn't moving anymore, her chin never approaching the bar. She willed her arms to move, to pull just that little bit more...

Instead she began to sink.

"No," she ground out. She had to do this, she couldn't fail.

She sank another inch.

He put his hand at her back. Not helping her—he'd promised, after all—but reminding her that he was there. That he believed she could do this.

She stopped sinking.

Allowing her core to loosen just a hair, she took a breath and re-centered herself. She could do this. Her body would obey her.

She began to move again, her chin rising inch by torturous inch toward the bar, her arms burning and shaking, her back screaming, and her shoulders begging for release. Her palms were burning too, as if the bar were made of live coals.

She pushed on.

Close. She was so close.

Summoning her very last bit of energy, of power, she gritted her teeth and gave one last mighty effort.

Her chin passed the bar.

Only for a half moment was she able to hold there—but she'd done it. Her body quit then, having done what she'd asked of it, her arms releasing with blessed relief. As she went for the floor, she only hoped her legs would catch her.

But it was Luke who caught her, laughing as he did.

She was laughing too, because it was just so damn... She couldn't even say. There was no name for this sensation—it could only be released through laughing. She panted and laughed and he held her and laughed with her and she wanted to hold to this forever.

So she kissed him.

It was so easy for all that they'd said that they shouldn't. That they mustn't. All she had to do was slide her hand along his jaw and meet his mouth with hers.

But what happened then was anything but easy. His lips were soft, surprised against hers at first, but then they firmed as he tested her lips, taking her lower lip between his, brushing his mouth against her upper lip, teasing the corners of her mouth.

He was exploring every inch of her lips, as if he'd already studied the map and wanted to see if her mouth matched his imaginings. Gently he nudged her mouth open and tested the softness of her lower lip, traced the contours of her upper lip.

She simply breathed as he did it, savoring the press of their mouths and bodies. She never would have thought he'd kiss like this, slow but not tentative, gentle but not hesitant.

When his tongue slipped into her mouth, she was ready, meeting him with her own tongue as she hooked her arm around his neck. Her nipples went to tight points, her breasts heavy and aching, and her pulse beat hard in her core, echoing throughout her entire body.

She began to kiss him back, testing his lips the way he had hers, tasting his mouth and tongue and teeth. He'd eaten something minty recently, her tongue tingling with the lingering aftertaste.

His body was warm and hard, and his scent was clean, reminding her of a summer afternoon.

Her pulse beat harder, awakening her clit and everything else around it. She tried to hook her leg around his hip so she could press her sex against him, but her leg just wouldn't obey.

But lovely mind reader that he was, he knew what she wanted and hooked his hand into the crook of her knee and pulled her leg up to his hip, holding it there. And opening her up so he could put his big body between her thighs.

She moaned as the hair on his legs scraped along the sensitive skin of her inner thighs. This was good, but it could be better. She'd bet it could be so, so much better.

Deepening the kiss, now devouring his mouth, she meant to kiss them to better and beyond. He kissed her back, his hips flexing against her, once, twice... but then he slowly went still. He lifted his mouth from hers and carefully set her leg down.

"Can I let you go?" he said, sounding as if his throat were gravel lined.

That didn't quite penetrate the haze in her brain. She closed her eyes and fought through to clarity. "Pardon?"

"Can you stand? If I let you go, will your legs hold?"

She put her hands on his chest and pushed. Instantly, he released her. She only stumbled a little bit.

Ana put a hand to her forehead, her arm muscles obeying her reluctantly. That had been a terrible idea. They'd agreed not to do anything physical. She couldn't even blame him for the lapse—she'd initiated the kiss.

And he'd run with it, with her encouragement.

She stared steadily at the floor, trying to think of something to say. He already knew it was a mistake—no point saying that. *This can't happen again*—yeah, he knew that too.

I'm sorry? She regretted it, even as she enjoyed it, but she wasn't really sorry.

"I'm sorry."

His apology made her pop her head up. He wore a grim expression, his mouth set in a hard line and his jaw tight.

She waved a hand at him, her fingers only slightly shaky. "I mean, it's fine." She didn't sound fine though. "Just some weird, awkward moment between friends." Maybe they could laugh this off. After all, they sent joking texts to each other, which was totally friendly and nothing but. "We are friends now, right?"

His expression softened but held its edge. "Ana, we are not friends," he said with deep resolve. "We've *never* been *friends*."

It was true, so she kissed him again. There was nothing like friendship between them, not ever. Annoyance, irritation, rivalry, rage, and now lust—friendship was an anodyne thing, and those emotions between them were anything but.

This time she took the initiative, trailing her lips over every inch of his and then going over again with her tongue. She wanted to *know* his mouth, to get the shape and taste of it under her skin. Her tongue touched his, but with less urgency than before. They'd gotten the need out of their system with the first kiss—this go-round was for the want still in their blood. But it might take forever to exhaust that.

"This is the worst idea ever," he muttered against her mouth after a time.

"I know, I know," she said, running her hands along his shoulders and down his back, learning the lines of muscle etched there. "I mean, I don't even like you, but I can't stop kissing you."

"I can't say I particularly like you either. Or at least I didn't used to. But goddamn if I don't want to get you into the nearest bed."

"Where we'll get caught by your sister." But it sounded wonderful to her too. Or maybe together in a shower. Yeah, that would be heavenly. Too bad it wasn't happening. "So what do we do?"

This kiss had been a long time coming; blowing it off as a onetime accident probably wasn't going to work.

"We keep training," he said. "We try not to get... distracted."

Easier said than done. But she nodded.

"And if we do get distracted," he finished, "try not to get caught up in our distractions."

"That's not much of a plan." There were way too many *try*s in there for her peace of mind.

"I have very little blood going to my brain right now. The old noodle isn't running at full power. You got anything better?"

She wished she did. "No. This is a pretty classic no-win situation."

"Yeah." There was a wealth of resignation in that one small word.

She swallowed hard, trying to be resolved. But she still couldn't bring herself to let go of him. "It's like you said: we have to do what's best. Not necessarily what makes us happy."

"I know. Too bad that in this situation, the best sucks eggs."

Ana couldn't agree more.

Chapter 13

ANA JOSTLED LORI WITH ONE arm, trying to get her to stop crying, and dialed Luke's number with her free hand.

Pick up, pick up, pick up. She didn't think she could tap out a coherent text message right now, not with Lori so upset, and she had to talk to him.

"Do you want some puffs?" she asked the baby. She tucked the phone between her shoulder and her ear and scooped up some banana puffs to offer to her niece.

Lori just turned her face into Ana's neck and screamed louder.

"Okay, that's a no." Ana bounced harder, finally thankful she'd done all those box jumps.

"Hello? Ana?" came from the phone. Luke was barely audible through Lori's screams.

"I can't go for a run today," she shouted at him. "I think you can hear why." The phone began to slip loose, and her neck cramped as she tried to keep it in place.

Luke was going to take this as an excuse for not wanting to see him after that kiss. That night, right after they'd agreed that the best sucked but before they'd let go of each other, Lil's voice had come from downstairs, calling to Adriano about something, and the mood had been shattered. Ana had escaped with quickness, not wanting to further hash out what had happened with him.

Kisses and distractions were to be avoided. They were agreed on that and there was no need to discuss it.

"Do you have a jogging stroller?" he asked.

"What?" Why would he think that? "No, I don't even have a baby. I mean, I have one right now, but she's not mine."

"Yeah, I got that part. Let me call some of my cousins—I think Kelly's got a jogging stroller she isn't using. We can run and Lori will calm down. I guarantee it."

"I don't know..." She bounced Lori harder. A screaming baby strapped into a jogging stroller on one of the back roads they ran on? It sounded like a recipe for disaster.

Although Ana already kind of felt like a disaster.

"You're clearly stressed," he said as if she didn't already know that. "You need a break. Remember how you told me I should ponder the burdens women with babies carry?"

"Yes."

"A long walk will calm her right down. I promise. Meet me at Boral Road and Creighton in an hour. I'll have the stroller."

True to his word, when she pulled up at the deserted intersection of the two dirt roads, way in the back country, he was pulling a stroller from the back of his truck, his arms straining under the weight.

"Good Lord, that's not a stroller, that's an SUV," she said as she got Lori out of the car. The baby had moved on to whimpering loudly.

The stroller had a thick metal tube frame like a bike's, and the wheels were only slightly smaller than a bike's. Ana could run someone over with that and not even feel the bump.

"It's more of a Humvee." Luke grunted as he snapped it open. "This stroller is ready for war."

"It's the kind of stroller Mad Max would use."

He held out his hands for Lori. "She looks like a road warrior. Don't you, you little chunky funky drool monster?"

To cover up how his cooing was making her feel deep in her ovaries, Ana said, "She's not fat."

"I didn't say she was fat. I said she was a chunky funky drool monster. Totally different."

He snapped the baby into the five-point harness. When he was done, Lori gave him a gummy smile as he tickled her chin. His fingers came away shiny with drool.

Of course he could charm babies. He could probably pull some princess magic and get the birds in the trees to sing as they perched on his finger.

But Lori was quiet for the first time in... Ana couldn't even remember. All that crying seemed to have wiped Ana's short-term memory. If Luke could keep the baby like this, he could charm away.

"Is Sara studying today?" he asked.

"No. Charlie Hernandez came up from Pala with his peon team, so we'll have a fiesta at the tribal hall tonight. Sara's good friends with his wife, so she went over to help set up and hang out. I offered to watch Lori so she could have some time alone. We'll go over later when things are in full swing and show the baby off."

"Peon?"

"Uh, it's a kind of game. With teams and there are songs that go with it."

"Do you play?"

"I have, but I'm not very good at it." She tried to think of how to explain it to him. "A team has bones, painted white or black, one color hidden in each hand. And the other teams have to guess the pattern a team is holding—that's calling out a shot. And you sing the peon songs as you do it."

That wasn't the greatest explanation, but unless he'd seen it, it would be difficult to go deeper than that. And then there was the fire and the fiesta that went along with it and… well, just everyone coming together. All that came along with playing peon.

"It requires strategy then?" he asked. "I'd think a crafty lady like yourself would be good at that."

She smiled at the jibe. "My cunning is limited to outflanking you." She shook out her arms and legs and rolled her head from side to side. Now that Lori was quiet, Ana's energy was surging back.

"Ready?" Luke asked.

Ana eyed the stroller. "Do you want to push or should I?"

He shrugged. "It's up to you."

"I'll do it."

It was harder than it looked, running while pushing a stroller, especially through the patches of sand in the road. Her abs began to ache after the first ten minutes.

"You okay?"

"Yeah, I'm fine." She grunted as they hit yet another patch of sand. "I just need to get used to this."

"How did you start running?"

She breathed through the effort it took to get through the sand, taking the time to think up an answer. "This place is so rural. I mean, you know exactly what I'm talking about. When you're a kid out here, there's literally no place to go unless you have a car. Which I didn't have, because I was a kid. I remember one day when I was about seven, I really,

really wanted to go down to the village store for some of that gum that came in the foil pouch—the one that was supposed to be like chewing tobacco? Do you remember that?"

He laughed. "I do. Jesus, can you imagine selling that to kids today? 'It's gum that looks like dip! Shove a wad in your lip.'"

She could almost taste it again, the chemical grapey purple taste of it, her jaw aching as she'd chewed and chewed and chewed. "I loved the grape flavor, and I'd always try to chew the whole thing at once. I have no idea why I did that since I'd go through the whole thing in about an hour and my jaw would ache like the devil. But I did."

Ana steered the stroller around another sand pit, Seth dodging it with her to keep close to the stroller. Lori was an awesome source of dropped food, so he stuck to her whenever he could.

"I did the same thing," Luke said. "Grape was my flavor too. And it wasn't even like you could blow bigger bubbles—it was just this unmanageable hunk in your mouth."

Her jaw moved with the memory. "Yeah, it was. I'm glad to know I wasn't the only dumb kid. Anyway, this one day I thought I'd die if I didn't get to the store and get some of that gum. Just die."

She still recalled the want that had flooded her mouth, the need to taste that awful grape flavor she'd once loved so much.

"But you had no car," Luke pointed out.

"No. And my mom was too busy to take me." She remembered that moment so clearly, the resolve in her as she'd realized what she could do instead. "So I decided to run there."

Luke whistled with appreciation. "How far was it?"

"Not that far, maybe a few miles. The other kids and I, we explored everywhere. The creek, the canyons, the rocks, the valleys—we used the outdoors as our whole playground. But this was a little different. I was going to do it by myself and I was going to run. Not walk, not meander, but *run*."

Just like she was doing now, with purpose, with effort.

"Why?"

When most people asked her why she ran, it was judgmental. They didn't like to run, so why did she like it so much? But his question held nothing but wonder. Almost needy curiosity. He really wanted to know *why*.

"I don't know. It just got into my brain." It was as simple and as complex as that. "So I ran to the store." She laughed. "It was not a good run. It was too hot, I had no sense of pace, my lungs felt like they were going to explode... but beneath that was something else. Something that just utterly hooked me. So I kept on running. And now here I am."

He didn't answer right away as they kept pushing forward, past the chaparral swaying in the wind, the sun warm but not fierce. A moment where they had to do nothing but keep going, all four of them.

After a time he said, "I remember seeing you running sometimes at Cornell."

Which brought up the notion that he'd been watching her, something she probably shouldn't dwell on. "Yeah, running there wasn't quite as much fun. Cornell was a great experience and I learned so much, but it was a good reminder that in the end, I always wanted to come back here. I guess I have you to thank for that."

"Me?" He frowned at her. "What did I have to do with it?"

Was he serious? She frowned back at him. "I went to Cornell because you were." She wanted to gesture at him to further press her point, but she didn't dare take her hands off the stroller. "I mean, we were already building the resort, and then you said you were going to Cornell, so I thought, *Well, now I have to. And I have to do better than him there*."

She didn't even care anymore how that made her appear. He already knew she was way too competitive. She was out of bad traits to hide from him.

He shook his head, an odd smile on his lips. "*I* went to Cornell because *you* were."

"What? That's impossible." There was no way that was true.

"No, I distinctly remember it. It was right after I graduated from Santa Barbara and I was trying to figure out what the hell I was going to do with my life. I did well enough in school, but I wasn't exactly focused." Regret threaded through his voice, as if he might like to go back and redo some of those years.

"Well, you didn't have to be."

He nodded. "I know. I was a dumbass. But I was talking to Jackson, and he mentioned that you were going to Cornell. And that planted the seed in my head. If you were doing it, it was probably the best choice."

"I swear I heard you were going first. I..." She thought back. Had she though? Maybe she'd only assumed he would do that once she'd heard about the hotel management program there. "I can't remember anymore."

She blinked at nothing, trying to reconstruct what had the sequence of events. But the details wouldn't quite form. Had it happened like he remembered?

It had only been one of the most important decisions of her life, and she couldn't be sure now why she'd really done it.

He shrugged. "Me either." He was clearly unconcerned

which version was correct. "But it worked out, didn't it? This rivalry of ours at least drives us to be better."

That was true. Not everything in her life had come about because she'd wanted to best him, but every time she pitted herself against him—or what she'd imagined him to be— she gained a success. Look at this charity race; even if they lost, she'd learned to do a pull-up. And kissed him. That was surprisingly awesome as well.

"Yeah. It has." She wouldn't call them rivals now though. She had no idea what they were turning into. Rather than ponder that, she asked, "How are things? How's Lil?"

"Still all lovey-dovey with Silva. It's getting kind of gross to watch. And Benedict's with Pilar, and Russ and Bea are... Well, I never see Russ anymore, so I guess that's going well. Everyone's paired off."

That sounded as if he was lonely. But he couldn't be. He was one of the most social people she knew. His popularity in high school had been proof of that. "That all sounds very romantic."

He smiled at her tone. "Yeah, I feel the same. Why is everyone getting so googly-eyed around here?" He shrugged as if to say, *What can you do?* but his smile was strained.

"It can be hard to feel left behind." When Lori had been born, Ana had felt more than a twinge of that. She knew she wasn't in a place to have kids or settle down and that school and her career had had to come first all those years—but her heart had still squeezed with *what if?* when she'd first seen Lori.

Luke wiped his forehead. "It's just that... Benedict has his own space, Lil's carving out a space for her and the baby and Adriano, I'm carving out a new space for Josh once he gets back... So I'm kind of wondering where my space is now." He laughed, but it was forced. "You know, the chronic middle child's lament."

This was the most honest, most unaffected she'd ever seen him, and it fascinated her. If you'd told her that Luke Merrill felt overlooked, squeezed out, she'd have laughed in your face. But hearing him say it—and to her—made her believe.

Although she wasn't going to coddle him. "You know, if you want your own space, you have more than enough resources to make it happen."

"You never let me get away with anything, do you?"

"Why should I?" He might be upset about being left behind, but he was still the most blessed person she'd ever met. "Okay, you're sad about everyone in your family pairing off, which is understandable. Then do something about it."

"What do you think I should do?"

"I don't know. Maybe get a place of your own for starters." He had the resources to do at least that.

"I've never lived alone."

"Me either." She hadn't inquired about his living arrangements at Cornell, but it sounded like he'd had a roommate too. She never would have guessed.

"Do you think you could?" he asked.

She imagined that, having a house all to herself. Not having to share with anyone. "No. It'd be too weird to come home and have no one there. To not have another presence in your space."

And lonely. She'd be unbearably lonely.

"Yeah. Maybe." He ran his hands through his hair, his agitation rising. He got twitchy when they discussed his family situation. "Maybe I'll find out."

"Let me know how it goes." She kept her voice calm and light, the better to bring him back down.

He slid her a look. "You sound skeptical."

"Like I said, I've never lived alone." Ana probably never would. Sara and Lori would move out once Joe was back, but that still left her mom, unless her mom got really serious with Ken.

"You know," he said in a musing sort of way, "I always thought when I reached this age I'd have everything figured out. And it feels like I should. Got a great career, a place to live... but lately it all seems out of focus. And then I look at everything you're doing, everything you're carrying..." He shook his head. "I *know* you can handle it, since I've watched you do it, but sometimes I still can't quite believe it."

So many of her interactions with him had been about impressing him, about *beating* him... and she had. He'd just admitted it. If she weren't pushing the stroller, she'd stop dead in the road.

If she'd won, if she wasn't competing with him any longer... then what was she doing here with him?

Running was the obvious answer. But this was more. Their relationship had shifted.

She took a deep breath and prepared to confess all. "Maybe... maybe I'm not handling it all so well." He deserved to know that she wasn't as all together as he thought, especially if he was beating himself up over it. "I look at the balance of what I've done and what I want to do... and instead of my accomplishments energizing me, all I can do is stare at what still has to be done and be exhausted by it. Maybe I've worn something out inside of me."

That was a terrifying thought, that she'd exhausted her well of enthusiasm and energy and drive. Because there was so much more she wanted to do, needed to do...

She couldn't be *done*.

"I'd say you probably need a vacation," Luke said, as if it was the most reasonable thing in the world. "Or to narrow your focus a bit. You've always been driven, ever since high school. That's fundamental to you. But we all need a break, even from what we love, sometimes."

Ana absorbed that as Lori cooed in the stroller. Luke had been right; getting outside had been exactly what the baby had needed. Maybe he was right about her taking a break. She certainly felt better having confessed what was truly bothering her these days. And she'd think about the vacation and narrowing her focus once she got home. Nothing needed to be decided now, and she ought to enjoy the rest of the run.

Ana checked her GPS. "We should turn around. Lord, but my arms and abs are going to ache tomorrow from pushing this."

He silently accepted the change in subject and reached for the stroller. "Want me to take it?"

He wasn't pushing her for more about her burnout or insisting that she take the vacation he'd suggested. He only offered to help with what she was struggling with at the moment.

"Sure," she said, slowing down so she could hand off the stroller. "You can give your abs a workout now." Not that his abs needed it.

"Always happy to help."

She didn't say anything else, only continued the rest of the run in silence, trying to find the cleansing headspace she needed.

But it never came.

ANA GINGERLY OPENED the front door, trying not to wake up Lori. The baby had fallen asleep on the way home, and Ana wanted her to take a good nap. A really long one.

Her mom came into the hallway as Ana shut the door behind her.

"Oh, did she fall asleep?" she whispered.

Ana nodded. "I'll go lay her down," she mouthed.

Lori, thank the Lord, stayed asleep when Ana put her in her crib. She backed out of the room, breathing a sigh of relief once she was clear. She loved Lori, but naptime was so, so sweet.

Ana made her way to the kitchen and found her mother there, unpacking some shopping bags.

"How was your trip?" Ana asked. Her mother had gone to the museum in Palm Springs.

"Oh, all right." Her mother set out a glass jar. "Margarita sent some of her yucca flowers with me."

"That was nice of her."

"It was. And I dropped off Grandma Teresa's ollas for the exhibition. Hers were in some of the best condition." Her mother paused in her unpacking. "But she was like that, you know: very careful about her things. She taught Mom and me to be that way too."

"I never met her." Grandma Teresa had been Ana's great-grandmother. Ana had heard her mother's stories of Grandma Teresa before, but she always loved hearing them again. Grandma Teresa's baskets were already in the museum as part of their permanent collection. Cahuilla baskets were justly famous, and Grandma Teresa's were some of the most beautiful ones Ana had ever seen.

"She was the most practical woman I ever knew. Being that practical is a hard skill you know; cultivating all the knowledge she had took decades," Mom said. Ana could just imagine how true that was. "She'd laugh to think of her olla in a museum. 'It's a cooking pot,' she'd probably say."

It *was* a cooking pot, but the fact that it had survived so long made it something else too.

"Where were you?" Mom asked, folding up the reusable bag.

"I went for a run with Luke." Ana had been doing just that for months now, but admitting it to her mother this time made her want to squirm.

"And the baby?"

"He found a jogging stroller we could use."

"That was nice of him."

Ana could sense something more pressing behind her mother's statement. It was there in the way she formed *nice*.

"It was." She opened the kitchen cabinets aimlessly, not certain what she was looking for. She wasn't hungry, but she couldn't sit still.

"Was that all it was?" Mom asked carefully. "I still worry about your being alone with him. That something deeper is behind your dislike of him, something that you don't want to share with me."

Ana definitely did not want to talk about this. As for the *something deeper* that might be behind her earlier dislike... she definitely didn't want to talk about that.

"We're training together for this race." She shrugged and stared at the breakfast cereal. "And once it's over, it's done."

"A man doesn't lug a jogging stroller out solely to win a charity event."

That was probably true. No, it was definitely true. Ana sighed and swung the cabinet door back and forth. "We just rub each other the wrong way. There's nothing beyond that, I promise. He doesn't like me. I don't like him. That's all."

Which wasn't really true. She used to not like him, but

she wasn't certain how she felt now. There was the long string of text messages and the uncomfortable confessions…

"If you're sure." Her mother let the silence stretch, clearly waiting for Ana to go on. "Has he tried to ask things about the casino?"

Not really. But Ana had volunteered things about the consultant… That wasn't anything sensitive though.

Instead she said, "Don't worry about him. It's just… Things are a little tense at work, with the consultant and all. And the time all this training is taking. I… I maybe took on too much here. Things will be better when this charity run is done."

Because she wouldn't be thrown together with Luke anymore, and all this confusing stuff would be swept away.

Her mother's expression softened as she patted Ana's arm. "I worry about you girls so much." There was a wealth of concern in her mother's words, present and warm and comforting.

Ana rubbed her temples, trying not to let her mother's words make her cry. "Why are you worried about Sara?"

Her mother raised her palms to the sky. "She's trying to finish school and there's the baby, and while she and Joe have a strong relationship, there will be some adjustments when he comes back."

It was a long list. Guilt snaked through Ana, that she was moping over some silliness while Sara dealt with all that. "I'm worried about her too. I wish I were here more to help."

"You help a lot. Sara appreciates everything you do. And Sara needs to learn to juggle school and the baby—she'll need those lessons in the next eighteen years."

"Yeah." Ana rubbed her arms, still wishing for more hours in the day. Or a better way to organize the ones she did have. Or something.

"Don't worry; you'll figure it all out too." Her mother smiled as she gave Ana's arm a squeeze.

Ana smiled back because Mom meant to reassure her... but until Ana really did figure it all out, she'd never quite believe it.

Chapter 14

LUKE WALKED THROUGH THE MEETING room at the resort, shaking hands and embracing his cousins as he made his way to a free seat.

Benedict had called a meeting—family only, no employees. So the cousins had been summoned from all over the state and were now assembled here. It was a hell of a lot of family in one place.

Luke had only heard about the meeting yesterday, although Benedict had clearly been planning it for a while. Not being an idiot, Luke could guess what it was about. He sat as far away from Fee as he could in preparation. Things between them had been strained lately. Professional, but strained.

Benedict was at the front of the room in sharply pressed jeans, a bright white button-down, and black jacket. He wore an expression close to a frown, his jaw jutting and his gaze narrow. He looked like he had a terminal case of indigestion.

So this was going to be fun then.

Luke's cousin Matt who was sitting next to him nudged him. "Is Benedict okay?"

"Yeah, he's fine. He usually looks like that—I think the stick up his ass has been growing these past few years. How was your flight?"

Matt shrugged. "The usual. Although SFO was fogged in —again—so everything was delayed. We barely made it on time." He checked his watch. "And while I'm always happy to see you guys, I'm going to need to head back to the airport in a few hours."

Luke squinted as he looked around. "I'm not sure who we're waiting for. Maybe—Nope, she's right there."

"Whoever it is, they better show up soon."

There was a bang from the back of the room as the door shut behind Leo—he was always late to everything. "Sorry," he said as he made his way to his seat.

Luke and Matt nodded together. "Leo," they said in unison. They should have known it was going to be Leo.

Benedict stepped forward and cleared his throat. The room went quiet as he set his hands on his hips and surveyed them all. "Thank you all for coming. I've called this meeting to address an issue that's come up."

Luke's pulse echoed through his ears. So they were going to do it like this...

"As you know," Benedict went on, "Josh is coming home soon. And by home, I mean he's planning on coming back to Cabrillo. He also wants to take a job on the ranch." Benedict gave a half sigh. "There have been... concerns raised in the community about this. And within the family."

A rustling went through the room as everyone adjusted to that. But no one spoke up for Josh. Not even Lil, who was sitting a few rows ahead of Luke, Adriano by her side.

Fine. Luke had wrestled steers before—he'd grab some

horns here. He crossed his arms and stared at Fee. "If anyone's concerned about losing Jasmine, we can get a new baker. In fact, we should have hired one by now."

He'd begun to suspect that Fee's refusal to hire a new baker permanently wasn't about the quality of the candidates—it was a protest against giving Josh a job.

A red haze crossed Fee's face, her mouth going tight. She was searching for something to spit back at him.

Before she could, Bea, sitting next to her, spoke up. "Really? Shouldn't you have brought this up before now then? You *are* the resort manager."

Aw, hell no. He understood Bea's impulse to fight for her sister, but she did not get to tell him his business when it came to the resort.

"I have brought it up. I do each week when I ask Fee for a status update on the hiring of the new baker."

"All right." Benedict put on his eldest-brother voice, which was very close to his CEO voice. "We're not going to argue about that right now."

"It isn't just about Jasmine. Or the business we've already lost," Fee finally said, addressing the entire room. "The Harper family—the entire family, not only her—is part of this community. We don't want to foster bad will with them."

"Our family isn't part of this community?" Luke asked. "We've been here for a long time."

"And the Harper family has been here longer. They aren't allowed to have concerns about Josh returning here?"

No. It was his instinctive response, and Luke knew it was wrong—of course they were going to have concerns. But Josh was family. "So they don't want Josh to come back to his home?" He leaned out of his chair, the better to pin her with his stare. "Tell us, Fee, since you seem to have a hotline to what they're thinking: if he doesn't come back here, to his home, his family, where's he going to go?"

The rest of the room was silent, wary—it was just him and Fee duking it out here. Goddamn cowards. At least Fee had the ovaries to tell him to his face how she felt, even if she was dead wrong.

"It's a big state," Fee said. "He could go a lot of places. Your parents are in Cambria, and the rest of the family is elsewhere. Some of them had to fly quite a ways to come here to deal with the problem of your brother. He won't be thrown among strangers. God forbid he actually have to survive like the rest of us."

Not a soul responded to that. They kept their mouths closed and stared stonily at Luke.

So they were all with Benedict then. Luke was alone in this. No one was going to speak up for Josh. Did they all hate his brother that much? Or were they simply worried about their precious trust funds?

There was still one person he might be able to count on. He looked to Lil.

Tears were running down her cheeks and her hand was tight in Adriano's, but she wasn't opening her mouth. Wasn't defending their brother.

Luke tore his gaze away and swallowed hard, his heart cracking. None of them understood what this really meant to him, not even Lil.

After what had happened that night, after he'd failed his brother and Leonora, Luke could never abandon Josh. If he'd only grabbed his brother's keys that night, worked harder to keep Josh from driving, none of this would have happened. He had to make that right.

But for all that emotions were rising and this was family,

it was still a business meeting. He couldn't pour out his soul here.

So he buried all that and went cold. The more professional he was, the more likely it was he could salvage something from this. "Has anyone bothered to tell Josh that the job he was promised isn't going to be happening? I mean, this is his company too."

"Actually, it isn't," Benedict said. "He gave up his voting interests. He'd only be an employee if he was hired on."

When the hell had that happened? Back when Benedict and Josh had their secret meeting? "So when he gets out, he'll have no job, no money, and no home?" Luke ticked the items off. "Am I reading this right?"

"He'll still draw from the trust." Benedict was as cool as ever. "But he has no say in the company."

"Was that your idea? I'll bet he has no hope of buying his way back in either." They'd cut him out. Just cut Josh out like... like he was superfluous and not their own flesh and blood.

Finally Benedict's facade snapped. "It was agreed we couldn't have a drunk holding a voting interest," Benedict snarled, his lip curling. "Trust me, it wasn't a pleasant choice. I'm not the asshole you think I am."

Oh, Luke wasn't so certain of that. Benedict might be a bigger asshole than Luke had ever dreamed.

"Oh my God," Fee snapped. "Did you really think he could waltz back in here with no consequences? Or maybe you did. You clearly think it's okay to have an affair with Ana."

Luke's vision went red. *What the fuck?* "What in the hell makes you think we're having an affair?"

Fee paled, but she pressed on. "You two were together at Gerry's the other night."

"And that's an affair now?" He wanted to shout that it was ridiculous, that there was nothing between them... except that there was. And he wasn't quite certain what to call it.

But it sure as shit wasn't an affair.

"Wait." Benedict held up a finger. "Are you sleeping with her?"

"No, I'm not," Luke got out, slow and furious. The accusation in Benedict's voice made him want to lie and say, *Yes, I am and I told her* everything *about our operations. Just like the idiot you think I am.*

What he said instead might have been worse. "And even if I was, what's so unethical about it? On a scale of one to 'fucking your secretary'?"

That... that might have been too low a blow. Benedict went a terrifying shade of red, and Luke instantly felt guilty, mostly because he really liked Pilar. She didn't deserve what he'd just said.

Penny Moreno, one of the cousins and the vet for the ranch, stood up then, holding her palms before her. "You've all got to stop this. This isn't why we're here. The issue is that hiring Josh could erode our goodwill in the community. We're looking at scales and trying to determine the balance here." She looked between Luke and Benedict and Fee, focusing on each of them in turn. "We need to decide: does our obligation to Josh outweigh our obligation to the community?"

Luke threw Penny a grateful glance. Finally some reason here. Finally someone else was reminding them that they all had an obligation to Josh.

Benedict drew a deep breath and let his fists fall from his hips. He rubbed his thumb across his forehead, suddenly looking weary. "Let's vote on it then."

He gestured to a few people and handed over a sheaf of paper and a handful of pens. Luke did a double take when he saw whom Benedict was handing them to. Nothing ever got Hank out of the house—calling him a hermit would be an understatement—but he was handing out stuff like it was no big deal.

"Write *yes* to vote to give Josh the job," Benedict was saying. "*No* to not hire him."

They all voted silently, pens scribbling and paper scraping as they recorded their responses, folding the paper and dropping it into the basket Bea was holding. Luke very clearly and decisively wrote *yes* and didn't bother folding the slip as he walked up to Bea. Everyone already knew his mind on this; he didn't need to hide his vote.

Once the last slip was dropped in—Leo's slip, late as usual—Bea handed the basket off to Benedict, who began to count the votes. He didn't announce a tally as he did, so Luke had no idea how the vote was going. And Benedict never gave anything away with his expression.

Finally Benedict examined the last slip. He blinked, once, twice, then said softly, "Well, that's that."

Luke couldn't tell much from that. He held his breath.

Benedict went on more loudly, "The majority of you are in favor of hiring him. Or if not in favor, at least willing to allow it."

Luke sat back but didn't relax. He knew better than to take this as a victory. This was only a first step—the real work would begin when Josh took on the job. But still, the job was his.

Little steps. They'd take little steps, and soon enough Josh would be back in the family fold.

Benedict dropped the last slip back into the basket. "But let me assure you all—this company is not a family charity, nor is it a family bank. I recognize that those of you who work for the company do a damn fine job. And that the rest of you take your voting decisions very seriously. I want to tell you that in no way is Josh getting a pass with this." He gave Luke a steady, unflinching stare. "He's getting a chance —just the one—and that's all."

Luke returned his brother's gaze, just as unblinking. Luke was going to make sure that one chance was all the chance Josh would need.

ANA WIPED her face with her towel, her arms rubbery as she did. It had been another day of box jumps and pull-ups with Luke, which had left her a sweaty, weak-limbed mess. Pull-ups were still difficult, but she'd fallen in love with them these past two weeks. She couldn't help but giggle a little each and every time she did one.

She still hated box jumps though.

Luke had gone to grab them some more water—Ana had chugged through her bottle of Lightning Blue pretty fast.

He'd been tense again today, but he hadn't said why. And she hadn't asked—better that they not share any more confidences. The further apart they kept their lives, the easier it would be when they came to the end of this.

She ran the towel over her arms, checking herself out in the mirror as she did. No wonder she'd gone through so much water; she had a "glow" from all her exertions.

She rubbed herself down with the towel, enjoying the rough scrape of the terry across her skin, pressing hard when she hit a sore spot. She slid the towel down her calves, then up to her thighs. She paused and cocked her leg. Huh.

That looked different. She craned her head to get a better look at her ass. Wow, she had a lot more muscle than before.

Had only a few months of lifting with him done this? She flexed her arms, checking out the new bulges in her biceps, the long line of sharply defined muscle girding her shoulders. That explained how she could do a pull-up now. That and the muscles in her back, which she couldn't see. But they probably looked amazing too.

She put forward her left leg and flexed so she could feel how tight her ass was. She ran her hand across it, testing the firmness with her fingertips. Goddamn, that was amazing. She repeated it with her right leg, found that side just as firm. The She-Hulk thing had been a joke, but she felt so strong, so powerful, as she looked at herself. Like she really could be a superhero.

Running her hands over her legs, she tested her calves, her quads, and her hamstrings. She'd always appreciated her body before, but now... now it was reaching a new level of awesome. Weight lifting wasn't so bad after all. Not if it could do this.

She ran her hands over her waist, testing the notches there, deeper than they had been before—

Luke appeared behind her in the mirror. A bottle of water hung from his fingertips, and his lips were parted, as if he couldn't quite get enough air. Her pulse picked up speed, all of her flushing with a heat that had nothing to do with how hard she'd been working.

She ought to be embarrassed being caught like this, feeling herself up in front of the mirror. Instead, the sensation of power lingered and then amplified. She completely and utterly had his attention here.

She held his gaze in the mirror, quite deliberately sliding her hands down her hips and over the muscles in her legs he had helped shape. The show wasn't entirely for him though; she wanted to keep exploring the new terrain of strength she was forging in this body of hers. And if he wanted to watch...

He dropped the water bottle, which gave a loud, wet pop as it hit the floor. She didn't even flinch, so mesmerized was she by the intensity of his expression, the leashed power in his stance. He stepped over the bottle on the floor and came up behind her, his hands lifting to fit over her own. The air between them crackled with all the things they'd tried so hard to ignore—lust, need, and something much more frightening than mere affection.

She held herself still as a bird in hand, waiting for his move. He watched her in the mirror, his gaze traveling over her with a weight she felt in her bones. And then he was guiding her hand to all the places that had changed.

"See here?" he whispered into her neck, their hands skimming over her shoulders, her arms, along her back. "Look at how amazing you are." His hands moved with hers, dancing together over her body. "I dream about you. You know that, don't you? You have to."

He'd dreamed about her.

Ana had a fairly realistic view of herself. She was pretty enough in an average way—but she wasn't a woman that men dreamed about. She was just Ana. Which was good enough for her.

How she felt when he said he dreamed about her was so much better than good though.

She turned her head and caught his mouth with hers, her arm snaking around his neck. This time the kiss started at intense and only went hotter from there. They kissed like that for long moments, him pressed against her back as they explored each other's mouth. It wasn't urgent so much as carnal, slow enough for them to savor each moment, deep enough to fulfill the need in both of them.

Then he turned her around and lifted her into his arms. She wrapped her legs around his waist and held on tight, cupping his face in her hands as she kissed him again. Devoured him and his taste.

Now the urgency was there. They were so close, so close... All they had to do was get rid of these horrible clothes and she could finally touch him like *she'd* been dreaming of. Instead, she ran her hands over every inch of bare skin she could find, his body scorching hot beneath her fingertips.

He began to thrust against her, tiny, almost involuntary motions of his hips. But she was so wound up, had been for so long, that even that pushed her close to the edge. All of her pulsed in time with his movements, bringing her close to a climax.

"Keep... Don't stop," she begged against his mouth.

"Jesus, you... When you ask me like that..." His thrusts slowed, went deeper, rubbing against exactly the right spot at exactly the right speed.

Her hands settled on his upper arms, her palms curving perfectly into the bulges of his biceps, and she dug in tight with her nails. His hips took up a quicker rhythm in response and she moaned, hooking her ankles into the small of his back, the better to hold on for this ride.

"I've wanted you for so long," he breathed into her ear. "So long. I watched you here, flushed, sweating, and wanted to lick every drop off your skin. And then I wanted to tongue you until you screamed. I bet you taste so good, darlin'."

She didn't scream then, but she did come, a lightning storm of pleasure making her every nerve crackle and sputter as she climaxed. Her thoughts went to white noise as she clung to him for dear life, waiting for the storm to pass and wishing it never would.

Her breath came hard and sawing, and she was hot enough to self-combust, but damn—*she felt so amazing.* Better than she had... well, since she'd started training with him and building up this vault of need. She gave a small, shaky laugh. Whoever said dry humping had gone out of style had never experienced something like that.

His face was nestled into her neck, and his lungs were working as hard as hers. Which was strange since he wasn't the one who'd just—

She blinked hard. "Wait, did you... Did you come too?" He was certainly acting like a man who'd had his crank turned.

His embarrassed laugh tickled her neck. "Yeah. God, I feel like I'm back in high school."

"Dry humping under your parents' roof is definitely very high school." Not that she'd ever done that, but there'd been a few fiestas where she'd made out under the stars with a cute boy.

"You all right?" he asked quietly, finally lifting his head. His eyes were dark, glazed with his lingering climax. He was disheveled and clearly kind of out of it, but still way cute.

"Yeah. Better than all right." But regret was sneaking in as she realized the implications of what they'd done. They'd broken their resolution not to do anything. And done it with an ease that scared her. "You?"

He released her to slide down his body and then caught her face between his hands. The regret was infecting him too. "What the hell do we do now? Because if this is how we deal with distractions, we're fucked."

She took his wrists in her hands and gently pulled them away. Needing space and some clarity, she stepped away from him and rubbed her arms, trying to steady herself. "We only have to last until this race. Which is a month away. Afterward, we won't even see each other. That solves our problem."

That hurt to say. To imagine not texting him or running with him or lifting with him. Or kissing him. But she had to do what was best. They both did.

"Until the race then," he said, solemn and sober.

She wasn't certain if he was agreeing to avoid touching her or if he was saying that whatever happened before then, it was over after the race. Whatever *it* might be.

And she really wasn't certain which one she wanted.

Chapter 15

IT WAS THE BEST RUN they'd ever done, Luke had to admit. They were only three weeks out from the race, and their pace, effort, attitude—everything was exactly as it ought to be.

Except for that thing between them, pulling at the both of them. Not pulling them back, the way the wind or fatigue might. It was pulling them forward, toward their trucks, where they both knew what would happen then. It had been inevitable since that first kiss. Or maybe even since she'd agreed to team up with him.

The irritation and rivalry they'd pushed on each other since high school had been a camouflage for something deeper, something worrisome that neither of them had wanted to admit to. But now that it was gone...

He sucked in a deep breath. Now that the mask was snatched off, they were going to act on what was beneath, even though that wouldn't change what had to happen in three weeks once they crossed that finish line.

It had been the dog that had given her away. Seth, who'd never warmed up to Luke, had not been with her. She'd always brought the dog before, and she hadn't mentioned anything about him being sick, so...

They'd find out in a few minutes. They were maybe twenty minutes from where they'd parked.

"So," he said, feigning casualness, "did you hear about the new fines the state is going to impose on hotels that don't meet the water restrictions?"

"Yeah. Are you guys worried?"

"No. We were pretty preemptive about implementing water-saving measures a while back. Mostly because I got sick of Benedict bitching about the water bill."

She laughed. "Yeah, from what I've seen of your brother, he's a bit much to take."

She didn't know the half of it. He was tempted to tell her about the family meeting, about how isolated he felt at the moment—but she didn't need his burdens too.

"Benedict is Benedict," was all he said.

"Anyway," she said, "I'm not too worried about the new fines. We've also cut back our usage, and those restrictions won't apply to us. Unless of course someone in Sacramento is looking for a new revenue stream and decides to try to tap the tribes again."

"Did you see the latest issue of *Southern California Weddings*? And the hot stuff for this year?"

She rolled her eyes. "The personalized gift bags for every single wedding guest? God, I hope that doesn't catch on. Can you imagine the nightmare of trying to coordinate that? The freak-outs the brides will have about it? Bad enough it's expected that the guests get something to take home. Do you know how many Jordan almonds we throw out each year?"

"Probably about as many as we do."

There was a lull, one that started out comfortable

enough because they *were* comfortable with each other now, and ramped up to charged as they came closer and closer to the end of the run.

The silence was absolute as their trucks came into sight, parked beneath some pepper trees lining the track. They'd chosen one of their more remote routes today, on a track that was less than a road but more than a trail. And pretty much deserted all the same.

She walked straight to his truck, her poise and confidence bringing the hint of a smile to his face. So he hadn't misread all this.

He took a moment to swallow hard. It was a terrible idea and they both knew it... and they were still going to do this. And that made him glad.

Without a word, he opened the passenger door of his truck for her. He'd already laid the backseat out into a bed. Hope springs eternal and all that.

She grabbed the jump strap, put a foot on the running board, and then paused. "Do you think anyone will come by?"

"No."

She glanced inside the interior. "You planned ahead. You know, you could have just brought some blankets to lay in the truck bed."

"I've never done this in my truck before."

She laughed. "Huh. An amateur. Don't worry, I'll teach you everything you need to know."

She climbed in and lay back. He left the door open as he climbed over her. And instantly saw the constraints of this setup. He wanted to have rough, athletic sex with her, sex that took up the whole bed. Hell, the whole room.

He couldn't even stretch out all the way back here, and if

he lifted his head even another foot, he'd whack it on the roof.

But she was beneath him, her eyes soft and her expression open. When she looked at him like that, he could make anything work. He kissed her, slow but not soft since he wanted her badly, but they had time. And he'd take it.

She shifted beneath him, trying to make space for him between her legs, and he lifted himself higher to help her. But her knees ran out of room halfway.

"Damn," she muttered.

"Clearly I didn't think this through."

"Should have brought the blankets," she said.

"I'll ask you next time." He pushed himself up even higher, the back of his head hitting the roof. "Unf."

She wriggled with him, and eventually they were situated with him pressed tight against her core. He could feel her heat even through their shorts, and his cock stiffened.

She gave him a look. "How are we even going to get our clothes off?"

He was wondering that himself. Man, he'd fucked this up. "Maybe we don't need to." He ran a hand up her torso and cupped her breast. "Oh shit, you're wearing a jog bra, aren't you?" Judging by what was under his palm, he'd need some goddamned pruning shears to get the sucker off.

"Of course I am. I can't let them just flap in the wind when I run. Do you know how much that hurts?"

This was the absolute worst place for this. They didn't fit, they couldn't even get undressed... but they had nowhere else to go. This cramped space was the only place they could be together.

But never mind that—they would make this work. They wanted each other too much to stop.

He pushed back, kneeling between her legs, his head hard against the roof. He crooked his fingers at her. "Sit up."

She rose up, pushing back her braid. He took hold of the hem of her shirt, his fingers resting against her belly. He savored the movement of her breath for a moment, her muscles fluttering with it, and then he tugged the shirt over her head as she shifted to help him free her from it.

When he saw her bra, he sighed. "Can you even get this off by yourself?"

"No, I call up my lady's maid to help me. Of course I can." She reached behind her and unhooked it. But it didn't release.

Great. They still had to pull it over her head. With the both of them twisting and tugging and banging their elbows on the truck frame, they finally got it off.

Luke had meant to pull off her shorts next, but he had to stop to appreciate her breasts. These had definitely been more than worth the effort to get her undressed. He cupped one, the skin there a lighter shade of honey than her shoulders and arms, her nipples dark. He rubbed his thumb across them, making a low noise of appreciation when they hardened at his touch.

"Did I look like this in your dreams?" Her voice was low and breathy, and he loved every syllable

"Darlin', this is so much better than my dreams." He gave her a crooked smile. "Even with our less-than-ideal situation here." He ran his fingertips all over her breasts, her upper chest, her shoulders, and her arms, her skin soft and smooth and so warm. So much better than his imaginings. And they'd only just started.

"Can I take out your braid?" he asked.

She did it for him, watching him as she pulled apart the strands and combed her hair out with her fingers, the atmosphere slow and thick between them. Once it was free, her hair came to her mid back, and it looked like the night itself was cloaking her shoulders so darkly gleaming was it.

"Jesus," was all he could whisper. Whether it was a curse or a prayer of gratitude, he couldn't say.

She raised an eyebrow. "You just going to sit there and stare?"

He never could resist a dare from her. He tugged off her shorts and panties with a rough quickness. Once she was entirely naked, he pushed her back and slid down her body. And realized that what he'd intended was going to be tough in this position.

The moment called for some improvisation.

"Hang on." He pulled her back up, lifted her off the seat, and with a powerful twist, reversed their positions.

She shifted above him, and he couldn't help but thrust slightly against her. He'd waited so long to get her naked, and his cock was screaming for her. She moaned as he did, and he had to think of anything but that noise to keep from exploding.

She braced herself against his chest and frowned at him. "How is this going to work? You're not even naked yet."

"Patience. We'll get to that. What I have in mind right now only needs you naked."

He gripped her thighs—damn, but she'd put on some muscle, which was so flipping hot—and pulled her up his body while scooting himself the opposite way.

"Oh my God," she started, "I don't think—"

"Brace yourself," he warned, then rubbed his face against her inner thigh.

She made a noise of needful protest. "Did you..." She gasped. "Did you not shave today?"

He only laughed softly and brushed his cheek against

the sensitive skin again. This time she grabbed his hair, giving something halfway between a moan and a hiss.

"I told you to brace yourself."

"You are awful. Horrid. A—"

He blew across the pink lips of her pussy, the dark curls surrounding it stirring with his breath.

She lowered her hips, still holding tight to his hair. He licked her then, slow and luxurious, savoring the tang of her as it spread across his tongue, her scent, her dense curls, and her slippery arousal his entire world at that moment. He traced her clit with his lips, felt it swell with his touch. He flicked it with the tip of his tongue and her hips bucked, her thighs tightening around his ears.

He sank his fingers into her ass cheeks and held her firmly in place as he licked and sucked and nibbled. Her cries grew louder, her movements more extravagant and abandoned as he urged her on.

When she did come, the truck cab could hardly hold her shout of release. Thank God they were so far out, because that could have been heard for miles.

She sat back onto his chest, her limbs trembling and her wet heat right over his heart.

"That was..."

"Good?" He gave he a cocky grin.

"Your ego is already too big for me to answer that."

"So it was."

She blew out through her lips. "I never said that."

"I heard what you didn't say. And your amazing—was that a scream? It felt more powerful than that—*noise* when you came."

She rolled her eyes even as her mouth tipped in a pleased way. "Are you going to get naked or keep fishing for compliments?"

He turned serious. "Help me, darlin'. Please."

Her chest rose and then fell, her eyes wide. She took her lower lip between her teeth and then inched herself down to his thighs. She was naked yet utterly powerful; she held all of him in her hand at that moment. Her fingers tangled in the fabric of his shirt, holding it as firmly as she was the rest of him. And then she peeled the shirt from him, baring him to her.

She made a noise of carnal appreciation, one that made him feel powerful. He lifted his hips, pushed against her, giving her the proof of his need for her.

"Do you want...?" She ran her hands down his chest, and his belly clenched when she hit his happy trail.

"No," he ground out. After all these months, any more foreplay would kill him. "Help me get the rest off."

Once more they wrestled to get him out of his shorts, heaving and twisting and tugging until they were finally both naked.

When he was, she wasn't a bit shy, fisting his cock with a bold intention that made his eyes roll back in his head. Never mind the foreplay—she was going to kill him like this.

"Ana." He managed to get a hand around one of her wrists.

"Please tell me you remembered condoms." All reedy and wanting and damn near bringing him to exploding again.

"The front console," he panted. If she needed more direction than that, they were in trouble, because his brain was short-circuiting.

With a rip, she had the foil package open, and he held the base of his cock for her as she rolled it on. Thank God she didn't try to tease him here, just got the thing on as quick as she could.

Then she was coming over him, her glorious breasts bouncing as she straddled him. He didn't bother waiting—as soon as her hot folds touched his cock, he pushed forward.

The angle wasn't quite right, but her head fell back anyway and her nails dug into his biceps, which made it *right*. She swallowed, shifted, and he thrust again.

Better, that was better. It went from *Man, that's good* to *Jesus, that's great.* She shifted again and he gripped her thighs to help her.

When he thrust the next time, they arrived at *Holy fuck, this is amazing.* They moved together, setting a slow, rolling rhythm. She opened her eyes, and that gaze of hers pierced him anew, just as it had when he'd first met her, held him in this moment they'd waited so long for.

"Ana." He couldn't look away from her, could never look away, not from something so beautiful, so necessary. "Ana."

He thrust hard, lifting her from the seat. She made a small, surprised noise, clenching around him.

"Luke." Her hands tightened on his arms, her eyes going wide. "Luke."

Slow was done. He thrust hard again; she gasped again. And then it all poured out of him, years of sniping, wanting, needing, his every thrust giving a little more to her.

Her hands left his arms and found his face, cupping his jaw. "Luke." She was begging him, a fracture of something small and fearful peeping through.

He swallowed hard. "I know. I know, angel, I know." Because this was more intense, more searing than he ever would have guessed. It scared him a little too.

He slowed his thrusts, turned them more rolling and

steady. "It's all right," he crooned. "I know, angel, I feel the same."

Her eyes slipped closed, and she set her forehead against his, her hands still framing his face. He held her hips as he increased his tempo, her shudders traveling through him each time he hit her clit just right.

She began to frantically nod against his forehead, a moan slipping between her teeth, and he knew she was close.

And then she was coming undone, clenching around his cock as heat flashed through her, threatening to incinerate him. His last bit of control went to ash as he climaxed, the both of them holding to each other as if they were the only stable points in a whirling universe.

ANA DIDN'T WANT this to end. Ever.

The truck was way too cramped, goose bumps were breaking out all over as the heat leached from her skin, and her knees were starting to protest... but Luke was beneath her, holding her close, breathing with her. When she pulled away, the moment would dissolve.

He kissed her hair, his big hand brushing along her back. She never would have thought he could be so tender. But she should have guessed—he was always surprising her.

"Can I tell you something?"

She nodded.

He didn't say anything right away. Maybe he'd changed his mind.

And then he said: "You infuriate me, you goad me, you push me to be better than I was. And you... you make me happy."

She'd been expecting something like that, but hearing the actual words, from his lips... She couldn't breathe for a time.

"You make me happy too." She shouldn't sound so sad when she said something like that. She pressed her lips against his shoulder. "Do you want to talk about it?"

He shifted beneath her. "How could you tell?"

"I've seen you or texted with you practically every day for the past five months. I knew."

He rubbed his chin along her hair, tangling the strands in his stubble. "The family gathered together to decide on the Josh question. Apparently more than just Benedict didn't want to give Josh a job. And the Jasmine situation spooked a lot of them."

The strain in his voice pulled hard at her heart. "I'm sorry." Not about the Jasmine thing, but that he was hurting because he was trying to help his brother.

"We had to take a vote on it. Everyone writing down their verdict on Josh's fate on little slips of paper."

She waited, but he didn't go on. "And?"

"They voted yes." There was no triumph or even relief in his voice. "*We* voted yes, although I'm not entirely sure who that *we* includes or how many there are. And they certainly didn't publicly stand up for him."

"But you did." She didn't put that as a question since she already knew the answer. "So now you feel all alone even though they voted yes?"

His chest moved under her, and she realized he was laughing silently. "You never let me wallow do you?"

"Why should I? Besides, you have already been wallowing. You did it Friday night when we..." She cleared her throat. Dry humping was a lot harder to say than she'd expected. "Well, when we did what we did. You told me about this now because you wanted me to snap you out of it."

"I needed to talk with someone outside the family about it. I needed to talk to *you* about it. And yeah, get snapped out of my funk. I'm not sure if I'm doing the right thing anymore. I never expected the family to be so against this."

He sounded lost, her arrogant, unstoppable cowboy. And it broke her heart. "For what it's worth, I think you are doing the right thing."

He kissed top of her head. "Thanks. It's good to hear someone say that. But especially you."

She was glad she could help him. But she wasn't here just to stroke his ego. Among other things. "I think you're doing the right thing, but you also need to decide where your line is in this. When will you say enough—how will you know when to let your brother go? And you need to have an answer to that if he's falling *or* if he's rising."

His hand drew languid circles on the bare skin of her back. "Yeah. I know."

Her mother had warned her to be careful of him, to watch out for his hidden, nefarious motives. But Ana should have been wary of this, of the personal confessions, of him opening up to her. Because she liked him. Liked his vulnerability. Liked how hard he was willing to fight for his brother.

She'd told her mother she'd be safe because she didn't like him. But what would keep her safe now that she *did* like him? And if he wasn't here to get sensitive information from her, to carry on their rivalry, did she even need to be kept safe?

Maybe he wasn't as *in like* with her as she was with him. Maybe she needed to keep herself safe from that.

She ran her hands over his chest. Breathtaking was such a trite word these days, but it was exactly how she felt when she looked at his body. It really was a living work of art. And for the next few weeks, she could touch it to her heart's content. Explore it and his desire for her. As well as her desire for him.

So she lowered her mouth to his again, to stop him from talking anymore and to stop her thoughts from lingering on the unsettling questions she couldn't answer.

Chapter 16

LUKE TOOK THE CORNER AT top speed, the grocery cart going up on two wheels as he careened around a display of tortillas.

Ana was waiting for him in his truck while he grabbed some of the energy drink she liked. It had to be the Lightning Blue flavor—she claimed that the Red Surge made her sick. So here he was, racing through the grocery store for her, praying that no one would notice her sitting in his truck.

They'd been at his house preparing for the race—which was the next morning—when she'd realized she didn't have any of the sports drink she liked. She was already close to vibrating out of her skin; apparently she didn't handle the night before a race very well.

So of course he had to offer to drive her to the store to get what she needed in an attempt to help however he could. But as they'd pulled into the grocery store parking lot, they'd looked at each other with the same realization.

"This isn't going to look good if we're seen," he said, swallowing hard as he held her wide-eyed gaze.

"Nope." She rubbed her hands on her jeans, her shoulders tense. He knew exactly how she felt.

It probably wouldn't have worried them so much if they hadn't spent the past few weeks hooking up in his truck every chance they had. They'd meet on a back road, run, and then jump on each other in the truck cab. It was still cramped and not ideal, but they'd take what they could get. And what they could get was pretty damn good.

No one knew they were sleeping together, but *they* knew, which made being seen together tonight that much more fraught.

So he'd parked in a deserted corner of the lot and told her he'd run in and get it. But every step away from her had his tension ratcheting up one more notch. If she was seen in his truck...

It probably wouldn't matter. Everyone knew they were doing this race together. It could be explained away. Probably.

But he didn't want to think too deeply on that. He rolled down the beverage aisle at a clip just short of a jog, looking for the familiar neon-blue color of the flavor she liked.

And had to stop dead lest he run down Jackson in the middle of the aisle.

Of all the people to run into...

"Hey." Luke kept that short. Not aggressive but not friendly.

"Hey." Jackson looked about as happy to see him as Luke was.

They stared at each other for a long moment, the air between them clogging with awkwardness.

But Luke didn't have time to sit there feeling silly. "I, uh, I just need to grab some of the Lightning Blue," he said. Although he still didn't see where it was.

"Yeah, Ana only likes that kind."

It had felt a little special, her telling Luke her preferred flavor and him going to these lengths to get it for her. But with the casual way Jackson indicated that he, too, knew this thing about Ana—suddenly it wasn't so special. Even though it was only a stupid sports-drink flavor.

He ought to simply say, "Excuse me," inch past Jackson, grab the drinks, and get the hell out of there. Ana was waiting.

Instead, he stood there and tried to think of something else to say. Which was insane since Jackson didn't want to talk to him.

He opened his mouth, his lips forming a good-bye—

"How's the training going?" Jackson asked. He shifted his weight to one hip as if settling in for a long chat.

Apparently Jackson did want to talk, which surprised the hell out of Luke. "Okay. It's tomorrow."

"I know," Jackson said. "Ana asked me to meet her at the finish line."

She hadn't told Luke that. And it was none of his business.

"Great," he said with a forced smile. "I'm sure she'll be happy to have you there."

"Good luck. To both of you."

"Thanks." This was getting stiff and formal, the two of them going through the motions of talking rather than really conversing. But what else could they expect? Except Luke did have one real question for Jackson. "How's Jasmine?"

He meant it with the best intentions. He liked Jasmine, a lot, and hoped she was happy in her new job.

"Good." Jackson nodded meditatively. "She really likes working at the resort."

"They're lucky to have her."

"I know."

There was a long beat of silence. The thing they were both circling sat between them like a recently doused fire—still hot, still smoking, but technically dead.

Ana wanted them to talk about it, to bring all their guilt out into the open and hopefully repair their friendship. But friendships didn't have to last forever. They were living things, and sometimes they died.

This one wasn't altogether dead yet though. Because Luke had one more real question.

"How are you?" Luke used to ask Jackson that question every day. But that was the first time he'd asked him in five years. He wanted to know: did Jackson carry the weight of their siblings' wreck as heavily as Luke did? Did he feel the same driving need Luke did to protect his sibling from whatever else life might throw at them?

Did he wish every day that night had turned out differently?

But Jackson didn't answer any of that. He only answered the question Luke put to him directly. "Okay. And you?"

Luke thought of everything he could tell Jackson—all about trying to ready things for Josh's return, the family's resistance to welcoming Josh back, his fears that Josh would fall back into his shithead ways.

And then there was everything going on with Ana. Jackson knew Ana better than anyone—he would be the perfect person to pour all this out to.

But Luke couldn't talk about any of it. Their friendship was gone, and he had to swallow down everything he wanted to say.

"Okay," he said. "I've been okay." Which was a lie, but

they were the kind of acquaintances now that required those lies. "Although I'm late to meet Ana."

Jackson moved aside. "Well, don't forget her drink. She's picky about that."

"Yeah. Wouldn't want her to hit me again."

The joke fell like a lead bar between them.

"Tell her I said hi." Jackson gave a wave and started off. "And tell her I said good luck."

"Will do," Josh said in farewell.

He turned back to the rows of plastic bottles, blinking for long moments to try to shake off that conversation. He needed to get his head together and get out of here.

A clerk passed the aisle.

"Excuse me?" Luke called.

The clerk paused with a questioning expression.

"Do you have any of the Lightning Blue flavor here?"

"Sorry. We sold out earlier today. But we have plenty of Red Surge."

Awesome. He hadn't gotten her what she wanted, and he'd run smack into the failure of his closest friendship. He was striking out all over tonight.

"Thanks," he told the clerk, "but she doesn't want that."

He grabbed the cart and went out to tell her that he'd failed. And prayed that Jackson hadn't seen her in his truck, which would be the cherry on this shit situation.

"WHAT DO YOU MEAN, they were out?" Ana demanded as Luke climbed into the truck.

She didn't mean to sound so shrill, but she needed that drink. She couldn't bonk tomorrow, and that was the only thing that didn't upset her stomach.

"We'll try the convenience store at the gas station," he said. "They probably have it."

His voice was low, his jaw tight, and he rubbed a hand across his face as if he was exhausted. He hadn't looked like that when he'd gone in.

"Did something happen in there?" she asked in a gentler tone.

"You didn't see Jackson come out, did you?"

Crap. "No. He was in there?"

Jackson catching them would be bad. She didn't want Jackson to know she was sleeping with Luke. Didn't want him to feel betrayed by what she'd done. Not that he necessarily would, but she didn't want to test that.

"Yep." He popped out the *p*, hard and humorless.

"Was it that awkward?" Maybe they had tried to talk, really talk, which was why he was so rattled. Although that would be an odd conversation to have in the grocery store.

"Don't get your hopes up. We didn't talk about anything. Well, anything except the fact that you like the Lightning Blue flavor."

"So he knows?" Her voice slipped out of her control and back into shrill.

"No. Sometimes I do nice things for people even if I'm not sleeping with them." The sarcasm in that was acid on her ears. "He knows that."

His hands were tight on the steering wheel now, the rest of him in shadow. They were in a dark corner of the lot, the better to hide themselves.

There'd be nothing to hide tomorrow. She had no illusions there; there would be nothing between them after the race, nothing but the memories. She didn't want those memories to be sour though, not for either of them.

"Sorry I snapped." She offered that quietly.

He released the wheel. But didn't reach for her. "It's okay. I'm sorry I couldn't get your Lightning Blue."

There was more there, more regret than simply failing to find something for her. Maybe the regret was because Jackson and he hadn't really talked. Or couldn't.

This was the point where she should push him, where she would have pushed him. He claimed to like it, to appreciate it. Well, she knew he did since he took her pushing with good humor. Beyond what would simply be his charm.

But she didn't push this time. She was too anxious about tomorrow, too sad about this being their last night together, and really, it was too late.

So she simply said, "It's okay. Let's try the convenience store if that's all right."

He nodded and started the truck.

When they got to the gas station, he parked on the side farthest from the road, dark and deserted. They didn't have to speak; she waited silently in the truck as he ran into the store.

The gas station was busy—it was a Friday night and everyone was bringing their toy haulers to the desert, passing through Cabrillo as they did. Headlights flashed through the truck cab every few minutes, blinding her for half a second every time they did. But no one actually walked by the truck; they were parked well out of anyone's path to the pumps or the store.

Her nerves were jangly, her lungs tighter than a drum. And it wasn't because she was worried about her drink.

The realization was sinking into her as she sat in the dark alone, headlights strobing every so often into the bubble of silence, the thought settling deeper than before, ready to reside for a long time.

This was it. This was the end.

They would see each other tomorrow, race together and probably win—but the daily workouts, the calls to each other, the intimacy—that would end.

But along with the aching understanding came her resolve, cold and gray and as immutable as granite. There would be pain, yes, but she'd survive and thrive. She always did and had through worse.

So she'd smile tonight and run her heart out tomorrow. And return to work on Monday and figure out her life. Without him.

Luke came out then, holding two cases of Lightning Blue high over his head like a boxer showing off his championship belt, his arms flexing with easy power.

It looked like he'd decided to get happy too. Or at least pretend.

"See, darlin'?" he said as he slid into the truck. "I told you I'd sort you out."

"And you did."

Some of the anxiety that was curled in her belly eased and released. She had her Lightning Blue, and they'd trained like champs, and she wouldn't be alone. At least not tomorrow.

They grinned at each for a moment, then she leaned over and kissed him. Tomorrow things would end, but tonight she could still thank him with a kiss.

He caught her face between his hands and deepened the kiss, their tongues meeting as their mouths joined. He was hungry, demanding, and she gave him all that right back.

When they separated, he set his forehead against hers and they simply breathed together for a moment.

"I should buy you that more often if that's the response I'll get." As a joke it was flat, but she understood his impulse. If they tried to laugh about it, it might hurt less.

"Yeah. We'd better go." She swallowed hard, then turned away from him.

And saw Chelsea Thomas staring into the cab, her eyes and mouth perfect Os.

Ana sucked in a hard breath, the air seeming to get trapped in her throat.

Oh shit. Chelsea couldn't know who Luke was, could she?

Her heart did a sickening skip into her throat as she glanced at Luke. Had he seen Chelsea?

He was fiddling with the keys, trying to start the truck, the motions of his hands unhurried and unconcerned. So he hadn't seen her then. He gave Ana a quick look and then did a double take.

"Hey, what's wrong?"

Ana looked back to the front of the convenience store, but Chelsea was already gone. Which seemed incredibly quick. She searched the shadows, looking for a thin slip of blond. Another set of headlights swept past them, blanketing everything in harsh illumination, but Ana saw no sign of Chelsea.

Maybe she'd imagined the whole thing. And even if Chelsea had been there, it was none of her business what Ana did in her private time. This was most definitely not related to work stuff.

Although that excuse only worked if Chelsea didn't know who Luke was.

Which she probably didn't.

Ana released a slow breath. She really, really did not need this tonight. But there was nothing she could do. She inwardly shook herself. "It's nothing. I thought I saw someone, but it was only a weird flash of light."

"Okay." He turned back to his keys, reassured by her

explanation. Which made her feel a smidge guilty. But it would be fine. "Ready to go home?" he asked.

She wasn't. She wanted this night to stretch out a little longer. But it was probably best if they went home. They had a long day tomorrow. "Yeah. We probably should. Can I leave this case of Lightning Blue in your truck and you can bring it tomorrow?"

He started the truck, the engine catching with a sputtering roar. "Sure thing. Anything you want."

She stared out the window as they drove away, trying not to let the regret and yearning in his voice catch at her heart.

Chapter 17

ANA WAS TRYING TO PUT her game face on, but it kept slipping.

Luke, waiting with her in the prep area of the race, didn't look much better. He'd look off in the distance, then at his feet, then at the other racers milling around them, but never once did his gaze touch on her.

She could guess why: after this, what was between them was over. That was enough to make her jittery too. That and this race they were about to run.

And Chelsea catching them last night. Not that Luke was concerned about that or knew. But the memory of it ground at Ana, made her heart feel sick. Especially Chelsea's wide-eyed expression of scandalized horror. As if she knew exactly who Luke was.

Or maybe Ana was just projecting.

She shook out her hands, willing her attention to turn to her body and away from all those anxious thoughts. She was really not in the right headspace to win this. And it didn't look like he was either. They both needed to get it together and quick.

She touched a hand to his elbow and instantly the fog between them lifted, his focus coming onto her with a sharp forcefulness. Okay, maybe he was ready and it was only her who was out of it.

"We, uh, we should start getting ready," she said. Getting their gear together should get their brains into the right frame. Or least give them something better to do than be uselessly anxious.

He nodded and starting going through their gear bag. He handed her the arm and leg sleeves, Body Glide, and a roll of duct tape. The sleeves were to protect them from any nasty bits on the obstacles, the Body Glide was for chafing—Ana could already tell a spot between her bra and her armpit was going to be a problem—and the duct tape was for their shoes, to help keep them on. They were both wearing old running shoes that could be tossed when they were finished. Although Ana did hope she could salvage hers—the waste of tossing them out bugged her.

Once they were all suited up and she'd double-checked that they had bottles of Lightning Blue in her pack and his, she looked him over. He ought to look ridiculous with the black Lycra sleeves clinging to his arms and legs and clashing with the neon green of his performance shirt and running shorts, and then the tape on his shoes...

Okay, so he did look ridiculous, but also amazing to her.

She knew how he looked beneath the silly clothes. How his hands felt as they ran across her skin. How his arms felt as they clasped her close. She knew intimately the hard ridges of muscle in his thighs as they contracted with his thrusts.

And she knew the way his eyes could be an utterly different shade of blue when he smiled at her and only her, without ever changing color.

She noticed then that his left sleeve wasn't quite in place. Reaching out, she tweaked it for him, tugging the material higher up his biceps. He caught her gaze, his expression intimate and fond. He was saying *thank you*, and so much more, with that look.

He shouldn't be looking at her like that, not where people could see, but she drank it in anyway.

"All better," she said after several heartbeats, letting her hands fall away.

He blinked and then looked past her, almost as if he were searching for something. His expression went sharp.

"Don't look now," he said in low tone meant to stay between them.

"What?" What had he seen? All of her itched to turn, but she held herself still.

"There's a couple over there who keeps staring at us."

Ana went cold. "Is it anyone we know?"

He shook his head.

Thank God for small mercies. But if the couple wasn't anyone they knew, why were they staring?

"Who could they be then?" she asked.

He shrugged with one shoulder. "I don't know. They're both in their thirties, I would guess. The dude is bald and the woman has brownish hair. Did you see them before? They've been giving us hard looks this entire time."

Ana frowned. She vaguely remembered a couple like that. Slowly, torturously, she angled her head so that she could see the couple from the edge of her vision.

They were both whippet thin with the kind of stringy, tough look that some serious runners occasionally got. Neither of them looked familiar. And they were both staring as if lasers might shoot from their eyes and obliterate Ana and Luke. What the hell?

Ana focused back on Luke. "What is their problem?"

"Maybe they think we're their main competition."

"Don't they know this is for charity?"

Luke gave her that fond look again, this time topped off with a smile. "I know. The nerve of some people, trying to win a charity race."

Okay, so it was a little hypocritical of her. Just a bit. "Well, we've got to disappoint them." A shot of adrenaline hit her heart, topped off with pure competitiveness. Finally, an opponent to set herself against. That was exactly what she needed to get her head together.

"I'm ready if you are," he said.

"I was born ready." She pulled a face to show how ready.

"That's an amazing look on you." His chest shook with suppressed laughter. But then his smile died into something more regretful. "Before this is over, I just wanted to say thank you. It was... No matter what happens, you're amazing."

She ducked her head. He wasn't supposed to do this right now. They were supposed to be getting into race mode, not telling each other they were amazing.

But it was still really nice to hear.

She cleared her throat, feeling suddenly shy. "So were you."

She couldn't admit to more, not with this race about to begin. So she kept her head down and left it at that.

An announcement came over the loudspeaker. "All right, it's time for the couples wave to line up in the starting area."

Ana took a steadying breath and shook out her hands. Doubt suddenly stitched through her. What if she hadn't trained enough? What if she wasn't ready? She knew how to run a marathon, but she'd never done this before.

The crowd of couples moved to the starting line,

carrying her and Luke along with them. His arm brushed against hers, light and accidental, but it gave her renewed strength. He would be with her. She could run; he was strong. They would get through this together.

There were about thirty teams in the group, with a wide range of ages and body types. Most of them were smiling, clearly eager to begin. They were probably there simply to have fun.

But that other couple was still watching Luke and Ana, their gazes cold and unsmiling. Ana stared back. If they wanted a horse race here, she'd give them one. And she'd beat them too.

"You gonna give them the stink eye the whole time?" Luke asked under his breath.

"Just letting them know they won't intimidate me."

I'm naming you two Mr. and Mrs. Stink Eye. She didn't know if they were married, or if Mrs. Stink Eye had kept her maiden name, but it was Ana's brain and she could do whatever she wanted in there.

"All right, Killer," Luke said. "I think they got the point."

"You're as competitive as I am. Don't act like you don't want to make them eat dust too."

"I do, but I'm more worried about getting you across that finish line."

"Hey. This isn't about your getting me anywhere. This is us doing it together. I'll be pulling my own weight here."

Something hot flared in his eyes, and she knew if they didn't have about a two hundred strong audience, he would have kissed her. She'd have probably kissed him back too.

The starting gun went off, cracking through the still morning air and setting some mourning doves into flight.

With that, Ana was snapped hard back into herself and the situation. Her legs started off purely on instinct, her eyes already searching for paths through the pack of runners. Getting clear of the seething knot of bodies, with everyone stumbling into their strides and trying to find their own cadence, was Ana's main priority. That and keeping Luke close.

Once they'd gained some breathing room, they could put their attack plan into motion. She caught sight of Luke immediately behind her and to her left. A space opened up before her as two women veered away from each other.

Ana burst ahead into that space, not waiting to see if Luke took advantage too. Hopefully he was right behind her, using her as a wedge to get through himself.

Another space opened and she could see the front of the pack. She surged forward and, when her path was blocked again, took a moment to mentally test the area behind her, trying to determine if Luke was there. She listened carefully to the rhythm of the steps, the weight of them as they hit the track.

It was him, right on her heels.

All right then. They only needed one or two more openings like that and they'd be clear of the pack. The group was already starting to naturally thin as certain teams fell behind and others sped ahead. Mr. and Mrs. Stink Eye were some of the ones speeding ahead. They weren't quite at the front but were only two or three lengths from gaining the lead.

If the couple attacked the obstacles the same way they were attacking the leaders here, Ana knew that she and Luke were in for a fight.

Bring it. She was ready. They were ready.

Another team in front of them began to fall behind, opening a lane for Ana. She put on speed, trying to slip through before the other team could cut her off.

But it wasn't the other team she had to worry about—it was Mr. and Mrs. Stink Eye she should have been watching out for. They swerved into the gap, blocking her in and forcing her to put on the brakes.

She bit back some nasty words as she pulled up, Luke almost smashing into her back as she did. Frustrated rage burned hot in her chest. She was going to make them pay for that.

But in the meantime, the Stink Eyes took off again, having done their dirty trick of messing up Ana's move to the front.

No, they weren't getting away that easy. Ana sped up, trying to catch them.

"Oi!" Luke called from behind her. "Remember to pace yourself. We've only just started."

He was right; she was letting them get to her and mess up her racing strategy. She slowed down until she was abreast with him, grinding her teeth to work out some of her anger.

"Sorry."

"They'll blow up if they keep doing that," he said, all reasonable calm. "Don't worry, we'll catch them. I doubt they're as well trained for the obstacles as we are."

He was right, so she let her jaw relax and made her legs settle into the proper pace. If they rattled her this early, they'd already won.

They went up a rise, then down again, and behind the next rise was the first obstacle: a cargo net.

Mr. and Mrs. Stink Eye were already scrambling up, their feet falling through the webbing in their haste to get up. Big mistake. Ana was going to take her time and not waste it trying to get up as fast as she could.

She and Luke hit the net at the same time, but he gradually pulled ahead of her, his superior strength and reach helping him there.

It was harder than Ana would have thought. A cargo net was basically playground equipment, but pulling herself up the ropes and not falling through was more difficult than it looked. And once she reached the top, she had to slide down the other side. She only hoped her clothes would protect her from the rope burn.

Luke reached the top well before she did. Before he was even fully on the platform, he was turning around and holding out a hand for her. She reached up and set her hand in his. He pulled her up the last few feet as easily as if she were a ten-pound kettlebell.

"You okay?" he asked as soon as he'd set her down.

"Great. Or I would be if we weren't behind."

They slid down the backside together, the knots banging Ana in the elbows and back and butt. But they were down quicker than they'd been up and off again.

As they settled into their rhythm, Mr. and Mrs. Stink Eye remained in front, close enough to watch but too far away to catch. At least if Ana wanted to keep to her planned pace.

Luke was right; she couldn't let them get to her. But she also couldn't shake the feeling they were taunting her, making sure they were always right in front of her and Luke.

Mr. and Mrs. Stink Eye disappeared behind a dip in the road. A few minutes later, the sounds of splashing floated back to Ana and Luke.

They looked at each other.

"A water obstacle," Ana said.

Luke nodded. "We knew they'd have something like it."

"Do you think we'll have to crawl through mud or swim through water?"

His expression was grim. "We'll find out."

The Stink Eyes weren't in the water when they arrived, but currents continued to churn from their passage. Judging by how the water was moving, they'd definitely have to do some wading to get through.

"Stay close," Luke said. "I don't think it's deep, but I don't want you going under."

Aw. How sweet. "You could go under yourself," she pointed out.

He grinned. "You'll have to rescue me then."

"Come on." They didn't have time to waste on flirting, as much fun as it was.

She waded in and shrieked when she suddenly sank to her waist. There was a wicked drop-off there.

He charged in after her. "I told you to stay close. Are you okay?"

"Yeah, just surprised." She grabbed his hand to brace herself and began to trudge ahead, shivering as she did. The morning wasn't that cold, but the water sure was.

He kept his arm taut, as taut as she was keeping hers. They used each other to lever themselves through the water, pushing each other forward. Ana was very glad he was with her for this part; she wasn't worried about going under, but it was so much easier with a partner.

Finally they clambered up the bank on the other side, panting and shivering. Okay, that had been a lot worse than the cargo net, and it was only the second obstacle.

"We're going to freeze," he muttered.

"Not if we start running. But it's going to chafe like a bitch soon." Ana shuddered to think about it.

"Ugh. I forgot about that. Why did we do this again?"

She laughed. "Because you're having fun." And it *was* enjoyable, even though they were both soaked and shivering. "Let's go and catch those two."

Running in sopping-wet clothes was a misery Ana had never really experienced before. She could feel herself slowing, her cadence never finding a sweet spot as her clothes flapped against her skin, cold droplets falling from them.

Luke looked about as miserable as she felt.

"The mud will be much worse, won't it?" she asked.

He nodded grimly. "I'm hoping they won't have a mud pit, but yeah."

Please let that be the last obstacle. Running with mud stuck in all her nooks and crannies was not something she wanted to do for several miles.

They came around a bend, a large pepper tree standing at the turn and spraying its branches into the trail. Dead ahead were Mr. and Mrs. Stink Eye, closer than ever before.

"We can catch them," Ana hissed.

"Are you sure? We're not even halfway."

True. But they'd have to make a move sometime. Now might be it. "How are you feeling?"

He shrugged. "Good. Except for my shorts rubbing my thighs raw."

Hers were too, although the urge to catch those two was much stronger than the discomfort of that. "Don't be a baby. Let's go."

But right as she sped up, the other couple disappeared behind another bend. They weren't really getting away, but Ana still gritted her teeth as she picked up her pace, pushing herself forward and faster.

Once she was around the bend, the Stink Eyes were nowhere to be seen. There was a long row of eucalyptus and another turn in the road—they must be behind those. She never let her pace flag as she went for the next turn. Luke kept close behind her, his steady breathing and the drumbeat of his feet pushing her forward along with her desire to win.

Just as she'd thought, the other couple was waiting on the other side of the eucalyptus. Along with another obstacle.

Not mud, thank goodness, but it was unlike anything Ana had ever seen. It was a pyramid made of high steps, almost too high to climb. They'd have to climb up five steps to get to the top, then another five steps to get down the other side.

Well, the box jumps were going to be good for something here.

Mr. and Mrs. Stink Eye were starting up, but they were struggling. Mrs. Stink Eye was screaming at Mr. Stink Eye to hurry up, to jump higher. When he finally made it up the step, bending over to catch his breath, she yelled at him to boost her up, damn it. When he did, Mrs. Stink Eye didn't even turn around to help him. The poor man had to jump himself up.

Ana almost felt sorry for him. But he was her competitor, and Luke was right: the other couple wasn't as prepared for the obstacles as they were.

They could catch them here.

Luke met her eyes, wearing the same sly, triumphant smile she was. He was thinking the exact same thing. "You can thank me for all the box jumps later."

She rolled her eyes. That wasn't happening. "At least you won't have to boost me up like that poor dude is doing."

When they reached the first step, without waiting for Luke to offer to help, Ana jumped for the ledge, catching it and boosting herself up. Her arms shook as she pulled herself up. This was harder than doing pull-ups in the gym.

Her clothes were still damp and adrenaline was making her shaky, but she made it.

Four more to go. She could do this. And she didn't want Luke's help—there were probably even worse obstacles up ahead, and he'd need his strength.

She looked up and saw that Mr. and Mrs. Stink Eye were only one step from the top, the jerks. And the way down would be much easier than the way up.

If they meant to catch them, she and Luke would have to go faster than this.

Luke had jumped up to her level and was about to jump up to the next step. "You need help?"

She shook her head and jumped, grabbing for the edge. Oh, this one was much harder. She pushed herself halfway up, then clung to the step for half a heartbeat before she could command her leg to swing over the edge. Using her thighs, she pulled herself to safety.

Three more. She panted as she gripped her thighs, summoning her strength for another jump. Three was nothing. Three was easy. And after three, she'd be halfway there.

Luke was already on the third step, having passed her a moment before while she was psyching herself up. He looked over the edge, a question in his eyes.

"Go," she said. "I'm coming."

Her legs burned with the next jump, her palms aching as she grabbed yet another ledge. She grunted hard as she pulled herself up, needing to get out the force of her effort somehow.

When she finally clambered up the step, he was waiting for her. "I can boost you up. It might be quicker."

"And then you'll get tired quicker."

She motioned him on, but the idiot man didn't move.

"Don't worry about me," he said, implying that he was the only one allowed to worry.

"We're in this together. I have to." She pulled herself up to the next step, her arms feeling like Jell-O that had been set on fire. "Come on, slowpoke."

She heard him laughing below her and then his grunt as he pulled himself up to her level.

One more step and this torment would be over. One more step and she'd have done it all on her own. She looked up at the step, gathering her strength for one more jump.

Hands slid around her waist, large, familiar hands, and Luke was boosting her up to the last step.

"Hey," she said but with little heat. She was too grateful to be finally done. Although there was still the part about getting down...

He boosted himself up. "We're in this together."

She gave herself half a moment to glow at his words, then went to study the backside of the pyramid, chugging some Lightning Blue as she did. There were another five steps to climb down, just high enough to make it tricky. She took a moment to consider a strategy.

But he was clasping her waist again before she could decide anything. "What are you—?"

"Trust me." He swung her down to the next step.

It was like riding the swings at the fair, her legs swinging free through the air in a great arc, the sensation of weightlessness making her giddy. When her feet hit the step, she was almost sad, the same way she'd been when she was a girl and the swings had come to stop, bringing her back to earth.

He hopped down. "This is quicker." And he grabbed her waist again.

This time she braced her arms against his shoulders and

watched his face. As he lifted her, his brows pulled together with the effort, but as he started his swing, a smile took hold of his mouth. She grinned back, because this was fun. Playful. Even if they didn't win, the memory of him swinging her from step to step like they were little kids would be reward enough here.

Although she still really, really wanted to win.

As soon as he'd swung her off the last step, she hit the ground running.

The other couple hadn't made it very far—their pace was clearly flagging. Ana had no doubt they'd catch them now and that they'd keep the lead. The Stink Eyes didn't seem to do so well when things got tough.

Ana didn't bother to see if Luke was following. She already knew he was.

Given the distance between the obstacles so far, they had about a half mile until the next one. Plenty of time to catch the other couple. And once they had, they'd let the obstacles keep putting the Stink Eyes farther and farther behind.

A little more speed. A little more and Ana would catch them. There was a hill coming up—they'd have to slow for that. Ana could keep her pace though, if she just pushed hard enough. Which she would. She was tired but not even close to bonking.

Then the mud pit came into sight. It was probably thirty feet wide with wire strung across it. They'd have to crawl under the wire to get across, bellies and elbows and knees in that muck. And probably their faces at some points as well.

Ana didn't allow herself to linger on the thought. The only way out was through, and she was going to barrel through that thing.

The Stink Eyes weren't quite as resolved as she was though and were pulling up as they neared the pit.

This was their chance. Luke was already at her elbow, so without hesitation Ana dropped down and started crawling.

It wasn't so bad... at first. The mud was cold and sticky and gritty, but Ana concentrated on moving forward no matter what. The sleeves on her arms and legs mostly protected her, but mud began to slip under her waistband. That was going to be a bitch to wash out.

Luke grunted next to her, pulling himself through with steady fierceness. He'd already passed her, and they were ahead of the other couple. Ana didn't think they were even in yet; at least, she didn't hear them moving behind her.

Ana hit a surprise deep spot then, her face going into the mud. She came up sputtering, dirt hard up her nose and her hair getting tangled in the wire above.

For half a moment she started to panic. Her hair was caught, she couldn't breathe, and she was trapped under the wire.

Don't panic. You can fix this.

She wiped a hand down her face, clearing most of the mud from her nose and mouth. There. Now she could breathe again.

Her hair would be trickier. She pulled slightly, testing how caught it was. Judging by the yank of it, her hair was pretty damn tangled up. She could just tear it out, but she didn't want to leave half her hair in a mud pit.

"Are you okay?" Luke was crawling toward her, panic splintering his voice.

"I'm fine. I just need to get my hair out."

He looked her over. "You're completely covered in mud. Hang on, I'll get your hair."

He began to tug the strands free, gently and slowly, taking tender care with her hair. But as he did, the Stink Eyes pulled ahead.

"Don't worry about my hair," she said, frustration making her voice gritty. "Just pull it out!"

"I can't hurt you." He tugged a little harder. But still not fast enough.

Oh crap, they were going to lose, and it would be all her fault. "Hurry," she urged him, pulling her head as far forward as she could in an attempt to speed up the process.

"Ana," he chided. But he tugged hard then, a muscle in his cheek twitching as he did, and suddenly Ana was free.

"Thanks. Let's hurry." She heard his exasperated laugh behind her as she crawled as fast as she could after the Stink Eyes.

She levered herself out of the mud pit only a second or two behind the other couple. Time to finally put them far behind her and Luke.

But as she straightened, a curtain of mud fell from her front and down her legs, the mud that had accumulated under her clothes sliding slowly down her thighs.

Running with sludge under her clothes was going to be as miserable as she'd feared, because she wasn't even moving and it already sucked.

She shook herself off like Seth after a bath, mostly to get rid of whatever mud she could and also to shake off any thoughts that weren't in the here and now. If she focused, she could fight past her discomfort and win this. She knew it.

Luckily, the Stink Eyes had stopped to scrape off the mud as well. Ana guessed that would slow them down; if she was uncomfortable, they were probably miserable.

That thought cheered her up immensely. She turned to Luke and scraped some mud out of his ear. "Ready?"

He raised an eyebrow. "It's time."

In unison, they took off. The mud slopped off their

clothes, chafed her thighs and arms, and itched like crazy... but Ana couldn't stop grinning. They were in the lead, her legs felt great, and they should only have two more obstacles to cross. Then the finish line and victory.

Luke was grinning too. He caught her eye at one point and asked, "Having fun?"

"Yep. Although this mud is awful. I'm sticking to road races after this."

"Not gonna look into a career as a mud wrestler then?"

She laughed. Oh yeah, they were both feeling good. They had this in the bag.

The wall came into sight then. She'd known there would be a wall obstacle, but the size of it was a shock. It was actually a half-pipe rather than a wall, but tall enough that climbing to the top was not going to be easy. They'd have to take a running start up the ramp, then jump from the highest point they could.

She was ready. Her body was ready. They could do this.

She climbed onto the ramp and judged the height. She'd have to get going pretty fast and explode into the jump. But there wasn't too much time to ponder; the Stink Eyes weren't that far behind.

"Hang on," Luke said. "I don't think we can just brute attack this. This is going to need teamwork."

"You boost me up and then you jump?" Hopefully Luke hadn't spent too much of his strength on the first part of the course. They would need it here if they were going to do that.

"Yeah. I don't think you can jump that high."

How would he know? "Well, maybe I can."

He gave a half sigh. "Maybe, but it's quicker if we do it my way. Come on, let's get up as high as we can."

They climbed about halfway up the ramp, until the slope was too steep for them to balance on.

"You've got no leverage here," Ana pointed out. Even with his strength, it would be difficult for him.

"Quit arguing and let me boost you up."

She positioned herself in front of him and looked up. The ledge she was supposed to grab was pretty high. Before she could tell him not to try, his hands were cinching her waist and he was lifting her up and up.

Reaching high for the edge, she tightened her abs and made her thighs rigid, trying to help him as much as she could. When his arms were fully extended, he wrapped one around her knees, pinning her legs to his chest, and set his other hand on her butt and pushed her even higher.

Her fingers found the very edge of the lip. She held tight, wishing he could boost her just a little bit more. Pull-ups by the very tips of her fingers were not something they'd trained for.

"Hang on," he panted, and with a heavy grunt, he pushed her up another few inches.

That was all she needed. She scrambled up as quickly as she could, ignoring the shooting pain in her knee when she banged it on the edge. Once she was safely up, she turned to watch him.

He was standing at the very bottom, hands on his hips and his head hanging.

Oh no. Had he run out of steam?

"Are you okay?" she called down.

He nodded without raising his head, his chest shuddering as he tried to breathe.

Crap. This was bad. She should never have let him boost her up.

She peered down the trail. The Stink Eyes were still coming, were maybe five minutes away.

But there was nothing she could do from up here. If she climbed down, they'd be in a worse spot than they were now.

Time to give him a shot of adrenaline.

"Come on," she yelled down. "Don't lose this for me."

He glared up at her. She simply raised her eyebrows. She wasn't there to coddle him or hold his hand—she was there to win, same as him. Besides, he liked it when she told him to buck up.

"I'm coming." He made it clear she was not going to like it when he got up there.

Whatever. As long as he got his butt up and they got going before the Stink Eyes.

He went to the edge of the ramp, then started running full bore, arms swinging, legs pumping, six feet of determined fury. He ran as far up the ramp as he could, exploded into a jump... and missed the ledge by a good foot.

Hell. They were in trouble. Her mind raced as she thought of how to help him. Yelling at him probably wasn't going to do it.

He went back to the end of the ramp, started off again, even faster now, climbing even higher up the ramp before jumping... and still missed.

She gritted her teeth. This was ridiculous. They'd never make it at this rate. There was one thing left that she could do. It might not work, but him brute-force attacking sure wasn't either.

She got down on her belly and hung her arms over the sides. "I'll help you up."

"You can't lift me."

"Yes, I can." Actually, she wasn't certain if she could. But she had to try. "We can do it together. Come on, they're getting closer."

He glared at her again.

"We don't have a choice."

"I could pull your arms out of their sockets."

She laughed in spite of the situation. "Hardly. How much do you think you weigh?"

"Fine." But he was clearly pissed.

He went to the end of the ramp and took off again. This time he was even faster, arms windmilling, legs churning, and she realized he meant to jump past her outstretched hands. She prayed that he would, even as she braced herself for his weight.

He leaped toward her, up and up, past her hands... and caught her forearms tight. Her fingers curled around his arms even as she grunted with his weight. He hadn't been kidding about pulling her arms out.

Hold on. She had to hold on. She pulled her abs in tight and braced herself. Pulling him up was going to be impossible for her, so she simply had to hold on until he could climb up.

He set his feet against the wall and began to climb his lower half up. As some of his weight was released off her arms, she was able to scoot back, giving him space to climb higher. It was downright ugly the way they did it, but finally they were together at the top. She took a moment to look him over, his muscles still quivering with the effort he'd just made. Their gazes tangled and he gave her a short nod. He was ready to finish this.

A quick check of where the Stink Eyes were—still at the bottom of the ramp and clearly at a loss for how to get up— and then she peered over the backside of the ramp to see how they could get down.

Stairs. Gloriously simple stairs. She could have cried in relief.

"I'll go first," Luke said. "You hang on to my shoulder so you don't trip. And catch me so that I don't trip."

That made sense. She stepped aside for him, then they went flying down the stairs, never stopping their headlong rush even when they hit the ground.

One more obstacle and they were done.

Another quarter mile went by quickly. She was tired and she could tell he was too—his head was lower than usual and his arms were held tight as if he were pushing himself solely through their motions—but they were keeping up a good pace, and there was no sign of Mr. and Mrs. Stink Eye.

By her reckoning, there was another quarter mile left. Maybe less.

They charged up a hill, or at least tried to charge up it. Okay, now they were definitely starting to flag. But they were so close to the finish; she just knew it.

And there it was. The finish line.

A smile took hold of her mouth. There wasn't another obstacle. They were done.

Then she saw a man standing next to... She squinted. Was that...?

A tractor tire. He was standing next to a tractor tire taller than she was. Oh crap. The thing probably weighed five hundred pounds.

They were going to have to pull that across the finish line. Or she might have to do it all by herself.

She sucked in a sharp breath. Everything else they'd come across had been doable. Tough, but doable. But the brute strength required to pull that across... She simply didn't have it.

"Don't freak out," Luke muttered to her. "Wait and see what they want us to do."

They slowed as they approached the man.

"Well, you're the first ones here," he called out happily. "But you're not quite done. The two of you—together— need to get this tire across the finish line. You get there first, and you've won." He held up a rope and some harnesses. "Here's everything you need to strap yourself in."

Ana didn't hesitate; she grabbed the harness and slipped it over her shoulders. Luke did the same.

As one, they started off, throwing themselves against the harnesses. The rope bit deep into her shoulders, all of her straining to get the massive circle of rubber behind them moving. Luke was straining just as hard, his body at a forty-five-degree angle to the earth, his feet digging deep into the dirt.

She heard a commotion—maybe the Stink Eyes finally arriving?—but she ignored it. There was work to do.

With a slipping sort of jerk, the tire finally started moving. She threw herself harder against the harness, trying to gain momentum. Luke's arms and legs were pumping, churning as he pulled too. The tire slowly began to gain speed, feeling lighter as they pulled it faster and faster.

Even if anyone was behind them, they'd never catch the two of them. They were moving too quickly now, the both of them running as fast as they could, in perfect sync.

And then she fell.

She wasn't quite certain how it happened; her toe somehow slipped in the dirt, and then her leg was sliding out from under her, and then she was face-first on the ground, dirt shoved into her mouth and nose and the skin of her palms.

Worst of all, she brought Luke down with her in a tangle of rope.

She pushed herself up, her arms burning with fatigue, and saw the Stink Eyes pulling their tire right past them.

No no no! She scrambled to her feet, ignoring the pain in her knee and frantically untangled herself from the rope.

Luke was already back on his feet, dusty, but uninjured. "You okay?" He held out a hand as if to grab her, but she waved him off.

"I'm fine. But I just lost this for us." Tears grabbed hold of her throat. So stupid of her to fall. So clumsy and just *dumb.*

She took a shaky breath and then threw herself full force into the harness, the tire jerking with the force of it as the harness cut deep into her.

They weren't finished yet. The other couple hadn't crossed the finish line; there was still a chance. And she wouldn't give up while there was still a chance.

He was right there beside her, pulling just as hard as she was, his entire body a study in sheer, determined force.

The tire juddered behind them, reluctant to move again, but Ana just pulled harder against its resistance.

This time, the tire began to slide forward with a hard bounce. And it kept on bouncing as they went along, thanks to how fast they were going, even faster than they had been before.

From the corner of her eye, Ana saw the Stink Eyes, watched as they passed them as if the other couple were standing still.

She and Luke crossed the finish line yoked together, exactly what she'd feared when he'd first offered to team up with her.

Except now that they were actually doing it, it wasn't unwanted or frightening—it felt perfect.

THEY'D DONE IT.

Luke pulled himself out of the harness, panting as he did. He swallowed hard, trying to catch his breath even as he grinned.

That had been amazing. And the way she'd pulled him up that wall... that had been hot as hell, even with her face all flushed and mud smeared all over her.

He turned and caught her eye. Her harness was falling away from her shoulders and she was grinning as crazily as he was and suddenly the distance between them had to be breached, and he needed to grab her up and kiss her—

"Hey." Jackson walked up to them, addressing himself to Ana and metaphorically throwing cold water on Luke's fantasies. It was for the best, but Luke felt himself getting pissed all the same. "You okay? I saw that fall."

She shook her head, her breath coming in great, sawing pants. "Yeah, mostly just scraped my pride."

"You did awesome," Jackson said.

Jackson's gaze flicked over to Luke for half a moment, and Luke had the sensation of being set aside to make space for just Jackson and Ana. Which was where Luke should be now that they'd crossed the finish line, but it still pinched.

"We did, didn't we?" Ana's smile took in the both of them, but then her expression went fixed. "We won." She didn't sound the least bit happy.

Luke's first impulse was to ask if she was okay. But that might give too much away. Instead, he clapped her on the back, bro to bro. "Yep, we did. Awesome job out there."

As if she were nothing more to him than a partner, to be left behind at the finish line.

"Thanks." She dipped her head and seemed to give herself a shake, but without moving. "You did good too." That was cool and a little pointed. More like how she used to talk to him.

So they were going back to how it had been before. It was for the best, if that's what she wanted. It really was.

Russ came jogging up to him then, dragging Bea along behind him. "Dude, you look like hell."

Luke looked down at himself, coated in mud, banged up, and worn out down to his very bones. "Yeah, hell pretty much covers it. But it was fun." He looked between them all. "Russ, do you know Ana and Jackson?"

"Hey, man, it's great to meet you." Russ came forward and shook everyone's hand. "I've heard so much about you. Both of you."

Ana and Bea exchanged casual hellos. If Luke was worried they'd all simply stare at each other in awkward silence, he didn't need to be. Russ stepped in with his usual friendly warmth.

"How was it?" he asked Ana. "You look like you had fun. Well, if you like mud. If you don't, it was probably miserable." He flashed her his "Everything's fine, ma'am, I'm a fireman" smile.

"No, it was great." She looked at Luke, uncertainty flashing from her eyes for a moment. "We had fun."

Russ looped an arm around Bea's shoulders and pulled her close. "Babe, we should totally do this. It looks awesome."

Bea gave him a fondly exasperated look, which was odd to see on her. "Really? You want to crawl around in the mud?"

Russ gave her a smile that was half-wicked, half-sappy. "What? You like to get dirty."

Bea smacked him in the belly, and Luke barely kept from rolling his eyes. He caught Ana's gaze, and he could see she was suppressing the same instinct.

Jackson cleared his throat. A little louder than he needed to. "Your mom and sister are waiting over there," he told Ana. "And I brought the thermal blanket you wanted. Do you need something to drink?" He held up a bottle of her favorite Lightning Blue.

That was Luke's cue. It was time to say good-bye.

Only, he didn't want to. He wanted to do what Russ was doing and sling his arm around Ana's shoulders and hold her close, mud be damned. Instead, he put his hand on her shoulder. That was friendly enough, but not too friendly.

"Thanks for doing this with me." He held her gaze, trying to say with his eyes everything he couldn't with his mouth. How much he'd miss their time together. How badly he'd want to text her when he'd had a bad day. How much he'd miss just being with her.

He wasn't sure if she heard all that though. She smiled back at him, an unfocused edge to it, and said, "Thanks for training with me. We won, which is what we wanted, right?"

"Yeah." He pulled his hand back. "Yeah, this was the best outcome. I'll let you get to your family."

Jackson tucked the silver blanket around her shoulders, then led her away.

She didn't once look back, which again was for the best.

But Luke didn't want what was best; he wanted to be happy. Watching her walk away from him made him anything but.

Chapter 18

ANA WALKED INTO WORK ON Monday feeling both enthusiastic and depressed—like a balloon that was slowly losing helium and bobbing halfway between the floor and the ceiling. She was enthusiastic because there was a half-page picture of her and Luke crossing the finish line in the Sunday paper. The best publicity was always free publicity.

And she was depressed because it was all over between them. He'd sent her a text yesterday—*How are you feeling today?*—which she hadn't answered. Oddly enough, it was the *today* part that convinced her not to answer. If he'd said, *How are you feeling?* without adding *today,* it would have felt more encompassing. More about their entire situation and how they were handling it.

But that one little word made it seem like he was only asking about her physical state: Could she walk? Had she foam rolled? Was she icing her legs?

She didn't need his help with that, so she'd tossed her phone aside and left it for the rest of the day. And yeah, she was foam rolling and icing her legs and she was just fine, thank you very much.

Cece was already at her desk, a pink box of donuts open next to her. "Hey! I saw you in the paper. Great job."

"Thanks." Not quite enthusiastic enough—Ana would have to try harder.

"Want a donut?"

Ana took a maple bar. "This was a very good idea for a Monday."

"I'm showing initiative. Are you sore today?"

Ana shrugged, then winced. "A little." Actually, she couldn't lift her arms over her head, which had made dressing herself quite interesting this morning, but she'd be fine.

Linda's office door opened then. "Ana. I need to speak with you."

Ana had never seen her boss look so grave. Her heart kicked into overdrive, adrenaline flooding her veins. "Sure."

She followed Linda into her office, trying to breathe through her panicked reaction. There was really only one possibility here, but how had Linda found out? Unless Chelsea *did* know who Luke was?

Or maybe it was something else entirely. *Please, let it be something else. Anything else.*

Ana arranged herself carefully in a chair, taking a moment to arrange her internal state as well. Panicking wasn't going to help. She needed a clear head if this was about what she thought it was. She swallowed hard. Well, she had no one to blame but herself.

Linda sat behind her desk, her expression sad and solemn. She released a weary exhale. "Congratulations on winning the race this weekend. I saw the photo in the paper."

Ana processed the disconnect between Linda's words

and her demeanor. She was *congratulating* Ana? While looking as if Ana had severely disappointed her?

"Thank you. I hope the resort benefits from the publicity." Ana waited then, knowing the other shoe had to drop soon.

"I got Chelsea's final report today."

Okay. This... this was not going at all how Ana expected. "That's good. I'm sure she had some... effective recommendations."

Am I about to be fired? That was crazy since Linda would never fire Ana based on some consultant's suggestions, but reality seemed to be suspended here. Linda certainly wasn't acting according to any rules Ana knew.

"She was very impressed by you."

Ana couldn't help her reaction to that. "Really? She... Well, I didn't think she liked me."

"That didn't preclude her from being impressed by you."

Ana felt that like a rap to her palm. Linda was right and Ana had tried to have an open mind, but she'd been annoyed by Chelsea all the same. Who maybe hadn't blabbed about Ana's illicit affair after all, which made Ana feel that much guiltier about disliking the woman.

"What were her recommendations?" Ana asked.

"With regard to your position? That you delegate more of your tasks to Cece. You're not doing that effectively."

Okay, that was reasonable. Ana was trying to do more of that anyway.

"And that when you do see an opportunity for community outreach," Linda went on, "you present it to the PR department first. You should work with them on these opportunities and not take it all on yourself. She wrote that you were a wonderful asset to the resort, but that in order to be a better asset, you need to manage your responsibilities more effectively."

It took a long moment to absorb all that. As Linda's works soaked through her ears and into her mind, Ana realized they were right. Her lack of focus, her exhaustion, her panic when she thought of everything she had to do... She *had* taken on too much, and everything was suffering.

She'd known that before—or rather, she'd suspected it. But now, hearing it from Linda and without the race hanging over her head, she *knew* it.

Ana released a slow exhale. "Is this why you're upset with me? Because I wouldn't listen?"

Linda's gaze dropped to her desk and she slowly folded her hands. "Are you seeing Luke Merrill?"

Ana couldn't help her gasp or her whispered "She *did* recognize him."

"Yes," Linda said, "she did."

And there was the other shoe, dropping right on Ana's head. The regret and shame boiling up in her was awful, and yet strangely relieving at the same time. There was nothing left to hide.

Except now Ana had to deal with the fallout.

"We... we had an intimate relationship," she said carefully.

Seeing each other implied that they actually thought their relationship might go somewhere. It didn't fit sweaty, frantic sex in his truck.

And what about all that emotional intimacy? But Linda wouldn't care about that. Only the salacious bits were concerning, which might have been funny, considering that their physical relationship had been the least of what had happened.

"How long has this been going on?" Linda asked.

"About a month."

Since high school. Because really, that was the ultimate truth—their rivalry had been all foreplay.

"Is it ongoing?"

"No." Ana swallowed down a bubble of grief. "No, we've agreed... Now that the race is over, it's finished."

She held Linda's gaze as she said it, willing the other woman to believe her. Willing herself to believe it.

"I have to ask: did you discuss sensitive matters concerning the resort?"

"Never!" Ana put a hand to her chest, the better to hold back her galloping heart. "I know that I screwed up here, but I never did that."

Linda shook her head. "You technically haven't done anything wrong. But I have to say... finding this out has been deeply upsetting. Ana, you don't hide things. And the fact that you hid this means that you knew exactly how inappropriate it was."

Ana had nothing to say to that. *We tried, we tried really hard not to do anything...* but that was just stupid. That was the excuse a high schooler would trot out when their hormones got the better of them.

"I'm sorry." Ana wiped her eyes, which seemed to have filled with tears. She didn't remember starting to cry. "Am I fired?"

God, to lose her job over this... But maybe she'd deserve it.

"Of course not." Linda's expression softened. "As long as you didn't give him any sensitive information, you haven't done anything you could be fired for. But I think you do understand that you made a mistake." She linked her fingers together, meditating on what she'd say next. "And I'm wondering if part of that wasn't related to how hard you've been working. How close to burning out you are. Maybe if you weren't juggling so much, you might not have done this."

Again, Ana had nothing to say. She was humbled and humiliated down to her very soul, and worst of all, she felt so stupid. She hated feeling stupid and ashamed and incompetent.

Linda was probably right about all of it. Had been from the very beginning, but Ana was too stubborn to listen. And look where she was now.

"You have plenty of vacation days accrued," Linda went on. "I suggest that you take two weeks off. It's not a suspension or any kind of official punishment. Just... just take a break, Ana."

She nodded jerkily. "You're right. Completely right. I need to... to reassess."

What she needed was to get her head together. Now, before she did something even worse than sleeping with a competitor.

"Thank you for not firing me," she said to her lap. And the floor. And her feet. And her self-esteem, which was rolling around down there somewhere, picking up dirt and lint.

"You really are a valuable asset," Linda said comfortingly. "Take some time, rest, and when you come back, we'll put this all behind us. And discuss Chelsea's recommendations."

"Okay." Ana felt anything but okay. Still, she forced herself to rise from the chair and put on a sickly smile. "I'll see you in two weeks then." A horrid thought hit her halfway to the door. "I'd appreciate it if you didn't tell anyone about this."

"Of course not." Linda's sympathy was slipping into pity now.

So Ana took the opportunity to escape to her vacation/punishment.

ANA STARED at her front door, trying to find the courage to go in.

Her mother's car was out front, which meant that Ana would have to face her.

If her meeting with Linda had been awful, this would be excruciating. Her mother had never done anything so stupid in her entire life.

Ana opened the door slowly, breathing hard as she did.

"Sara?" her mother called from the kitchen.

Ana shut the door behind her. "No. It's me."

Her mother came into the hallway, wearing an apron with flour streaked across it. She must have been making tortillas. "Why are you home so early? Are you sick?" Her mother laughed as if that were ridiculous. "Did you get fired?"

Ana felt her face go cold. "No. Not exactly."

Her mother put a hand to her mouth, her mirth instantly dissolving. "Oh my. What happened?"

Ana tried to suck in a breath. Where to even start? Probably with the worst. "You remember how I said that there was nothing between Luke and me?"

Her mother's expression went from shocked to stricken as she nodded.

"Well, things did happen," Ana said. Of course, her mother had probably guessed that from the moment Ana mentioned Luke's name.

"When? And where?"

Oh, there was her mother's "Wrath of God" voice. Not angry per se, but when she used that voice, you did not want to lie to her.

But Ana definitely didn't want to get into the particulars. "We managed. It hasn't been going on very long—only a month—and now that the race is done, we're done. Totally and completely." Ana slashed her hands through the air to indicate just how totally it was over. "But Linda found out."

"Ana, Ana, Ana." Still not angry, but the gray disappointment in that hurt like hell.

"I know. I know it was stupid and reckless and you warned me to be careful. I knew." Ana rubbed at her forehead.

"What did Linda say?"

"That I hadn't done anything fireable, but that I should take some time off. It's not a suspension, and I'll still be in touch with Cece so she can handle things... But I've got the next two weeks to figure things out."

"But you said it was over. What do you need to figure out?"

"I..."

Her mother was right. It was over, Ana would never be alone with him again—what was left to decide?

Yet Ana had the sense that a ragged, unfinished edge was hanging from her heart. Maybe she needed these two weeks to snip those threads off. Although she had no idea how to do that.

Her mother clucked her tongue at Ana's continuing silence. "This isn't like you. This boy... I don't know anything about this boy except that he's our competitor and you've disliked him so long..." She turned her palms up. "And now you tell me you've been seeing him in secret? How am I not supposed to worry when I hear this?"

Ana opened her mouth, ready to defend Luke from... from what? He *was* their competitor and she *had* disliked him since high school. Of course her mother would think that Ana getting involved with him was a terrible idea.

"I know," she said, to everything her mother had brought up. "I'm going to spend this vacation pondering all of it."

"Hmm. Well, we'll find some other things for you to do too." Her mother tapped her first two fingers against the counter. "Have you told Sara?"

"Not yet."

Her mother caught sight of her expression and put a hand to Ana's cheek. "Oh mija, it will be all right. We all make mistakes."

Ana rubbed at her eyes. "Okay, but you never make mistakes."

Her mother started laughing. "Ana..." She laughed some more. "That's not true. I worry so much about you, not because you make mistakes, but because you're so terrified of anything less than perfection. No one can be perfect."

No, Ana was pretty far from perfect. Because even though she'd said it was over, she still wanted to call him, to send him a text asking if he wanted to go for a walk, because he needed to recover and she needed to recover—oh, and she needed to tell him about almost losing her job thanks to their hookups.

He'd understand better than anyone. Her mother would help her fashion a plan, redirect her energy toward something useful—but Luke would simply listen. And remind her to do what was best.

Ana wanted both of those things—someone pushing her forward and someone just to listen.

"I know I'm not perfect," she finally said. "But I can be better. I can always be better."

Her mother only sighed.

"I'm going to go lie down." Ana's head had begun to pound, and she could hear the siren of an oncoming migraine. Which wasn't surprising, given everything she'd been through today.

"Call if you need anything." Her mother's sympathy was warm but firm. She'd help Ana if she asked, but she wouldn't coddle her.

Ana nodded and made her way to her room. She threw herself down on the twin bed she'd had since middle school. She'd never bothered to buy anything bigger since she was the only one who'd ever been in it.

She tossed an arm over her eyes, and her forehead throbbed against it. Yeah, she had a killer headache coming on. Some ibuprofen would be a great idea, but she couldn't bring herself to get up. She only wanted to lie here and...

And call him. It might be wise, simply letting him know that they'd been spotted and that the story might be all over town soon. Chelsea probably didn't have anyone other than Linda to tell, and Linda wouldn't tell anyone, but rumors had a funny life of their own in Cabrillo. And if Chelsea saw them, that meant someone else might have too.

Warning him was the right thing to do, even if calling him was the wrong thing to do.

Ana reached for her phone and pulled up the last number in her recent calls.

It only rang once before he answered: "Hey."

His voice was throaty, rough, and it licked at every inch of her skin.

She swallowed. "Hey."

"How are you?"

When he said it that time, without the *today*, she heard everything that had been missing from his text. "I'm... I'm not good."

There was a rustling on the other end as if he'd sat up suddenly. "What's wrong?"

She could almost imagine him, jaw squared and hands fisted, ready to ride off to right whatever wrong had beset her. If only it were that simple.

"We were seen at the convenience store."

"The...? Oh, shit. Jackson."

She drew a deep breath. He was going to be rightfully pissed when she admitted to not telling him about Chelsea. "It wasn't Jackson. That consultant I told you about? It was her."

"What's she look like?"

"Blond. Straight out of *Style* magazine."

"Oh, yeah, I remember her in the store. Crap. If only you'd seen her and warned me."

Here it came. God, she was getting out all kinds of painful confessions today. "I did see her."

She could almost hear him frown over the line. "When?"

"Right after we kissed."

"Why didn't you say something?" Yeah, he was not happy.

"I figured she wouldn't recognize you. And the race was the next day. You didn't need to worry. Besides, the damage was already done." Her head throbbed and her voice went thick as her throat closed.

"So you took it all on yourself, as usual." His anger had ebbed, and now he sounded resigned.

"Funny story about that..." She pushed out a laugh. "Chelsea, the consultant, was going to recommend that I take on less. And that I get an assistant." She closed her eyes and pushed her fingertips hard against her forehead. But that didn't help with the pain building under her skull. "There's more. Linda asked that I take some vacation time. Think all this over."

"You're suspended?" Resigned and guilty—wow, she was really hitting the trifecta on bringing out the shitty emotions in him today. But he couldn't feel any worse than she did.

"No. I technically haven't done anything wrong." She bit her lip. She still felt awful though.

"Darlin'... God, I wish I could help you."

Hang up on me. But she couldn't ask that. She needed his voice.

"What are you going to do?" he asked.

"Take my two weeks of vacation and then go back to work." She shrugged, although he couldn't see. "I mean, this is over, right? It's already been decided."

She held her breath as she waited for his response. Would he agree? Would he do it reluctantly?

Did he want it to be over?

"Yeah," he said. "It has."

Okay, well, that sounded pretty final. Which was what they both needed. She nodded, resolved, even as her throat started to close. She gathered up the comforter in her fist. "I only wanted to warn you that the story will probably start to spread. I imagine it won't be any better for you."

"When Fee hears, she's going to go nuclear. I'm already on her shit list because of the Josh stuff."

"When's he coming home?"

"In a week."

She could hear the smile in his voice. "Awesome. I'm really glad for you."

And she was. Things would be tough for him—they already were when it came to his brother—but he'd be so happy to have Josh back. She only hoped Josh wouldn't hurt Luke any more than he already had.

"I don't think it's going to be like I'd planned," Luke said. There was a long beat of silence. "I thought about what you said. About when to let go... I think I might need to do some letting go before he even comes."

"Yeah? How'd you come to that?"

"He's said something about needing to work stuff out on his own. About needing some time alone. And maybe I've done everything I can do. Maybe now it's up to him."

That was all very reasonable and exactly the conclusion she'd hoped he'd come to. But— "You're still going to worry."

"Yeah. Probably." There was a long beat of silence, thick with regret, sadness dripping from it. "Ana, if there was anything I could do..."

"I know." She could barely get that out. "The best thing you can do is stay away." She rubbed her nose. Time to hang up before she started sobbing into the phone. She'd done what she needed to in warning him—it was time to end this. "I've got to go."

"Okay. Call me or text me if you need anything. They're not tracking your phone, so you can at least do that. Promise me."

"I promise."

She hung up then and tossed the phone away. Curling around her belly, she closed her eyes and tried to sleep. Tried to escape the pain swamping her.

It took a long time for that to happen.

Chapter 19

LUKE PULLED HIS STRESS BALL out of his desk drawer and squeezed it as hard and as fast as he could.

Fee sat across from him, scowling. "I've hired a new full-time baker," she said, each word inched out through a tight jaw.

He squeezed his ball, then released. Squeezed and released. He had a lot of tension to work out.

Fee had been abrasive ever since the meeting about Josh. Not to the point where it was actionable, but enough to irritate him. Sometimes he wished he could leave all this family and business entanglement bullshit behind.

But today he had to try to talk Fee down rather than tell her off. "Great. I'm sure she's awesome. When does she start?"

"In two weeks. The part-time baker will handle anything until then."

He didn't bother to ask more. Fee was in a mood. "All right." He squeezed his ball. "Listen, can we discuss this"—he gestured between them—"stuff going on?"

"Do you have a complaint about my job performance?"

Her expression was blank, her tone flat. As if she were a robot and not his cousin.

"No." Because he really didn't, and even though she was his cousin, she was also his employee. If she'd been anyone else, someone not related to him, he'd find out what was bugging her and try to rectify the situation.

He knew exactly what was bugging Fee, and there wasn't a damn thing he could do about it. Not without opening up the festering mess the meeting about Josh had stirred up.

He'd called Bea and apologized for the tension of the meeting and explained more calmly his position. Explained that he was going to be the one in Josh's corner since Josh needed that. Bea hadn't really changed her position—although he didn't think she felt as strongly as Fee did—but they'd come to an understanding.

Luke had figured he'd talk to Fee sometime at work and hammer things out like he had with Bea. But he realized now that wasn't going to happen. Their jobs were straitjacketing them.

He sighed inwardly. He wanted to step out of his role as head of the resort and shake off all the baggage from it right now. He wanted to be a cousin and nothing more, just for a moment with Fee.

Actually, scratch that. He wanted to step away from being entangled with the family for a lot longer than only a moment. He wanted to simply be a brother with Benedict when they butted heads over Josh again, wanted to be just a cousin with all the other family who felt as Fee did... He wanted the trip wire of his role in the family business gone, since the rest of it was already such a minefield.

And he wanted to be something other than a rival to Ana. Maybe him being just Luke and not her competitor wouldn't solve the issues between them, but he wanted to try.

Josh was coming home in a week though. This wasn't the time to have an existential crisis about his job and how it was fucking up every single meaningful relationship in his life.

"Is there anything else you need?" Fee asked.

"No. Thanks for keeping me updated on the baker situation." *And thanks for* finally *hiring someone.* "Let's meet next week to discuss the wedding schedule for the next few months. Also, did you get the e-mail I forwarded you from that winery? They're offering us a discount for weddings."

If he wasn't going to have a crisis of confidence about his job, then he might as well keep managing the hell out of this resort.

"I did. I'll look it over and let you know what I think." She gathered her things and went for the door, never offering a farewell.

"Hey, Fee."

She paused and looked at him over her shoulder.

"I'm sorry." He didn't elaborate. He only wanted to offer something small across the breach between them. Not nearly enough to mend things, but maybe they could slowly get back to where they'd been.

She shrugged. "It's... it's all pretty complicated, huh?"

He gave a short, humorless laugh. "Yeah."

Her mouth twisted as if she might say more, something as bitterly resigned as he felt, but nothing came and she left without saying more.

He gave the ball a few more hard squeezes. The urge to work this out physically rose in his muscles, tugged on his bones. A run sounded really nice right now.

A run with Ana sounded amazing. He could pour all this

out to her and she'd tell him to buck up. She might even have some suggestions on how to unravel at least some of this.

But he couldn't call her either. He couldn't do a damn thing except keep on with his work. So he that was what he did.

ANA SLID the last freezer bag into the chest freezer and closed the lid with a decisive whomp.

"That's the last of it," she said to Mrs. Hernandez.

"Thank you, sweetheart. I appreciate it." Mrs. Hernandez smiled as she slipped off her apron.

"No problem. I've wanted to help make we'wish for a while now."

We'wish was an acorn dish that had been staple of her ancestors, a dish that few people even knew how to make any longer. Ana used to love to help make we'wish—it made her feel connected to the women who'd come before her in a way few other things could—but she'd had so little time for it since she'd started at the resort.

That was one thing Ana had been neglecting in her efforts to make the resort as successful as possible and support her people and her heritage—her personal stake in it all. The more people who learned to make we'wish, the more likely it was to survive. She could be one of those reservoirs of knowledge.

Yes, her work at the resort helped to bring in the funds for classes and cultural preservation, but she should be in the classes herself. That had gotten lost for her along the way.

Not that she was entirely happy on her little forced vacation. There was still an itch deep within her to be doing more, now. Only, not really for her work at the resort specifically. More like just meaningful work in general. Work like what she was actually doing on her break, being with her people and helping and all that, but *more* of that.

Even so, her time off was going really well. She'd rattled about the reservation and found more to do than she'd thought. Slower work, but still vital.

She took up the food processor parts lying in the sink and began to scrub the bits of acorn off them.

"Perhaps next season you can come gather acorns with us," Mrs. Hernandez said. "Our families used to share the same gathering spots, you know."

"I didn't know that." Ana had missed Mrs. Hernandez's expeditions two years in a row thanks to work. She really shouldn't do that again. "I'd love to go next season."

Ana finished up the rest of the dishes, wiped down the kitchen, and gave Mrs. Hernandez a hug and a promise to visit again later that week before leaving.

She turned her truck toward home, although there wasn't really anything pressing waiting for her there. Sara and Lori were at a mommy-and-me thing in the valley, and her mother was at Soboba, touring their school. Ana had thought about going with her mother—she would have loved to see how their tribal school operated—but then Mrs. Hernandez had called and asked if Ana could help her out today.

Her mother had put out the news that Ana was home for the next two weeks, so Ana had been getting calls right and left from people asking if she could come visit or help with this or that. It felt good to be needed, to be drawn back into her tribe. There was nothing like knowing everyone and having everyone know her. And no one had mentioned why she was home—everyone just seemed to assume she really had taken a vacation. Which was a relief.

The truck bounced as she went down the road, past Jerry Torres's place and his collection of old fire trucks parked out front, past the cluster of boulders that she and the rest of the kids used to play on, and on and on past all the places she'd known since before she could even remember.

Her phone rang on the seat next to her, and for half a stupid moment, she thought it might be Luke. It was a silly thought, but it was one she had every time the phone rang. Only it was never him.

This time it was Helen Contreras.

"Your mom said you were home this week?"

"Yep." Ana didn't get into the reasons why.

"Could you drive me to the tribal office before it closes?"

"Sure thing."

Ana turned the truck around with relief. Now she wouldn't have to try to find something to do at home.

But after taking Helen to the tribal office, waiting there while Helen finished her business and shooting the shit with everyone in the office, then taking Helen back home, Ana was back right where she'd started.

She wandered through the empty house, trying to work off her excess energy. Today had been great—the whole week had been pretty good considering she owed this break to doing something monumentally stupid—but all that *doing* just made her want to do more. TV was out. There was nothing good on. She didn't think she could sit still long enough to read. And she'd already gotten bored with *Angry Birds* after only a week.

A run was exactly what she wanted, but somehow she couldn't bring herself to lace up her shoes. It was ridiculous since she had Seth and she used to love the solitude of her runs, but... she wanted Luke with her. She wanted to tell him about her day, about how it was good, but also about her never-ending itch to do more. About how she was beginning to understand that she needed a speed between the one she'd been going at and the one she was at now.

But she couldn't.

She stared at her phone, the dark screen staring back at her.

She could text him.

No, that wouldn't be fair. They'd both agreed not to contact each other, and since her phone call to him last Monday, they'd held to that.

Although his brother was coming home soon. Did he have someone to talk to about that? It was probably weighing on him.

But it wasn't any of her business.

She stuck her head out the back door. "Seth!"

He thumped his tail at her.

"We're going for a run. Just the two of us."

And she wasn't going to be sad about it. About any of it.

LUKE SLOWED as he went down the beverage aisle at the grocery store, the rainbow of sports drinks catching his eye. There was plenty of Lightning Blue this time, not that he would be getting any. He didn't like that particular flavor, which he tried to take as proof that he and Ana shouldn't be together.

Along with all the other reasons.

He needed every reason he could get these days, a week after their race, since the urge to call her was growing stronger each day. He ought to just delete her number from his phone, but he couldn't bring himself to do that. Some man he was.

"Looking for the Lightning Blue?"

Luke turned to see Jackson coming up the aisle toward him.

"Fancy meeting you here," Luke said, trying to keep his voice light. This was the absolute worst way to experience déjà vu.

"You okay?" Jackson tilted his head, his gaze probing. "You, uh, don't seem yourself."

You haven't really talked to me in five years. How would you know?

Luke gave a jerky shrug. He wanted the conversation over. "Just tired."

"Ana's been tired too."

Luke went very still. "Oh?" he said, falsely casual. "When did you talk to her?"

"About two days ago."

That wasn't jealousy rising in him—it was something much deeper, more painful. Jackson had spoken to her just two days ago, and Luke was dying to talk to her but couldn't.

But it was what it was.

"I hope she can get some sleep," Luke said and started to turn his cart the way he'd come.

"Look, I can tell something happened between you two." Jackson's words stopped Luke dead. "I've only known the two of you since forever."

Luke almost laughed. Ana had wanted them to talk, but he guessed she didn't want them to talk about *her*. He slid Jackson a look. "Are we really going to talk about this in the middle of the grocery store?"

Twenty minutes later, they were sliding into a booth at Gerry's.

"Taking me on a date?" Jackson asked as he settled in and grabbed his beer.

"Only the best for you."

"Aren't you a sweetheart?"

"You know it."

They shared a smile that was half sarcastic, half amused. Maybe a touch more amused. Just like old times.

Jackson looked away and cleared his throat. "So, about Ana. Should I be worried?"

Luke studied his soda. *Worried*. That was a loaded word. If Ana was feeling half as terrible as Luke was, then yeah, Jackson should be worried.

But she probably wasn't. He gave Jackson a level stare. "There's nothing going on between us."

Jackson said nothing. Man, Luke had forgotten how much Jackson could put into a silence. "But you wanted there to be," Jackson said finally.

Luke shrugged. "Yeah." No point denying it, not now. "Turns out that all that rivalry between us was covering something else."

"I might have guessed. I did warn her away from you."

The edge to Jackson's statement had Luke snapping out, "It isn't like that. I don't have to tell you this, but she's awesome. She wasn't a notch on my belt or anything like that."

Jackson held up a hand, his mouth twitching. "Okay, okay. Your intentions are totally pure." He sobered, the lines around his mouth drawing down. "But Ana's got a lot of responsibilities. Stuff that you or I will never have to deal with. Stuff that she'll always have to carry. And carry isn't even the right word, because she's happy to shoulder it."

"I'm very aware of all that." He stabbed his straw into the flotilla of ice in his drink. "But she still needs to slow down. She's going to burn out."

"That's what she's spent her vacation considering."

The sardonic twist Jackson put on *vacation* got Luke's attention. "So you know why she's taking a vacation?"

"Yeah."

Great. Apparently Luke was the only one keeping his damn mouth shut about all this. "Then why ask me what's going on?"

"I wanted to see if you'd lie about it."

"You know me better than that." After a lifetime of friendship, for Jackson to insult him to his face like that... He shook his head. "Frankly, it's really between me and her."

"According to you, there's nothing between you and her. Not anymore."

Shit. Wasn't that the truth?

Luke shrugged and spread his hands in a gesture that said *What more is there?* "So there's your answer. You don't need to play the heavy or threaten me since Ana and I are done. Are *we* done?"

Jackson could go poke some other former friend of his. Luke was finished here.

"Yep," Jackson said. "We're done."

So this was how a lifetime of friendship ended. Not with one big bang, but with sputters and spurts. Little pops of resentment and flashes of their former closeness... until finally not even those were left.

Luke found himself wishing he could step outside his role as Josh's brother, just for a moment, just to assure Jackson that he understood why it was all over.

He sure did spend a lot of time these days wishing he were someone else.

He pondered his half-full soda. He wanted to simply leave it, toss some money down for the waitress, and slink away. Go home to a house that seemed to have less and less space for him.

Make your own space. Ana wasn't here, but her words came to him clear as when she'd spoken them to him. And even though she wasn't here, she was still right.

Fuck it. He was going to look online for apartments tonight. Maybe he couldn't have Jackson back as a friend and he couldn't have Ana as a lover, but he could stop being a whiny baby about his living situation.

He reached for his wallet. "Well, I'll be seeing you then."

"Hang on." Jackson held up a hand, looking uncomfortable. "Your brother's coming home soon."

Here they went again. Might as well plumb the festering depths of that too. "In a couple of days."

"I know that things... that I have no standing to ask you this. But as your friend—as someone who used to be your friend—I'm asking you, in light of all that, could you promise me one thing?"

"What?"

"Promise me you'll keep Josh away from Leonora."

Luke sucked in a breath, remembering Josh's insistence that he needed to make things right. That he'd wronged her and was intending to make amends. Luke had thought it a bad idea then and he still did.

"My sister doesn't need any apologies," Jackson went on, "or closure or any of that. She's getting on with her life, and I don't want Josh to derail her. Please. Swear to me you'll keep him away."

If Jackson hadn't invoked their friendship, their lifetime of almost brotherhood...

Jackson was right. No matter what fantasy Josh was spinning in his head about having to make amends, Leonora didn't need it. She deserved to be left alone.

"Sure. I can do that." Luke tapped his fingers on the table. "Actually, I will definitely do that. I swear you won't have to worry about Josh contacting her. I'll make it clear to him that he can't. And there will be consequences if he does."

Ana had told him to set a limit, to know when to let Josh go. That then was the first limit. When Josh came home, Luke would have to tell him that he couldn't contact Leonora.

As for the consequences, Luke would leave those up to Benedict. Their eldest brother probably already had an entire brimstone-and-fire program ready to go.

"Thanks, man." Jackson stared at the table as if embarrassed to meet Luke's gaze. Well, it was kind of an awkward situation all around.

"No problem." Luke tossed some money onto the table and grabbed his hat. "See you around."

Chapter 20

IT WAS THE MOMENT OF TRUTH.

Luke watched his brother take in the apartment he'd fixed up over the garage, his throat tight.

They'd picked Josh up yesterday—the entire family, even Benedict. After a one-night stay in Cambria at their parents' place, they'd come back to Cabrillo today.

His brother was home.

That didn't feel as good as it should have though. Josh was like a newly arrived cat—skulking around the edges of things and generally looking like he wanted to bolt.

But now Josh was looking over the space Luke had made for him. Things would get better once he'd settled in. They would.

"The place looks good," Josh finally said.

Luke could only nod, unable to look away from his brother. Of course he'd seen Josh—at least once a month over the past five years. But seeing him back in their home, away from the walls of the prison, he was struck with how different Josh really was.

His brother was thinner of course, yet his muscles were

harder, giving him a tough, sinewy look he hadn't had before. His brow had half a dozen creases, and the laugh lines around his mouth had hardened into something sad. Josh's hair had always been on the lighter side, closer to a real true brown than the darker shade the rest of them had. But now there were streaks of gray sprinkled throughout, making it even lighter. Even farther from the color the rest of the siblings had.

Luke had hoped that prison would mature his younger brother, but Josh looked more than matured—he looked old.

"I hope you like it," he said, tucking his hands into his back pockets. "Anything you don't like, we can change."

"No," Josh said quickly. "This is already too much."

"Do you need to go shopping before work tomorrow? I'm not sure if you'll need clothes or whatever."

As part of his probation, Josh wasn't allowed to drive. Which meant anywhere he needed to go, someone would have to haul him there. Luke was already taking him to the ranch tomorrow to start his job.

"No, I'm good. My old clothes still fit. Just have to tighten my belt." Josh's smile was wan.

"Good." Luke nodded, trying to think of more to say. Awkward silences had never been a problem for them before. They had a shared lifetime of jokes and memories to call on. Except for the events of the past five years. They hadn't shared that. "Dinner's probably ready if you want to go down."

"I'll stay up here actually."

"What?"

Josh inhaled, exhaled, then inhaled again. "I don't think I'm up to socializing tonight."

"You don't have to talk. Just eat." That was easy enough.

"Yeah, even that..." Josh rubbed at the lines on his forehead. "Lil looks like she could have the baby tonight, and I don't know this Adriano dude at all and—" His jaw went tight, as if he was biting back anything else he might say.

"I understand. You need some alone time." Luke would have thought Josh had gotten more than enough of that by now, but he wouldn't push. He could come down to dinner tomorrow instead.

"That's not really it," Josh said slowly. "Being back here... I feel like my skin doesn't fit anymore. None of this fits. *I* don't fit."

"Stop being melodramatic. You just need some time."

It looked like Ana had rubbed off on him; that was exactly the kind of thing she'd say.

Josh, to Luke's surprise, began to laugh. "I think that's the first time you've called me on my shit in... ever."

Was it? That wasn't really Luke's role in the family. He was the charmer, the one who got along with everyone. Benedict was the enforcer. But Josh never had listened to Benedict. And Luke had never tried to make his brother listen to him.

Maybe if he was really determined to disentangle himself from the family business and make a space all his own, Luke could rethink his role in the sibling pecking order too.

"About calling you on your shit..." He swallowed. He hadn't wanted to broach this so soon, but the opportunity was there. "I promised Jackson you wouldn't go near Leonora."

Josh went very still, his whipcord leanness somehow coalescing around him. Yet he wasn't diminished—if anything, he was steely. "You and Jackson agreed to something concerning me and Leonora? All on your own?"

"Come on. You have to agree it's best if she doesn't see you."

His brother had better agree. Luke didn't think he'd be able to stop Jackson from going after Josh if he didn't. And Luke didn't think he'd *want* to stop his former best friend if it came to that.

"Leonora gets to decide that."

The resolve in Josh's voice, the way he clenched his fists, but most of all his utter control—Luke was getting spooked.

"Oh, and have you talked to her?" Somehow Luke didn't think his brother had.

"Have *you*?"

"What are you going to do, jump out of a bush at her?" How the hell was this running off the rails? What the fuck was Josh playing at here?

"No." Josh's facade suddenly crumbled as he shook his head. "Benedict already warned me I'd be out of a job and out of the house if I looked sideways at her."

Luke hadn't been wrong about the fire and brimstone from Benedict then. He hated to admit it, but it was a relief Benedict was going to continue to be the asshole here.

"So you're going to stay away?" Luke pressed him.

"I'm going to do what I need to."

Fuck. That wasn't promising. "Josh…"

"You've made yourself clear. You and Benedict."

Wow. Well, beyond making themselves clear, Luke wasn't sure what else he could do here.

He also found himself in the odd position of being on Benedict's side. "Good. I'm glad. I'll leave you to it."

Josh merely grunted in farewell.

Luke walked stiff legged to his room. That was… He worked his jaw. He'd been anticipating Josh's return for so long, and Benedict had tried to warn him that it wouldn't be easy, but that was worse than he'd been expecting.

The fact that Josh already had a bug up his ass about Leonora was bad news. If the threat of losing his home and his job didn't convince him...

Luke shook his head. That was the line he'd drawn. Now it was up to Josh not to cross it.

He pulled out his phone, calling up the one number that he knew he shouldn't, knowing it was crazy and against their rules—but he didn't hesitate in hitting the Send button.

That was something he and Josh had in common, involving themselves with women they shouldn't.

But he didn't care in that moment. He needed to talk to her. Hell, he needed to see her, to touch her.

"Luke?"

Fuck, the way she said his name... She wanted to hear from him. She wanted *him*.

"Can you meet me? Somewhere. Anywhere."

"Yes."

THIS WAS A BAD, bad idea. But Ana was still there, parked on a back road, waiting for Luke.

She drummed her fingers on the steering wheel, her pulse loud in her ears as the darkness pressed on her.

She knew what he wanted. It had all been there, in his rough demand to meet him, the low urgency of his words as he told her where to meet him. That same demanding urgency had taken hold of her at the sound of his voice, so here she was.

But it wasn't only desire. She missed talking to him too.

Afterward, after they'd worked out all their lust, she'd pour out everything she'd been holding in for him.

She wasn't sure what she was looking forward to more: the sex or the talking.

Headlights swung across the road and over her truck, blinding her for half a second. Her heart kicked into overdrive.

The truck pulled up behind hers and the lights cut off. Everything was dark and quiet. She waited, still and shivering. A door opened and footfalls sounded on the road, coming closer and closer. Still, she waited.

Her door opened, sharp and sudden. She stared at him for half a moment, his limbs and hair silver and gray under the moonlight, and then she was falling out of the truck and into his arms, her mouth catching his.

He framed her face with his big, callused hands, devouring her mouth with a carnality that made her all liquid breathlessness. She slipped her hands around his waist, pulling his hips into hers. She moaned against his mouth as they pressed together, his body so solid, so present.

God, she'd missed him.

They kissed for long moments, desperate, consuming. Trying to cram as much sensation as they could into that short span of time.

"Come to my truck," he said finally.

He didn't take her into the cab; instead, he led her around to the bed. She laughed when she saw the blankets there. "You've learned your lesson."

"I take what you say to heart."

That kind of melted her.

He unlatched the tailgate and handed her in.

She climbed on her hands and knees through the pile of

blankets, sinking deep into the softness with each move-ment. For all that it was a truck bed, there was a sense of luxury there. A sense of comfort and concern.

She stretched like a cat in the blankets, simply savoring being in her body and in this nest of softness.

Then he climbed over her, and she savored being with him again.

He didn't kiss her right away. Instead, he smoothed her hair from her face, ran his fingers down her cheeks and along her jaw, all with an expression of hungry wonder.

She ought to deflect that look with something—maybe "See something you like?" or a kiss—but she felt like she kind of deserved that adoration. Or if she didn't deserve it, she ought to just bask in it.

"I missed you," he said, totally unnecessarily.

"I missed you too." She ran a hand through his hair, giving him back some of that affection.

He kissed her, slow but deep. She ran her hands along his arms, shoulders, chest, claiming every bit of his gorgeous body once more. The weight of him against her, the hot slide of his tongue in her mouth, the way he smelled like sunshine even in the middle of the night.

Her fingers found his shirt lapels, the hard, cold snaps going bump, bump, bump under her fingertips. She fisted her hands in each lapel and pulled.

His shirt opened with several satisfying cracks as the buttons gave, revealing his well-muscled chest and the dark curls covering it. Praise the Lord for snap-front shirts.

She tested the pad of his muscle with her nails, savoring his sharp inhale. Her nipples tightened in response, and heat gathered between her legs. She was already getting amped up, and she hadn't even taken off her clothes. Or the rest of his.

With a jerk, she tore his shirt from his shoulders and arms and frantically reached for the button of his fly. She'd meant to take things slow, but in the moment, with him between her legs and his breath hot in her ear, she wanted it hard and immediate.

"Hurry," she urged him.

"Anything you want, darlin'."

He helped her shuck off his jeans and boxers, his erection springing free. She ran a hand down it, so smooth but so hard.

"Hang on there," he grunted.

Her laugh was an evil tease. "What's the matter? Can't keep up?"

"With you? Just barely." But his next action belied that as he whipped off her shirt with a ferocity that left her breathless. His mouth caught hers as he shoved off her jeans. She shivered to feel him so frantic, so wild. And all for her.

By the time he reached between her legs to find her clit, she was swollen with want. His touch sent waves of sensation through her that crested into rising need.

"You're drenched," he muttered against her mouth, as if it were the most impressive thing ever.

Which only made her that much more frantic. Her fingers curled around his biceps as her hips rocked into him. "Please tell me you brought a condom," she begged.

She sensed him rooting around behind for something and then came the familiar tearing sound. *Thank God.*

He rolled it on, then pulled her up so that she was in his lap, facing him. His hands sank into her ass as he lifted her and entered her in one long, thick glide.

She set her hands on his shoulders, the better to balance, and rolled her hips to bring him even deeper. His pubic bone caught her clit and she had to moan.

Something like curses were coming from his mouth, so low and quick as to drop away before her ears could catch them. He thrust again, slow and steady, stretching her almost beyond bearing.

She dug her fingers into his shoulders, the muscles there bunching and gathering, trying to hold on and urge him on. *More. Now.*

He heard her, pumped into her with a steady, urgent rhythm that was just on the right side of frantic. Her pleasure built at a dizzying pace until she was nothing but compressed, coiled *need...* until all at once, it released, stars sparking behind her eyes.

His climax came right behind hers, his thrusts slowing as he held her tight against the shudders running through him.

They fell back together into the blankets, breathing hard and hearts racing. He pulled her into his shoulder as he tugged a blanket over the two of them.

The aftershocks of her orgasm washed over her along with the night and the scents and sounds and presence of him. Sex in the back of a truck might sound uncomfortable, but this night, with him? Well, it was pretty amazing.

And it wasn't over yet.

"Can we talk now?" she asked.

He settled her a little closer, all of him shaking as he laughed silently. "Sure. I have so much to tell you."

"Me too."

But they lay together, quiet and content for several moments more. The stars glittered overhead, thick in the night sky. And the moon... the moon was full and bright and almost blinding. Toads called, filling the silence with their deep, rumbling songs.

"Josh came home today," he said finally, his words somehow adding to the night, rather than diminishing it.

"I know. Are you okay?"

His tone had been studiedly flat, which meant she couldn't really tell if he was or not. Or maybe the fact that he'd called her was all the evidence she needed to know things were definitely not okay.

"He's not what I was expecting."

"Oh Luke." Her fingers tripped along his chest, a weak answer to the tight pain in his voice. "You knew he wasn't going to be."

"I did. But I was still hoping."

So that's why he'd called her. Because that hope was gone now. She wished he'd been more clear-eyed about his brother's return, but the fact that he hadn't been, that he'd still wished for his brother to be fixed... It was endearing.

"Is he...? What happened?" she asked.

"Did I tell you I talked to Jackson?"

She hadn't been expecting that. "No. When would you have done that?"

He flinched at the reminder that they weren't supposed to be speaking. "I promised him I would keep Josh away from Leonora. And apparently Benedict threatened Josh with all kinds of stuff if he went near her."

"Banishment?"

"Pretty much."

"But Josh wouldn't listen," she said.

His brother had been home one day and already Luke was trying—and failing—to save him. This would be the moment to remind Luke that he couldn't save Josh unless Josh wanted to be saved. But Luke had to come to that realization on his own. And it sounded like he might be.

"Remember how you told me I needed to have a limit?"

She nodded against his shoulder.

"I think I'm going to hit that limit a lot sooner than I'd thought."

She swallowed. What he was going through was necessary, but she still hurt for him. "You did what you could," she reminded him. He'd done more than that, actually, with the job and the apartment and pushing back against the entire family. "Now it's up to him."

"Yeah." His chest rose as he filled it with a deep inhale, her hair catching on the dark curls there. "Fee's still pissed at me though. Along with all the rest of them. Dealing with the family and the business—it's too stuck together for me, with Josh coming back. I just want it to be family again and not business."

She couldn't quite believe what he might be saying. "Are you going to leave the resort?"

His family ran the ranch. That was what they did. True, not all of them did—there were plenty of them off doing their own thing—but she could hardly imagine Luke not being part of the resort.

"I don't know." His words were rough with confusion and indecision. "But I am going to move out."

Her heart took up a ragged beat. They could be together if he left the resort. But he hadn't said anything about that. It had all been about his family, not her.

So she exhaled slowly and tried to push those thoughts away. "But your gym," she teased shakily.

"Yeah, I'll have to work out with everyone else. Maybe I'll see you at yoga."

She really hoped not. Coming across him in workout clothes, watching him bend himself into poses... That would wreck her.

"Maybe," she said. "So you're having a midlife crisis then."

She guessed if anyone could, he could afford to. Although she still thought it a little ridiculous of him. Well, she'd always known he was spoiled.

And then she'd discovered that he was a lot more than that—loyal, funny, and yes, competitive. And the person she wanted to turn to most when things got tangled.

She could wish she could go back to thinking him as only a spoiled rich boy, but then she'd miss out on all the rest of him. Which would be a damn shame.

"Hey, the midlife crisis is proud white-dude tradition." He brushed his lips over her hair. "Besides, you're going to tell me to get over it and that'll be that."

She couldn't help but smile. "You know me too well. But yeah, get over it. You got a place then?"

He hadn't said anything about leaving, but if he was thinking of leaving the resort, he could move out of Cabrillo. He could go anywhere he wanted. Frost collected under her skin at the thought.

"I'm looking tomorrow at Buddy Whitman's old place. Do you know it?"

"Yeah," she said. He wasn't leaving then, at least not yet. She tempered her gladness at the thought. "It's a little run-down."

"It's got land and a barn, and I don't mind doing repairs."

"I hope you like it."

"Me too." A beat passed. "Are you going to talk, or should I take advantage of your being naked again?"

"Again?" She poked at his chest. "I thought you were middle-aged."

"You won't be teasing when I'm through with you."

"Big words."

"And I'll back 'em up with my big... libido." When she stopped snickering, he asked, "How's your vacation? Feeling better about work?"

Better. She supposed she was, but it was way more complicated than that. But hey, she'd wanted to unravel all this with him. "It's good. And yes... and no."

"What's the yes part?"

"I'm itchy to get working again." Only her itch wasn't exactly centered on the resort. Being away from it made her realize that yes, it was important, but it wasn't the be-all and end-all of what she could do for her tribe.

The question, the one she still couldn't answer, was: what should come next then, if it wasn't to be the resort?

"You always were the most driven person I've ever met," Luke said. "Even more than Benedict."

"More than Benedict?" She whistled. That was high praise from him.

"Yep. What's the no part?"

Here came the tangle. "I'm loving just being present on the reservation." She said that slowly, recalling everything she'd done the past week. "No time card to punch, no work breathing down my neck. I've had the time to be with my people in a way I haven't in a long while. But like I said, I'm also a little itchy to do more once my vacation's up. So I think I need a speed somewhere between where I was and where I've been the past week."

He didn't speak for a long time after that, for so long that she worried he'd fallen asleep. Or had nothing to offer her in response.

But he finally said, "I knew you'd figure things out. You're a smart woman."

"But I haven't figured anything out!" She pushed up to

her elbow and stared down at him. "How do I get to this ideal speed?"

His expression was amused and unconcerned. "Take it day by day. Give more work to Cece; you said she's ready to take on more. Give more work to the PR department; that's what they're there for."

She flopped back down. "You sound exactly like Chelsea." He knew how Ana felt about her.

"Even though she ratted us out, she's right. And man, get them to hire you an assistant. You deserve that."

That was something to chew on. Linda had said something about hiring someone to help Ana, or at least she thought her boss had. That last meeting of theirs was a little blurry in her memory. "They might not give me anything when I get back. Maybe Linda will still be angry."

"Was she really angry? Or more shocked?"

Ana tried to remember, reconstructing Linda's expression and tone in her mind. "I guess more shocked. And this here"—she gestured between them—"isn't really going to help matters. I promised it was over, and now I'm a liar."

"No one will know. And it won't happen again." There was steel in his voice, but whether he meant that warning for her or himself, she couldn't say.

"We've said that before. Many times before."

"Once you're back at work, you'll stick to it. You probably only came out here because you're bored."

She wanted to protest that, to remind him that she'd wanted to talk to him all week. But he was giving her an out here, an excuse not to pick up the next time he called. She'd need that excuse and her fortitude for the next time. "So you're planning on calling me again?"

"Nope." He took a strand of her hair and rubbed it

between his fingers. "But I wasn't planning on calling you tonight or any other night, and look what happened."

"Delete my number from your phone."

"You first."

She made a low noise of resigned amusement. "Yeah. We're kind of in a lot of trouble here, aren't we?"

"Maybe. But we'll get through it. I'll stay strong, you'll stay strong, and after some time, this will only be an intense memory."

That answered any question she might have about him seeking her out if he left the family business. He wasn't thinking of leaving it for her—for all that he'd called her when he needed someone, he wasn't going to call her again. He'd just flat-out said that.

She pushed away from him, her stomach suddenly sour. "I need to get home."

He let her go. The light was too weak for her to see his expression, but he said nothing as she gathered her clothes, put herself together, and walked back to her truck.

She took his silence as agreement. And deleted his number from her phone once she was safely in her own truck, wiping silent tears from her cheeks as she did.

Chapter 21

THE MERRILL FAMILY was all collected for dinner once more.

Well, not everyone, Luke reflected. Their parents weren't there, but all four siblings were arranged around the dinner table.

Lil was dishing out chicken potpie, which struck Luke as an odd choice considering how hot the weather was. But she was also one day past her due date, so he kept his mouth shut and ate what she put in front of him. Otherwise he risked getting his face clawed off.

Luke had suggested a week ago that Lil might want to think about letting someone else cook, at least until after the baby arrived and she was ready to take over the kitchen again. What he'd thought was an innocent, kindly suggestion had started a tirade about how she was perfectly capable of seeing to her own kitchen and just because she was pregnant didn't mean she needed to be coddled.

Adriano had come in to rub her back and murmur about how of course he thought she could do anything and if she wanted to keep cooking she should, all the while shooting dark looks at Luke.

The whole scene had made finding a place of his own that much more pressing.

Right then Adriano was watching Lil closely, no doubt ready to spring into action if she needed help. And *he* wasn't going to get his face clawed off if he offered it.

"Thank you," Benedict murmured as Lil dished out his food. Having Benedict at the table was rare. Usually he ate in his hidey-hole in the pool house or with Pilar. He must be here to observe Josh, although what trouble Josh could get into at the dinner table, Luke couldn't see.

Josh was staring at his plate, as quiet as... well, as if he weren't even there. He'd been home for four days now and only spoke when spoken to and only came out of his room to work and to eat. Which wasn't at all worrisome. Josh had asked for some space and time to fit back into the real world, but this didn't seem like fitting in—it looked like floating through. Although it was still early days.

"All right, does anyone need anything else?" Lil asked.

"Only for you to sit down." Adriano caught at her wrist and pulled her into the chair next to him. The look she gave him in return made Luke roll his eyes.

"How was work?" he asked Josh before anyone else could start a conversation.

"Good."

"How's Rusty working out?" Rusty was the ranch horse Luke was loaning Josh.

"Good."

Luke nodded and tried to think of something that might get Josh to say anything other than good. "You, uh, need to run some errands or something? I can take you."

"Nope." Josh didn't look up from his potpie, which he

was eating with steady concentration. He'd be done in a few minutes at that rate. And then he'd probably race back to his room.

Well, Luke had tried at least.

The table fell into silence. Lil looked close to miserable and definitely not inclined to talk. Carrying a full-term baby must be sapping all her energy.

Benedict was quiet too, but that was usual for him.

Well, if no one else was going to talk, Luke might as well drop his bomb here. "I'm thinking about moving out."

There was dead, utter silence as everyone's forks went still. Luke kept on eating though, as if it were a totally normal thing to say in the middle of dinner.

Adriano shrugged. "Bye."

Lil dropped her surprise long enough to send him a look. He simply shrugged again.

Luke smiled. "You know, Adriano, I think I'm going to like you a lot more when we're not living together."

An amused gleam lit Adriano's eyes. "Me too."

"What's all this about?" Benedict said through a tight jaw.

"The baby'll be here soon, and I don't want to share space with an infant. No offense," he said to Lil. "It's time for me to have my own place and leave this one to Lil and Adriano. And Josh."

Josh's expression was studiedly neutral. As if he was afraid of being punished for showing any emotion.

"Oh," Luke went on, as if he'd just remembered, "I'm going to resign my position at the resort too."

The look on Benedict's face was the greatest thing Luke had seen in a long time. Shock, surprise, and utter befuddlement—it was all delicious.

"Is this because of Ana?" Benedict got out.

Now it was Luke's turn to be surprised. "What?"

"You have a shitty poker face," Benedict said. "When Fee said something about you and Ana, your expression gave it away."

He looked to Lil, who nodded. "It was pretty clear something was going on."

Well, hell. And he thought he'd been stoic about the whole thing. He cleared his throat. "I'm, uh, sorry about the crack I made about Pilar. It was out of line."

"Yeah, I decided to forget about that in the interest of family harmony." But it was clear from the ice in Benedict's eyes that if Luke did it again, there'd be no forgiveness the next time. "I'm going to assume you haven't shared any sensitive information with her?"

"No corporate espionage was committed," Luke said dryly.

"I fucking well hope not," Benedict said. "I can't say that I'm happy about this, and I still think she might be up to something."

Luke gritted his teeth, but his earlier crack about Pilar meant he couldn't hit back as hard as he wanted here. "Well, since I'm quitting, you don't get a say anymore. About her or me or any of it."

Goddamn, but that was going to feel good, getting Benedict's nose out of his business.

"Does Ana know you're giving up your entire life for her?" Benedict asked.

"That's a little melodramatic," Luke said.

Josh smiled at that.

"It really isn't about her," Luke went on. "Or at least not entirely about her. I've been thinking about leaving the resort for a while."

"If it's not about her," Benedict said, "then what is it about?"

Me. You. Our sister. Our brother. Our cousins. "I want this to just be a family to me again and not also a business."

For a moment, Benedict looked as if he'd like that as well. But Benedict would never dream of resigning.

Suddenly Luke felt sorry for his brother, stuck as he was in his role as eldest sibling and CEO. He was glad Benedict had ended up with Pilar; she made him happier than Luke had ever seen.

"I'm moving into Buddy Whitman's old place," he went on. "And I'm going to become a consultant. I know a lot about hotels; no sense letting all that go to waste."

There was silence after that. Benedict looked... well, as inscrutable as usual. If he was pissed or happy or indifferent, Luke wasn't able to say.

"Good luck, man," Josh offered.

"Thanks." Luke smiled at him, and it was just like they were kids again, the youngest two conspiring to piss off their older brother.

Their older brother shook his head. "Fine, you're leaving then." But there was quiver of something like regret beneath the curt words. Maybe Benedict would miss him at work. "Who's going to replace you at the resort?"

"Fee," Luke answered without hesitation. "She'd be great at it."

There was also the matter of keeping her happy; Luke suspected some of her recent discontent stemmed from the fact that she wanted to move up at the resort but would have to take his position if she did.

"All right then." For a moment sadness might have flickered in Benedict's eyes. But Luke couldn't be sure. And then his brother was saying, "Good luck from me too. When are you moving? Do you need help?"

"I'm moving this weekend. And yeah, some help would be great. I'll make sure to have some pizza and beer."

"I can help too," Adriano said gruffly. "Unless the baby comes."

"You'd better hope this baby comes," Lil muttered darkly.

Josh picked up his water glass. "To new beginnings then."

They all raised their glasses to that. Luke gave his brother an extra salute, one meant just for the two of them.

ANA WAS SURPRISINGLY unexcited about returning to work the next day.

It was Sunday night and she was cleaning up the kitchen. From upstairs, she heard the sounds of Sara giving Lori her bath. Sara was singing a little song as Lori splashed around, repeating the words so that Lori would learn some Cahuilla.

Their mother had sang them the same song when they were little. And now Lori was learning it too.

Her mother knew Ana had gone out to meet Luke earlier this week but hadn't said anything. Things between them had been... not distant. That wasn't right. More that her mother knew what she'd done and was perhaps puzzled but not exactly sad. Ana couldn't quite make out her mother's reaction.

Ana couldn't quite make out her own reaction either. But there was no need to parse it or put a proper name on it —she'd deleted his number from her phone. It was done and she was going back to work tomorrow. Back to her real life.

Her mother came into the kitchen then, her expression grave. Ana's heart went for her stomach.

"Mija, there's something I need to discuss with you. About work."

Ana nodded even as her breathing went shaky. The last time she'd had a talk about work, it hadn't ended well.

"Joe is going to retire from the Intertribal Federation," her mother said.

Joe was their representative to the federation, an organization of tribes from across the state. If he was retiring, they would need to nominate someone new, someone who'd be able to travel all over the state for the federation's work.

"Are you going to take his place?" Ana asked. Her mother would be perfect for it. But oh, Ana would miss her when she was gone. And how would her mother fit that in with her work on the tribal council?

Well, she'd find a way was how. Her mother was the most capable person Ana knew.

"I wasn't thinking of myself as a replacement," her mother said. "I was thinking of you."

If Ana was fluttery before, she was utterly still now. "Me? But... what about the resort?"

"You'd have to leave that job. But perhaps it's best."

Ana's mind began to sift through the possibilities. If she left the resort for the Intertribal Federation, she'd still be working for the betterment of her people—for the betterment of all Natives—and there would be no obstacle to her relationship with Luke.

Her heart kicked against her rib cage. Maybe... maybe he did want a relationship. Maybe she only had to ask him.

"You might slow down a bit," her mother went on, "if

you were doing something other than working for the resort." Her mother wet her lips. "And with all the travel, you could get away from *him*."

Ana started. "What?"

"I know you met him this week. I know you're depressed because of him."

Her mother was suggesting this so Ana could get away from Luke. Or at least avoid him more than she could at the resort.

Her mother was offering this as a way to help Ana. Which was touching and a little painful all at once.

"Is this only about getting me away from him?"

"No." Shock lit her mother's expression. "I think you'd be wonderful at it. But it has the added benefit of lots of travel."

When Ana had talked about finding a new speed and figuring out a different path in life, she'd thought it would come organically. That the choice wouldn't have thorns no matter where she grasped it.

She could remain at the resort and keep doing what she'd been doing. A little more slowly, with more delegation of authority, with more time taken to simply *be*.

Or she might just fall into her old habits. Maybe she did need a clean break. And if she were away more, perhaps she'd slow down and appreciate what she ought to when she was here.

If she did take the position at the federation, that left the question of Luke wide open. She could resolve to not see him again, and if she wasn't in Cabrillo often, it would be that much easier. With time, she'd forget him. Perhaps even meet someone new as she traveled around the state.

Or she could rekindle things with him. Although rekindle was maybe kind of fudging, since what was between them had never really died out. Without her job as an obstacle, they could pursue a relationship. She couldn't just bring him home right away—she'd have to ease him into her world. But it could be done.

But did she want to give up her job for him while he gave up nothing? He was already so spoiled. The fact that most of her wanted to go to him didn't make the situation any less palatable.

Assuming he even wanted a relationship with her. She might be jumping the gun in more ways than one here.

It was all a muddle, an even worse one than Linda finding out she'd been seeing Luke.

But first she had to explain to her mother. "I... I might have misrepresented him to you. I know you don't know him, that I've only ever said horrible things about him... but I was wrong about him." She swallowed as she confessed this ugly bit: "I was jealous of him."

"I don't understand. You're so smart, you went to all those wonderful schools, you work so hard... Ana, when I look at you, I have to blink against your brilliance."

Oh God, now she'd really start to cry. "No, you're the brilliant one," she insisted to her mother. "I worked so hard for all that. And he made it look so easy."

"So you don't hate him?" Her poor mother sounded so confused.

Ana rubbed her face with both hands. "No. I don't know." She let her hands fall. "No, I don't. How long do I have to decide about the job?"

"Well, you don't have to tell me right now." Her mother's confusion had multiplied.

But there wasn't time to fix it. Not until she knew his feelings for certain. Ana grabbed her purse from the side table. "I have to go talk this out with him."

Her mother put a hand to her chest. "I didn't think it was that serious."

"It's... Look, I know I can't just bring him into our lives like a freight train crashing in. He needs to ease into our world here, because this is my world. And if he's going to be part of my life, he needs to fit here. Or at least try to fit. But I also need to see if this is something I should even worry about. If I don't talk to him, if I don't feel things out, I'll always wonder."

Her mother didn't look entirely convinced, although Ana had thought that a pretty good speech. But she said, "I trust you to do the right thing. I only wanted to help you stay strong in what you thought was right."

Ana drew a deep inhale. "This might not be right. Or maybe ending things with him is right. But I'm going to go find that out. Because..." She blinked hard. "This sounds so silly, but he's such a good listener. And sometimes I need that. Just to be heard. And I know that you and Sara and the rest of the tribe do that too, but... but you are all part of me. He's outside me. And he listens."

All that felt clumsy coming off her tongue, but it also felt true. Which was why she had to go talk to him.

"A man who actually listens? You shouldn't throw away a treasure like that," her mother said dryly.

"When you get to know him, you'll like him. I think. He's very charming."

"Charming and a good listener? Why did you dislike him in the first place?"

Ana nibbled on her lip. "Well, he's also spoiled and tends to feel sorry for himself."

"The fact that you see his flaws makes me feel better about all this. A little." Her mother sighed. "If you're going to see him, you'd better go. You have work tomorrow."

Ana pressed a kiss to her mother's cheek. "I won't be too late. And thank you, Mama, for listening."

"Anytime, mija."

Ana smiled, then dashed out the door to discover what awaited her next.

Chapter 22

MAYBE THIS WAS A MISTAKE. Maybe Ana ought to have never gotten into her truck and come here.

Or maybe they'd been building up to this since... since high school, really. She'd chased him or he'd chased her—or maybe they'd been racing each other to this very destination all along.

Her current destination—or place—was Buddy Whitman's front step. Or maybe Luke's front step.

It was probably his front step since his truck was in the driveway. She'd deleted his number, so she couldn't call and ask if he was here.

She blew out an impatient breath and knocked again, louder this time. If he never opened the door, they'd never find out if they were meant to be. Which would be a damn shame, especially after that speech to her mother.

A chaos of barking dogs erupted on the other side. She sighed. Of course the dogs hadn't heard her earlier knock but decided to freak out now. Well, if he was home, he was definitely coming after that racket.

The door opened with a hard rattle as the lock came undone. When he saw her standing there, he broke out in a wide, slow grin. As if she were the best possible thing he could find waiting for him on his doorstep.

"Hey." His voice was husky and amused.

"Hey yourself." She wrapped her arms around herself, suddenly shy.

He stepped aside. "You coming in?"

"If you'll have me."

"You already know the answer to that."

She stepped inside, looked around. It looked typically bachelorish with some furniture, nothing on the walls, and a massive TV. "It's nice."

"It's okay. I've only been here a day." He closed the door behind her. "Do you want anything to drink? I think I've got some Lightning Blue."

She smiled. "No, I'm good."

They stared at each other for a long moment. Then he grabbed her face and kissed her. She melted into him at the first touch of his lips on hers. He lifted her, never breaking the kiss, and hauled her to the couch.

They kissed frantically for long moments. Ana slid her hands under his shirt, finding all the hot skin and thick muscles her fingers had been craving. That all of her had been craving.

"Are we ever going to do it in a bed?" she said, low and rumbly, because she wanted to tease, but she also really just wanted him.

"Maybe." He braced himself above her. "Is that all that you came for?"

"No."

His expression brightened into delight, as if he'd been

waiting to hear that. "I guess this would be a good time to tell you that I quit the resort."

She gasped and shoved against his chest. "Really? I kind of never thought you would."

Although he had said something about it the last time they'd met. Only she hadn't realized he was serious.

Oh God, had he done it for *her*?

She froze up so hard at the thought, she couldn't get that question out.

"It was time," he said, as if it were just that easy. "I'm thinking about taking up consulting instead. That way I can stay in the hotel business and only be a brother and a cousin to my family."

Okay, so it wasn't for her. Or it wasn't *only* for her. Somehow that made her feel loads better about this. "Good. I think you'll be great at it."

And of course that changed things. Changed how she was going to come at this.

Because she wouldn't be the only one giving something up to have what was between them. Not that working for the federation would be giving anything up.

"I guess this would be a good time to tell you that I might quit my resort," she said, as casually as he had.

"What? How could you do that?"

"I haven't quit quite yet." She twined her fingers in his shirt, tugging the fabric toward her and letting it ride up and expose his abs. "But there's an opportunity for me to work with the Intertribal Federation. Going all over the state, meeting with other tribes, still helping my people, but helping out other Natives too."

"When did this happen?"

"Just today."

"Are you going to do it?" His tone was sharp, as if he

either really wanted her to do it... or really *didn't* want her to do it.

"Well, I kind of thought I'd talk to you about it first."

"Ana..." A wicked smile crossed his face. "Are you asking me to be your sidepiece? Because if you're going all over the state, and I'll have all this free time as a consultant..."

She laughed. He was... he was funny and never let her rest on her laurels and was a great listener and...

And she loved him. She hadn't wanted to, she hadn't meant to, but it had still happened. Funny how these things ended up. Maybe in a few months, once they were further in their relationship, she could confess. If a relationship was what they were heading for. She should probably clarify that at some point.

"I didn't know you'd quit when I came over here," she said. "It looks like we had the same idea at the same time." She twisted her fingers so tightly into his shirt her knuckles went white. "Do you think... Are we heading toward a relationship here?"

"What?" He reared up, tearing his shirt from her grip as he blinked down at her. "How could you ask that? I mean, I love you—"

"Wait." She held up a hand and tried to catch her breath. What had he said? "You can't just throw that on a person."

"You smashed me in the eye with a kettlebell. I think I can throw the word love at you."

"Are you throwing the *word* at me or...?"

This was kind of her whole future at stake here—a little clarification would be good. Also, if it was more than the word, she could give her heart permission to go into overdrive like it wanted to.

He cupped her face and brushed his mouth across hers. "No, it's more than just the word. It's the real thing. I met you in the middle of the night on a dirt road to make love to you in a truck. How could you doubt my feelings after that?"

That really wasn't the greatest proof, but coupled with everything else he'd done for her—everything he *was*, really —that was more than proof enough.

She told her heart it could finally go crazy, then said, "I... I love you too. I thought I hated you, or at least I wanted to beat you at everything, but I think that's just how we are. We'll be competitive, yes, but in the end, we're better people for that competition. We hone each other into our best forms."

Wow, she was just speechifying all over the place tonight.

"That's very poetic," he said with mock solemnity.

"I also like telling you to shape up and stop whining."

"And I love hearing that from you."

"Also, you're a great listener. In that you just listen. You never meddle."

"Because I know you're smart and capable enough to solve stuff on your own."

To hear that he had that much trust in her, that he didn't have to charge in and try to solve everything... Her mother was right; he was a treasure she shouldn't lose.

Even so: "This won't be easy." Even with love, they had a long way to go to Happily Ever After.

"I know. But we're not afraid of hard work."

That was definitely true. "We can't just move in together," she said. Not that she even wanted to at this point. Another thing they'd have to work toward.

"As if I'm that kind of floozy," he teased. Then he sobered. "I'm going to follow your lead on this, darlin'. You tell me when and how you want to invite me into your world. Okay?"

She nodded. She could do that.

"We'll figure it out," he said. "Slowly, but we'll get where we need to be. Look how long it took us to get here from high school."

"Yeah. It'll take some more time to get this"—she gestured between them—"dialed in. I can't just leave the reservation. And you can't just move out there."

"I know. How about you come visit me here whenever you want? And we'll take baby steps toward more. Toward dialing things in."

That sounded good. She'd still have plenty of time to help Sara with Lori and to spend time with her mom and to do everything else she wanted to do with her life.

As for him... "What will you do when I'm not here?"

"You might not have noticed, but there's quite a bit of family shit going down right now." His voice went dark, his brows drawing together. "Josh is avoiding everyone, Fee's still pissed at me, Benedict... well, he's Benedict. Oh, and I just got a text from Adriano—he and Lil are on their way to the hospital. It looks like my niece finally decided to show up."

Why hadn't he said so right away? "Oh my God, how exciting! Do you need to go too?"

"No, I'll go visit once the baby's actually here. I'll save the hospital waiting room routine for my own kids." He winked at her.

"Huh. As if your wife wouldn't want you there so she could tell you in great deal how it was all your fault and you did that to her." She tried to play it off as sarcasm, but the blush on her cheeks gave her away.

"I guess we'll find out, won't we?"

It was the *we* that dissolved any last worries she might have. Yes, it would be tough and it would take a lot of figuring out—but that *we* said that he saw them doing it together. Just as they had the past few months.

"Yeah, we will find out," she said.

She had no doubt that what they'd find together would be nothing short of pure joy.

Epilogue

LUKE PUT HIS TRUCK INTO park and killed the engine.

"Is it always this... big?"

He looked out at the crowd gathered near the tribal hall. There were well over a hundred people here. Maybe two hundred. A heavy plume of smoke rose from a barbeque trailer.

This was a serious party.

Ana peered out the windshield. "It's not always this big, but this isn't unusual." She grinned at him. "There's no party like a rez party." She popped open the truck door. "Don't worry; most of them are probably here to check you out."

"Yeah," he muttered under his breath. "That's not at all deflating."

He got out and followed her. She waved to her mother first.

Mrs. Chacon was going to start at the Intertribal Federation in a few weeks. Ana had decided to stay at the resort after all—she'd said something snarky about not wasting her education, unlike *some* people—and while people occasionally gave them odd looks, most of Cabrillo was getting used to it.

He still hadn't introduced her to his family, but his niece's christening was coming up in a few weeks, and she was coming with him to that. Even Benedict would have to smile at her there. And once Benedict got to know Ana, he'd love her. People who took no shit were favorites of his.

Ana's mother came up to greet them as they approached. She remained reserved with him, so he gave her his best smile and was at his most polite. He couldn't blame her for being wary—after all those years of Ana claiming to dislike him, her mother probably thought he was hiding horns somewhere. She only wanted to make certain her daughter was safe with him.

Once they'd said hello, Sara came up to greet them. Luke scooped Lori from her arms with Sara's laughing approval.

Lori instantly tried to jam her fingers into his nose. That was her favorite trick lately.

Luke ducked his head just in time, getting wet, sticky baby fingers shoved into his ear instead. Which might have been worse.

He gently pulled the baby's hand down. "Little girl, you got to stop doing that."

Ana leaned in and tickled the baby. "You get him, kiddo. He deserves it."

"Thanks for the support."

She never passed up an opportunity to yank his chain. It was part of why he loved her.

"Hey, I see Cece," she said, waving to someone in the crowd. "I'm going to go talk to her. If you want, the dudes are all gathered at the barbeque. You should go meet them. Watch some meat cook."

When he went over to the barbeque, a line of unsmiling men met him, their arms crossed over their chests.

Aw hell. This must be the welcoming committee.

"Hey," he said.

None of them said anything. They were good at the whole stare-down thing, he had to give them that. Not even Lori blowing spit bubbles was breaking them.

"So you think you're going to date Ana," one of them said.

Luke guessed that this might be one of her cousins she had told him about. Although she was related in some way to pretty much everyone on the reservation, so it wasn't a bad guess to assume anyone was her cousin.

He knew better than to say he was already dating Ana. "She's a great woman. Better than I deserve."

"That's for damn sure," another man said.

Okay, that wasn't really working. Maybe he should try to get Lori to do something cute. Also, was he *supposed* to agree with the man about his unfitness for Ana?

"You should know," the first man said, "we know a lot of quiet places in the desert. Places no one ever goes. Where nobody would ever stumble across anything."

Great. Now they'd moved on to threatening him with an unmarked grave in the desert. This was going just awesome.

"Uh, yeah. I'm not planning on doing anything that would require you to murder me. Ana pretty well keeps me in line."

That surprisingly got a laugh out of them.

"Yeah, you should probably be more scared of Ana than us," the second man said.

"I am."

"But you should still be scared of us," the first one said.

"I am."

That really got them laughing.

Finally the second man stuck out a hand. "I'm Ken."

"Luke." He gave a firm shake.

The rest of the men introduced themselves, some still giving him hard looks. He understood. He knew it would take time.

Ana came over then, taking Lori from him. "Do you need saving?"

"From her or from them?"

That made them laugh again.

"I'll take pity on you," she said with a wink. She grabbed his hand. "Come on. There's some people I want you to meet."

"Who?" he asked as she led them away, her steps bouncy and the baby firmly tucked against her hip. She looked really good like that.

"Oh, everybody."

And she pulled him toward the crowd, pulling him deeper into her world, setting the pace just like he'd asked.

WANT MORE HOT COWBOY ROMANCE? Pick up *Reunited with Her Cowboy,* the next in A Cowboy of Her Own! Keep reading for a sneak peek!

About the Author

Genevieve Turner is a *USA Today* bestselling author of western romance. She loves cowboys, the rural life, and happily ever afters. She lives in beautiful Southern California with the perfect number of kids, dogs, and turkeys—and probably too many chickens.

You can find her on the web at www.genturner.com.

Genevieve's Newsletter

NEW RELEASES, SALES, AND A *Free* STARTER LIBRARY WHEN YOU SIGN UP!

CLICK HERE